*For my parents, Mary and Alfred Long
who like Regencies best of all*

CHAPTER 1

Means of Escape

The existence of the ill-used and sorely troubled Lady Malvina first impinged on Alys Weston's consciousness in a nightmare, which she later ascribed to the roast duck she had eaten at dinner (sent over by the squire), and the sip of Papa's port she took to fortify herself for the ascent to her chilly bedchamber.

However it was, she awoke very early next morning with the whole plot of a gloriously Gothic romance in her mind. Springing out of bed, she lit a stump of candle, wrapped herself in an old shawl and, tossing a long plait of dark chestnut hair over her shoulder, proceeded to get her ideas down on paper before the prosaic light of day could dispel any of the thrillingly dark miasma filling her imagination.

> *Her captors travelled night and day with scarcely a pause, save for such meagre sustenance as they carried in their packs, through countryside that grew ever more craggy and mountainous.*
>
> *The few sullen, sheepskin-clad peasants they met spoke in the language her mother had used to her in childhood, and Malvina came to realize that she was within the borders of Galbodia, beyond all reach of friends, family . . . or her beloved Alfonz!*

The tall, raven-haired and sinister villain of the piece came to life on the page, rapidly followed by Malvina's angelically fair betrothed, Alfonz. Then she added a ghostly, monkish figure, the plot and characters unfolding before her hurrying pen as she sat, frozen and exalted, before the little campaign desk that her papa had carried with him throughout his soldiering days. (It had fared rather better than he did, being battered but at least still all in one piece, which was more than one could say about Major Harrison Weston.)

The candle had guttered and died, and the sun long since weakly dragged its sorry self into the leaden sky over the Yorkshire moors, before she was disturbed. Miss Laetitia Grimshaw, once Alys's governess, but now occupying a nebulous position somewhere between under-housekeeper and companion, popped her head around the door, looking quite distracted and with her muslin cap over one ear.

'Alys? Are you ill?' she called softly, then on catching sight of her seated before the desk, came right into the room.

'Ill? No, of course I am not ill!' Alys said, blinking away Malvina and her perilous situation . . . and *especially* the image of her tall, dark, harsh-featured and fascinatingly villainous abductor, Raymundo Ravegnac. 'Why should you think so? I am *never* ill!'

'Well, you did not let the hens out, and it is not like you to be late for breakfast, my dear.'

'Perhaps not, but I had the most brilliant idea for a novel in the night, Letty, and thought I had better get the bones of it down before I forgot it – and then it was so engrossing that I had no notion of the time passing.'

'It was remiss of me not to notice your absence sooner, only the washerwoman is here and I was much engaged in sorting and counting linen.'

Her general air of damp dishevelment and coarse cotton apron finally registered. Alys said remorsefully, 'I had quite forgotten that Mrs Clarke was coming today to see to the laundry. Let us hope my blue cambric does not run out any more, for it is getting to be sadly grey. And you *did* remind her to take care with the sheets we have not yet turned?'

'Oh yes – though she is so vigorous at pounding them that she gets quite carried away. I had best get back to her. Shall I leave you to compose the rest of your little story, or will you come down now?'

'This is not just a story, Letty, but is to be an entire Gothic romance along the lines of Mrs Radcliffe's wonderful tales, which I am sure we must both know by heart. I will read the outline of it to you later, but for now I suppose I had better hasten to get ready.'

Letty looked relieved. 'That would indeed be best, for although Saul has seen to the hens, I am afraid the major is having one of his *better* days.'

Their eyes met in mutual comprehension and Alys exclaimed, 'Oh no!'

Letty nodded her head, a strand of mouse-brown hair, sadly out of curl from the steam, escaping from under her cap. 'Yes, the news the squire brought to your papa yesterday, of the terrible tragedy at Priory Chase, has so enlivened him—'

'*Enraged* him,' amended Alys.

'Rage does enliven him,' Miss Grimshaw pointed out. 'So much so that he awoke early, ate a coddled egg and dry toast and then sent down for the brandy – which he accused me of watering. I was quite quaking in my shoes, but I told him straight I would never dream of doing such a thing.'

'No, for I do it myself, so your conscience is quite clear on that score,' Alys assured her.

'I don't really know if it answers anyway, Alys, for if it tastes weaker he just seems to drink the more. And now he has finished the bottle, called for his boots and pistol, and gone into the garden.'

Alys sighed, for Major Weston, a feverish, emaciated invalid generally under the influence of intoxicating beverages, only now left his room when the fancy suddenly took him to shoot off his pistol in the garden. Since he lost his left arm, and the sight of one eye, during the disastrous retreat of the Duke of York's army through Flanders in '94, and suffered frequent tremors due to a recurrent fever, his aim was not what it once was.

'Let us hope Saul remembers to stand well back, once he has loaded for Papa,' she remarked, for the young servant, though amiable and obliging, was not noted for his high intelligence. 'He will not be of much use about the garden if he has a hole blown through him.'

Miss Grimshaw shuddered. 'I am sure he learned his lesson that time the major singed his hat.'

There was a sudden explosion from the garden below and the tinkle of broken glass, followed by a noisy mass exodus of startled rooks from the trees that divided them from Squire Basset's park.

'Oh well, I suppose using empty bottles for targets at least gives them *some* use, even if we are picking glass out of the flowerbeds for ever afterwards,' Alys said, then advised Letty to get back to the laundry. 'Send Mary up with the hot water and I will be down directly.'

But by the time she had got downstairs the explosions and curses from the garden had ceased and Saul, grinning as though he had just enjoyed a high treat, was assisting Major Weston back to his chamber, quite exhausted.

'Good morning, Papa,' Alys said dutifully, stepping aside to let them pass.

'Well, Miss Slug-a-bed!' he returned, his hollow-eyed face cadaverous in the dark passageway and his one, sunken dark eye burning with fever or drink . . . or possibly both. There were traces still of the handsome man who had captivated her mother into an imprudent runaway match with him so long ago, Alys thought, even though he was now quite pared down to bones, selfishness and bad temper.

He grasped her shoulder suddenly with a skeletal, shaking hand. 'You have heard the news that Lord Rayven and his heir are dead, girl?'

'Yes, Papa,' Alys said cautiously, for she could not see that the accidental death of two people she had never met, tragic though it might be, could concern her.

'And now the son of that cheating blackguard Hugo Rayven is to inherit all!' His face grew dark and twisted with anger and his grip on her shoulder became painful. 'You will have nothing to do with him, do you hear?'

'Of course not, Papa! How should I? Our paths are unlikely to cross in the extreme.'

He stared at her for a moment as if he had forgotten who she was, then his hand dropped and he pushed past and went on up the stairs.

'Now what maggot has got into his head?' Alys muttered, as the stumbling footsteps passed overhead. Even Squire Basset, papa's cousin, by whose kindness they were established in the modest Dower House on the estate, was not on visiting terms with the

Rayvens of Priory Chase, which was situated miles away, near Harrogate; though he might, she supposed, have occasionally shared the hunting field with one or other of them.

Alys broke her fast with tea and bread and butter fetched from the kitchen herself, since Mary, the one maid of all work, was by now engaged in helping Letty spread the first sheets to dry over the lavender and rosemary bushes.

Alys had taken full control of the housekeeping before her fourteenth birthday, and mastered the art of driving a hard bargain in the bartering of chickens and eggs long before that, but it was Letty who seemed to find all the tedious little household tasks quite engrossing. A timid and self-effacing woman originally engaged by Squire Basset's first wife as Alys's governess, she had quickly and almost imperceptibly slipped into the role of general factotum to her strong-minded charge.

Due to Major Weston's reclusive tendency, chronic invalidism and a selfish determination that his only child should devote her life to his care, Alys's social circle was largely constricted to Sir Ralph and Lady Basset, his son James by his first marriage, and the Rector and his good – *too* good – wife, Mrs Franby.

The nearby village of Little Stidding did not provide much in the way of amusement either, except for the weekly market, and although there were monthly assemblies in the nearest town she had as much hope of gaining Papa's permission to attend them as of flying to the moon.

Other than that, there was an unlimited supply of bleakly beautiful moorland to roam over, and a lot of sheep . . . among whom, of course, she did *not* include her dear Letty, to whom she was most sincerely attached, despite her being some twenty years her senior and quite scatter-brained.

So it was perhaps not surprising that Alys had found her only means of escape from this trammelled and unexciting existence in the world of novels and her own imagination. And now that she had set out on the writing of an entire novel of her own, she possessed a whole new world she could, god-like, create for her own amusement, peopled by creatures that must dance at her command.

Soon the squire would send down yesterday's paper from the Hall and she would have to read it to Papa, when he had recovered from his exertions, though at least he did tend to be meek as a lamb for some hours after these sessions which was one good outcome. Meanwhile, alone in the dining parlour with a half-eaten slice of bread and butter, Alys sat turning over possible pen names – *male* pen names – until eventually she fixed on Orlando Browne. She had no idea where the notion came from, but liked the sound of it very well.

Orlando Browne. Yes, he could take liberties with his characters and plot that a mere *Miss* might not, especially in the way of scenes of passion and violence, which she intended to sprinkle liberally throughout Lady Malvina's history.

And her heroine would not be some frail, fainting creature – or even worse, a pious bore – but a woman of sense and fortitude who would be undaunted by the supposedly supernatural terrors that would beset her, for Alys was at one with the great Mrs Radcliffe in believing only in the rational.

Later, walking across the park to the Hall, Alys reflected that it was odd that the warm-hearted, good-natured, but undeniably vulgar second wife of Sir Ralph should have formed her literary tastes.

Lydia Basset had been an actress before her elevation to her present position and loved melodrama, adoring any tale that smacked of the Gothic. Alys, frequently called on in the afternoons to read to her until she fell asleep, soon found herself eagerly carrying each new novel home for a more earnest perusal once Lady Basset had finished with it.

She read and re-read them, especially those of Mrs Radcliffe, who had, for some reason, ceased to produce any more after *The Italian*, and became quite an expert on *Udolpho* and an intimate of the Castles of *Otranto* and *Rackrent*. In fact, she could probably have found her way around either blindfold.

This had been her apprenticeship and she now felt fully ready to embark on her own novel. As to those other vital requisites of the genre, romantic scenery and gloomy mansions – well, there were rocky and precipitous outcrops enough to please anyone in Yorkshire. And, if she had not actually visited Priory Chase, the family seat of the Rayvens, romantically built among the ruins of an abbey, she had heard enough about it to fire her imagination.

Caves too ... Alys adored caves, and had several times persuaded the owner of a local one to let her descend into the Stygian gloom where, lantern in hand, she would examine the pallid and interesting accretions formed by the slow dripping of water from the roof.

Emerging with a sudden start from her reverie, Alys recollected that both Lady Basset and Sir Walter Scott's newly published *Marmion* awaited her at the Hall.

Picking up her pace, she cut through the wilderness past the hermitage, where old Jethro, in a hooded robe, was gloomily seated on a rock whittling something and did not even look up to pass the time of day when she called out a cheerful greeting.

It showed a rank ingratitude for the many fresh eggs she had bestowed on him, but she supposed a surly and reclusive nature was a requisite for the position.

CHAPTER 2

Pursuits

The air seemed to move about Malvina and she could have sworn that the ghost of a kiss lightly touched her lips. Her eyes flew open: the monkish figure stepped back from the moonlight that came through the narrow windows, the dark shadow cast by the cowl of his long robe rendering him eerily faceless.

'Pray, sir, who – who are you?' she whispered. 'And what do you mean by me?'

The Travails of Lady Malvina by Orlando Browne

Alys found Lady Basset lying upon her daybed as usual, her exceedingly plump form enveloped in a dashingly diaphanous pink négligé quite unsuited to her figure, languidly eating sugarplums and reading a letter. A glass of brandy, with which she dosed herself against all manner of imaginary ills, stood on a little table at her elbow.

She had developed an interestingly delicate constitution as compensation for a life of unrelieved tedium, for Sidlington Hall was isolated and her husband's interests largely consisted of estate management and hunting. Although rather snubbed by the wives of the half-dozen neighbours within visiting distance, she was good-natured to a fault and always happy to see her stepson's friends, even though she found them rather serious young men, disinclined to fun and frolic. Her husband's hunting cronies also voted her a very good sort, for she kept an excellent table and always retired immediately after dinner, leaving them to their carousals.

'Has *Marmion* arrived, Aunt?' Alys asked eagerly, as soon as she had greeted her.

Pug, who had sat up and barked at her in a token sort of way, settled back down again next to his mistress and began trying to lick powdered sugar off his snub nose with a triangular pink tongue.

'Yes – it is there on the table, together with some book about the Lake District which I have *no* recollection of ordering,' Lady Basset said, without much interest, for while a thrilling tale filled her with such fearful pleasure that she could resist the enveloping vapours of sleep for quite as much as an hour, poetry set her yawning in a trice.

She resumed the reading of her letter, for she maintained a voluminous correspondence with an old friend from her days on the stage who lived a life of much greater interest in London, though in Alys's opinion Lady Crayling's letters only served to make her aunt the more dissatisfied with her lot.

'Do you know, Alys, that although Eliza is received in several great houses and married a lord, some of the nobility are still too high in the instep to acknowledge her – Titus Hartwood, your maternal grandfather, among them,' she said now. 'She writes that the widow of his younger brother – and I daresay there were twenty years between them – has gone to live with him in Albermarle Street, together with her daughter, Arabella. *William* Hartwood married late, so Lavinia Hartwood must be about my age, and her daughter still in the schoolroom. There is a son, too, whom Eliza says is exceedingly handsome, besides being his uncle's heir, but he resides in bachelor lodgings near St James's Street.'

'Oh?' Alys said, looking up from the table where she was eagerly examining the new books. 'How odd it is to have such close relatives about whom I know nothing, excepting only from hearsay.'

'I believe your grandfather had a partiality for me at one time, for he would haunt the green room when I was there,' Lady Basset said complacently, 'but a greater nipcheese in these affairs there never was, and so several of the girls warned me, so I—'

To Alys's regret, she broke off before she could impart any more interesting insights into her grandfather's character or, indeed, her own scandalously exciting past.

'Might I borrow this book about the Lakes, if you do not like it?' Alys thought that the volume might give her ideas for the background of her novel, which was to be set in the imaginary kingdom of Galbodia at some nebulous time in the mists of antiquity.

'Yes, do take it . . .' Lady Basset agreed, once more returning to her letter. She heaved a great sigh, dislodging a sugarplum from the filmy drapery covering her massive bosom.

'How lucky Eliza is! She goes to routs and masquerades, drives her own carriage in the park and can go shopping whenever she pleases . . . and indeed, when Sir Ralph asked me to marry him, I thought my life would be much the same. But no, here I have been stuck in this wilderness ever since.'

Even Alys had heard of some of the doings of the notorious Lady Crayling, since Miss Grimshaw had a numerous family circle in London who, though quite genteelly engaged in professions rather than of the *ton*, were sufficiently well-connected to hear the latest *on dits*. She was not in the least surprised that Sir Ralph refused to allow his wife to visit London with him on his infrequent visits to that metropolis.

'Just listen to this!' Lady Basset said now, for she often read passages of her letters aloud, entirely forgetting that her audience was a green girl of eighteen. Alys had learned the most scandalous things, for Lady Crayling appeared to have no moral scruples about anything.

Remember what larks we had in the old days, Lydia, when his lordship used to ferry us up the river to his house at Kew, to dance for The Brethren in that heathenish underground temple he had constructed? We thought we would die of cold, changing into those thin veils in the shell grotto! Well, you would stare if I told you what goes on when most of the girls leave, except that now I am a Sister of the Order (no Covent Garden nun!) I am constrained to secrecy under threat of the direst punishment should I betray their—

Here she seemed to recollect her audience, for she stopped suddenly and laid the letter aside for later perusal, leaving Alys filled with curiosity to know more about this mysterious Brethren.

A mere two pages of *Marmion* sufficed to put her aunt to sleep, and then Alys could not resist picking up the letter and, with wide eyes, reading more – though she was disappointed to discover that the rest of it was filled with Lady Crayling's complaints about her husband's 'bits of muslin', addiction to gaming and the prowess of her young lover.

She was just puzzling over the precise nature of *Blue Ruin* and *Cribb's Parlour* when Lady Basset gave an unladylike snort and muttered something. Guiltily, Alys laid the letter down again – but really, she *needed* to know more of the wide world, especially now, when such worldly knowledge could add a new dimension to her work.

Lady Basset and Pug snored on obliviously as Alys utilized her aunt's papier-mâché desk and violet-scented notepaper for the next exciting instalment of Malvina's adventures:

'He will never marry me while you live,' hissed the woman, her beautiful face wild with jealous anger. 'My birth is too lowly – I cannot give him the advantages he seeks through an alliance with you . . . or from your death. So, let it be death!' The curved blade of a great knife flashed angry light from the wall sconce as she flung herself upon the hapless captive, her intention writ clear upon her livid countenance. . . .

On leaving her aunt some time later, Alys had the good fortune to encounter her cousin, a stolid, worthy and rather pop-eyed young man some few years her senior.

'James, the very person of all others I wished to see!' she exclaimed, her luminous large grey eyes lighting up, and immediately begged him prettily for some paper.

He always had a ready supply, since he had a keen interest in – if little understanding of – modern scientific advances and so maintained a large correspondence on the subject with numerous likeminded acquaintances and learned societies.

If James somehow gained the impression that she and Miss Grimshaw were compiling recipes and household hints, he was fortunately too stupid to be surprised at the volume of manuscript required. However, he was always kindly and generous when asked for such little favours, so in return Alys let him hold forth about his current pet subject of magnetism for quite a half-hour before making her excuses and returning to the Dower House with her booty.

'Letty,' she said, ruefully, when she got home, 'I am afraid I have agreed to let James try a little experiment in magnetism on us tomorrow, when he has set up the apparatus in the small summer house.'

'Magnetism?' Letty echoed, looking up from the handkerchief she was hemming.

'Do not worry, from what I can discover, it will not harm us in any way and may even do us some good.'

'Well, if you say so. What have you there?'

'A large quantity of paper and a book about the Lake District, which came to my aunt by mistake.'

'And did you ask Lady Basset if she knew why any mention of the Rayven family, especially the new heir, rendered Major Weston so irate?'

'Yes, as I was coming away, for she was asleep most of the time I was there. She thought, from something Sir Ralph once let drop, that Papa and the father of the new Viscount Rayven were in the army together and fast friends, until they fell out. Crooked play was mentioned, so I expect it was gaming: I know Papa was an inveterate gambler, or we would not be living in such reduced circumstances now.'

'But I believe, Alys, that gambling is a fever in the blood and those in its thrall cannot help themselves.'

'And *I* believe it is a great piece of self-indulgence that can lead to nothing but hardship and misery for the families of those concerned,' Alys declared roundly. 'Excuse my father's nature as you will, but you will *never* succeed in convincing me of the worth of his character, for you can't make a silk purse from a sow's ear, embroider it as much as you please.'

James had omitted to inform Alys that he had also invited one of his friends to be present at the experiment in magnetism, though since Mr Yatton was cast in the same stolid and commonplace mould as himself, this discovery did not send her into transports of delight.

But Mr Yatton, on being introduced, took an unaccountable fancy to her and paid a morning call at the Dower House next day.

It was unfortunate that Mrs Franby, the wife of the rector, had also condescended to pay one of her rare – and unwelcome – calls at the same time, for she scented a clandestine romance and immediately sent the rector up to tell Major Weston.

'Papa, the young man came to call from courtesy only, and Miss Grimshaw was present throughout,' she told him when the inevitable rage ensued. 'Pray, do not fret yourself into one of your fevers over it, for I assure you I found him as staid and uninteresting as my cousin James.'

But, of course, the major, fired by a purely selfish fear that she would leave him, ranted on until he quite wore himself out. A moment's sane reflection would have told him that the chance of a serious suitor turning up at the door, prepared to overlook Alys's penniless state, lack of ladylike accomplishments and lowly situation, was hardly worth mentioning.

It was not even as if she was a great beauty, Alys reflected later, examining her face critically in the mirror. Her abundant hair was a dark and glossy chestnut and curled without any help, it was true, but her eyes were an unremarkable grey, her mouth too wide and she was quite tall – nearly as tall as her cousin, a grave defect in a woman.

Still, at eighteen most girls have *something* of beauty about them, she supposed, if only the dewy freshness of youth, and if they are going to get a husband had better do it before the bloom rubs off. Unless their papas decreed that their destiny was to flower and fade alone. . . .

Only in poetry and novels did perfect, gentle knights beat a path to the beleaguered maiden's door.

The Travails of Lady Malvina advanced apace and Miss Grimshaw, impressed if rather appalled by the worldly and passionate tone of the story, said she did not know where Alys got the half of it, but she was sure it was much better than anything she had read in print.

Alys believed it read well, but resolved to send a sample of her work to Sir Walter Scott, whose *Lay of the Last Minstrel* they both so much admired, for his opinion.

'Though perhaps, being a poet, Sir Walter is not the right person to send such a work to?' suggested Letty. 'Might not some genteel lady novelist be more suitable?'

'But I would value *his* opinion above all others, and I daresay even if he does not *write* novels, he reads them.'

So Letty wrote out the first few chapters in her best copperplate on the paper so unwittingly provided by James Basset. These she enclosed in a package with a covering letter to her nephew, Thomas Grimshaw, an attorney in a good way of business in London, to forward to Sir Walter – a quite circuitous way of doing it, but the only one that would not raise eyebrows in Little Stidding. No one would be surprised at letters and packages passing to and fro between Letty and her kindly London relatives.

Of course, Major Weston knew nothing of Alys's writing. He probably assumed that she and Miss Grimshaw spent all their days in the wholesome and healthy pursuits of housewifery, needlework and perhaps a little ladylike rambling about.

And in fact Alys *did* ramble about: she walked for miles and quite often at a furious pace for, full of youth, vigour and a yearning for action of some kind – *any* kind – she was so restless that exercise was the only way to calm her disordered spirits. And now that her novel and its characters had so taken over her mind, she muttered and occasionally even *gesticulated* as she walked, pouring into the novel all her longings for romance, travel and excitement.

Up on the moors, under the boundless and ever-changing skies, her imagination was free to soar like a hawk, even if in reality she was forever confined to run about a constricted world, like one of her own chickens.

CHAPTER 3

Cut to the Quick

The door by which her jailer entered the tower squealed hideously when opened: so how could the sweet music that had lulled her to sleep the first night of her sojourn in this place be rationally explained, or the glimpsed, monkish figure silently descending the stair into the windowless chamber below?
The Travails of Lady Malvina by Orlando Browne

'And listen to *this* part, Letty!' Alys raged, indignantly brandishing the longed-for letter from Sir Walter Scott in the air, for the blinkered pride of the new author had left her in daily expectation of receiving only the most lavish terms of admiration and encouragement.

Instead, he gently pointed out those faults of the amateur – such as overwriting, a veritable thicket of exclamation marks and a derivative reflection of the works of others – that had been quite obscured to Alys's fond eye until that moment. Having them quiveringly exposed to the light of day made her feel both defensive and angry, however well-meant the advice.

In short, my dear young lady, much as I may admire the inspiring works of Mrs More, or the particular genius for sweeping vistas and picturesque settings so excellently employed in Mrs Radcliffe's novels, in general a woman's mind is not fitted for the task of earning her living by her pen.

'Oh . . . oh dear!' Letty murmured inadequately.

'He understands *nothing* about novel writing,' Alys exclaimed, striding about the room in a most unladylike way. 'If Lady Malvina is "*devoid of many of those tender and pious qualities that would engage the reader's sympathies with her terrible plight*" then I am glad of it! Oh, I should have known better than to send my work to a poet, for ten to one, now I have put the notion into his head, he will steal my plot and write a novel himself!'

'Oh no indeed, Alys – I am sure you are wrong.'

'Ha! We shall see,' Alys said, taking another hasty turn about the room, reminding her companion of nothing so much as a caged beast. 'And the next passage adds insult to injury!'

A woman's sole and most beautiful design should be to support and nurture the spiritual and physical comfort of her family, and to this end you must put aside any ill-judged yearnings for fame. Do not dim and sully that pure vestal light with longings for which Nature has not fitted you. . . .

'Pah!' She crumpled up the letter and hurled it away with some force. 'What, pray, can he know about my situation? My vestal light will be quite burnt out in ministering to Papa while he selfishly drinks himself into an early grave, leaving us all but penniless.'

'He knows nothing . . . you are quite right, dearest Alys,' agreed Letty. 'I daresay Sir Walter was liverish, or does not have a taste for the Gothic, or some such thing. And I am sure that caring for your poor papa as you do is *just* as much a noble duty as being a helpmeet to a husband, for were it not for your patience and firmness he would not be with us now.'

This was true, but with no control over Sir Ralph, who saw nothing amiss in supplying his invalid cousin with wines and spirits from his own cellar, her influence was limited.

Letty plied her with cups of weak tea and comforting platitudes until eventually she calmed down enough to retrieve the letter, smooth it out and re-read it in a calmer frame of mind. And if she was soon scrawling her own angry comments over it, she was also starting to realize the sense of most of what he had said on the subject of writing.

'And it was kind of Sir Walter to answer your letter at all, don't you think?' Letty ventured. 'He probably receives so many of them.'

'I suppose so – and in retrospect I am *deeply* thankful that I did not also send him some of my juvenile attempts at verse. And it may be perverse of me, but I fear I may never again read any of his verse without a feeling of distinct aggrievance.'

But she soon began to revise her novel for, while she could not make her heroine nauseatingly good and pious to suit Sir Walter's tastes, she could and did attempt to expunge all borrowings from the novels of other authors and strive for a more original tone.

Upon request, Letty's nephew in the city managed to find out Mrs Radcliffe's direction and, in due course, Alys forwarded a much humbler and wiser letter and a few pages of rewritten manuscript to her for an opinion.

In due course Mrs Radcliffe wrote back to Alys briefly, but very kindly, saying, since this time Alys had mentioned her family circumstances, that she believed writing would provide much solace in her lonely situation, as she performed the loving and unselfish duties of a daughter.

But Alys could not agree with her opinion that her work showed an almost *masculine* tone of assertion – or if it did, why this should be a bad thing? Besides, since it was being penned by her *alter ego*, Orlando Browne, she was sure any tone of masculine assertion was perfectly natural.

Mrs Radcliffe's confession that she had only turned to writing novels in order to add to the family coffers struck Alys quite forcibly: for although publication alone had first been her dream, what if she could earn a living by doing something that she so much enjoyed?

But then, any such fruits of her labours would go to line her papa's pockets and he would inevitably use them to hasten himself to the grave – just as Mrs Radcliffe's money was her husband's to do with as he would. She hoped for her sake that he was not in the least like Major Weston.

It began to be plain that Lady Basset's increasingly poor health and palpitations had become more than imaginary, for her lips occasionally turned an alarming bluish shade as she gasped for breath, and the dabs of rouge stood out on her plump cheeks.

Sir Ralph could not understand illness: he thought his wife could be better if she would, and was quite cross with her for not being so.

'The doctor has advised a reducing diet, but has also suggested that the waters of Harrogate might prove beneficial,' Alys told Miss Grimshaw after one visit.

'I believe some of the waters have medicinal properties,' Letty said. 'I am sure I have heard of many people having been made better by taking them.'

'I daresay, but I expect the change of scene may be enough to make the invalid feel better in most cases – I am sure it would do so in Lady Basset's. Let us hope Sir Ralph will accede to the scheme.'

'Perhaps James will help persuade his father, when he returns from his visit to friends near Halifax,' suggested Letty.

'He may do so, for he is always kind to his stepmother in his way. Indeed, his kindness is one of his more attractive traits, though it would be more attractive were it not frequently coupled with a belief that he knows what is best for everyone to do, which he most manifestly does not.'

'But, dear Alys, men *must* know so much more ... they are so much wiser, don't you think?'

'No, I do not! And it often seems to me that James's benevolent impulses would be better directed if he asked *my* opinion first.'

'But he has persuaded his father to perform several charitable acts,' Letty protested. 'Only think of the new almshouses on the Green, for example.'

'Yes indeed, and do you recall when he had the tenants forcibly removed from their old cottages? Poor old Boswell said to me that day, 'Young master *means* well, but my family've lived in that there cottage for generations and I never thought to die nowhere else.''

'But James did it for the *best*.'

'I am sure he did, but Boswell was dead within a fortnight. *That* is what comes of misdirected good nature. I could have told him how it would be, if he would but have listened.'

CHAPTER 4

Stygian Depths

Resolutely Malvina took up the candle, descended into the lower chamber and looked about her carefully. Though bare except for a tattered arras depicting in faded colours some long-past battle, faint marks of footsteps in the thick dust led from the stair. . . .
　　　　　　　　The Travails of Lady Malvina by Orlando Browne

Her inspiration kindled afresh and her resolution strengthened by the hope of possible remuneration, Alys threw herself into her writing at every conceivable moment.

Thus it was that she carried a near-completed novel with her in her valise, as she embarked on her first visit to the nearby watering place of Harrogate in the company of Lady Basset, when the squire, having a dislike of all such places, refused to go.

How Lady Basset had endeavoured to persuade Major Weston to let his daughter accompany her, leaving only Miss Grimshaw to minister to him in her place, Alys could not imagine.

Perhaps the fact that he owed to the squire's generosity the very roof over their heads and, if not precisely the food on the table, most certainly the bottles in the cellar, may have had something to do with it.

However it was, Major Weston, fixing his daughter with a sunken and glittering eye as he reluctantly informed her of the treat, added dampeningly, 'But you need not be in too great an excitement over it, miss! The rector gives me to understand that Harrogate is a place of decorum and taste, inhabited mainly by aged valetudinarians in search of a cure for rheumatic disorders.'

That it sounded unlikely in the extreme that she would be in much danger of being carried off by a young suitor seemed to cheer him a little. Still, he forbade Alys to do anything more adventurous than attend on her aunt while she took the waters, went to church, or engaged in any other similarly innocuous pastimes. She was not to dance, or go to balls – but that would have been impossible in any case, since she did not have any suitable gowns and Lady Basset was clearly in no fit case to keep late nights.

'Oh thank you, Papa! Indeed, I will do just as Lady Basset wishes,' she promised, quite dizzy with delight, for even this, compared to the daily round that had continued with monotonous regularity for as long as she could recall, was the height of dissipation.

'You had better, for Mrs Franby has friends there, so I am bound to hear if you misbehave.' He looked at her doubtfully, then added reluctantly, 'Go to the corner cupboard and bring me the small wooden box on the middle shelf, for I suppose you had best have your mother's trinkets – trumpery stuff, but she wanted you to have them.'

'And it was the first *I* had heard of it,' Alys said, showing the little box inlaid with strange figures to Letty as soon as she had quitted her papa's chamber. 'You know how he will never talk of Mama, except to complain that my grandfather would not give her her portion once they were married, and did not even reply when informed of her death.'

Letty exclaimed over it. 'It is a very fine box – from the East, you know. I saw another such a one as a girl.'

'It is pretty, and since it was my mama's I must value it, since it is the only memento of her that I have, though I am very sure that once she must have had more jewels than these strings of glass and carnelian beads, and that Papa has sold them.'

'Perhaps there are more in the *other* compartment?' Letty suggested and, with a dextrous twist and a light pressure, she revealed a hidden cavity.

'Good heavens, Letty. I would never have known that was there.'

'Nor would I, I am sure, had I not been shown the trick of it. And look, there are one or two papers and something wrapped in a bit of silk.'

Unwrapped, the treasure trove proved to be a large and rather bizarre pendant ornament of gold, inset with a medallion encircled by seven emeralds. A sizeable and very ugly baroque pearl was suspended from it.

'Good heavens!' Letty said faintly, peering over her shoulder. 'And is that a naked man in the centre of it? Perhaps you should let me—'

'How interesting, Letty. This central part looks to be quite ancient, and I believe the figure holding a trident must be Neptune – or Poseidon, as the ancient Greeks called him.'

'Did they?'

'Yes, for I read it in some old book up at the Hall. It is just as well *some* of the Basset ancestors did not neglect the library, or my education would be sadly limited.'

'And it would be *my* fault,' cried Letty remorsefully. 'My lack of accomplishments and learning has meant that I have failed you most dismally, Alys.'

'What rubbish is this, Letty? *You* have practical skills of much more value, besides firm principles and a loving heart: what better qualifications could you have?'

Letty sniffled and dabbed at her eyes with a wisp of muslin. 'You are very kind. But I feel that any gaps in your education must be put at my door – and I do not know how I will contrive to find another situation if – when – the necessity arises. I . . . I find myself thinking about it sometimes, for though I am sure my nephew and his family would take me in, I should not like to be a burden, dependent on them for every crust.'

'We will cross that bridge when we come to it, Letty, so do not worry your head about it in the meantime,' Alys said, embracing her fondly. 'As to my education, I have gleaned what knowledge I need from books, and if there are gaps, I am not aware of them.'

'Well, it is certainly clever of you to recognize the figure on the medallion,' agreed Letty, 'and if it is Roman or Greek, I expect that explains why he is not wearing any clothes, for they do not seem to have had much idea of modesty in those times.'

'It is not done in such detail that it would make you blush anyway,' Alys said with a twinkle, holding up the ornament so that the green stones caught the light. 'The setting is not as old, do you think?'

'No, but I am sure it is a fine old piece, even if to our modern eyes it seems a trifle barbaric. I remember my dear mother telling me that men used to wear such ornaments, suspended on gold chains.'

'There is no gold chain here,' Alys said regretfully. 'Well, this is very odd, is it not? Papa can have had no notion of its existence, or I am sure he would have sold it long since. I wonder if Mama knew of it? Perhaps it is an heirloom of the Hartwoods – but if so, why should it be hidden away in Mama's jewellery box?'

'Perhaps the papers beneath it will shed some illumination on the matter?'

'Oh yes, I had forgotten those.' Alys unfolded them and read the few pages with knitted brows, before looking up. 'Well, *Mama* certainly knew about the jewel, for these are the notes Papa sent her before they eloped, which she must have hidden in here. They are very terse and unloverlike – how can she have been so easily taken in?'

'She was but seventeen when she met Major Weston, and I daresay he was very handsome then *and* in his regimentals. Besides, there is no saying but that he really loved her, Alys.'

'From what he has let fall, he loved the notion of marrying an heiress the more – he certainly can't have considered how such a sheltered young girl was unfitted to follow the drum. But, of course, his hopes came to naught.'

'And the poor lady dead of a fever not a fortnight after you were born,' Letty agreed. 'It is a great tragedy.'

'Yes, and it is quite unfair of Papa to suggest my grandfather might have come round and done something handsome for us, had I been a *boy*, not a girl,' Alys said bitterly, returning the papers to the secret compartment. Then she took a last look at the jewel before wrapping it up and popping it back on top.

'Should you not tell the major of our discovery?' Letty suggested timidly.

'Certainly not! If I did so, he would just sell it and squander the money. Besides, if it does turn out to be a family heirloom, it ought to be returned to the Hartwoods; so for the present we will keep it just as our secret – and you must look after the box until my return from Harrogate.'

'From . . . Harrogate?' Letty quavered, and Alys broke the news of her projected holiday, and the less glad tidings that her companion was to stay at home and try and fill her place during her absence.

The anticipated day of departure finally dawned and Alys put on one of the new dresses fashioned by Miss Grimshaw's nimble fingers from muslin bestowed on her by Lady Basset.

At parting the squire kindly gave her a few guineas, saying she was bound to want something to spend on feminine fal-lals in the shops there, which led her to kiss his cheek and thank him sincerely, which seemed to please him.

James was in London, or he might have escorted them, but Sir Ralph sent a manservant in his place and they set out in very good time.

It was a very easy day's journey and Lady Basset appeared to revive amazingly the very second the steps were put up and the horses given the office to start. So when Alys tentatively suggested that since they were to pass the very gates of Priory Chase, the ancestral home of the Rayvens, it would be quite *criminal* not to catch a glimpse of it, she winked conspiratorially and agreed.

Indeed, they were almost equally agog to see such a romantic place, built as it was on the site of a former abbey and reputed to have a monkish, ghostly figure haunting the original cellars running beneath the house.

The house proved to be an impressive pile built of warm, almost amber stone, but the adjacent ruins had been reduced to a crumbled and pierced wall or two. Romantic enough, Alys supposed, especially on a moonlit night, but in the broad light of day not in the least sinister.

The housekeeper came out and, informing them that none of the family was at home, kindly begged them to enter. She conducted them around the very fine public rooms, elegantly furnished and hung with portraits of tall, dark and glowering Rayven menfolk and their ringleted, simpering ladies, until finally Lady Basset declared she must rest for a while.

'While you do so, I wonder if it might be possible for me to see something of the cellars that run under the ruins of the old abbey?' asked Alys, greatly daring. 'Only I have heard so much about them.'

'I'll be bound you have, and all the young ladies are mad to see them,' the housekeeper replied indulgently. 'They think it romantic, or some such nonsense. But they come out again quickly enough, miss!'

However, she sent a servant with a lantern to conduct her through the vaulted and eerie subterranean depths of the building and Alys thought it quite delightfully atmospheric. The further they went, the danker and more interesting it became, and the more she felt the weight of the old house, constructed of stones taken from the abbey, pressing down on them. She did not see any bats or chained skeletons, of course, but the imagination of an author can supply those with the greatest facility.

She was enchanted – the lantern lit up carved faces grimacing in the corners, fluted pillars, strange stone channels, some running with water – and even the occasional large cobweb when they ventured deeper. But eventually, when the long-suffering servant seemed to be convinced that his lantern was about to go out, Alys had reluctantly to retrace her steps.

Lady Basset had been given tea and macaroons while she engaged in a long gossip with the housekeeper and looked so rosy and animated that Alys was in hopes the change of scene alone would improve her aunt's health considerably.

They set off on the last few miles of their journey and Lady Basset repeated to Alys all the details she had elicited of the fatal carriage accident that had wiped out the last Lord Rayven and his heir at one stroke, elevating Serle Rayven, member of a cadet branch of the family, so unexpectedly to title, fortune and family seat. A soldier, he had been obliged to sell out just as things were becoming eventful on the continent and return home.

This was interesting, but for her part Alys was delighted to find inspiration for the setting of her novel – and probably further novels to come – from her visit to Priory Chase. She felt she could have developed quite a taste for visiting mouldering ruins, had she freedom enough.

They bowled into High Harrogate in the late afternoon, passing an open expanse of green with people promenading upon it, one or two fine hotels – and such houses and shops as Alys had never seen in her life.

'It is a candle to the sun, compared with London,' Lady Basset said,' but the nearest I have come to civilization in many a year. I hope we are to be given a good dinner – I have been quite famished this last hour and more.'

Alys looked at her in astonishment, for she had not ceased eating sweetmeats throughout the journey, except when being shown over Priory Chase. (And even there she had consumed most of a plate of macaroons.)

In a trice they were pulling up outside their lodging, found for them through the good offices of Mrs Franby's friends, and Alys dutifully helped Lady Basset to settle into their very comfortable chambers.

Her maid began unpacking immediately, while Alys did the same for her own modest belongings in the small adjoining bedchamber. Then they changed and dined below with the other inhabitants of the house – a strange experience in itself. The long table was organized not by rank, but by seating the newest arrivals at the foot of the table – but so apparently was the custom there, and a very sensible one it seemed to Alys. She exchanged shy smiles with a fair young lady seated a little way above her, who looked to be about her own age.

Lady Basset was by now quite done-up and retired immediately afterwards, and Alys of necessity went with her, but they were to rise betimes tomorrow and take the water at the Sulphur Well.

'And after that, we will explore the shops, perhaps,' Lady Basset said, when Alys went in to say goodnight. 'We must put our names in the visitor's book, go to the library . . . perhaps even promenade in the rooms at Low Harrogate.'

'So long as you are not quite exhausted, Aunt.'

'I am sure, from what I have heard of the curative effects of the

Sulphur Well, that I will soon be quite restored to health,' Lady Basset said optimistically. 'Besides, the lady next to me at dinner was telling me of a milliner that I quite long to visit.'

Alys, still full of restless energy, abstracted two of Lady Basset's candles from the candelabrum on her mantelpiece on her way to bed, for her small chamber was much less luxuriously appointed and she feared to run out.

Then, in nightgown and shawl, she wrote long into the night, revising several passages in the light of her new experiences:

Her lantern illuminated grinning and malevolent faces carved on the crumbling stone columns of the cellar and clammy fingers brushed across her cheek. . . . She gasped, then took herself severely to task, for it was but a cobweb.

The humble spider, spinning here in solitary darkness, would not harm her. Only mortal man was to be feared, if she did not find a way to leave this place. . . .

CHAPTER 5

Villainous Appearances

The dank stone chamber had the chilliness of the tomb about it, while beneath the window the sea threw itself with stupefying violence at the base of the tower, as if trying to dash it down and consume it entirely. She could admire such a spectacle, but not draw comfort from it.
          The Travails of Lady Malvina by Orlando Browne

The next day at breakfast they made the acquaintance of Mr Pullen, an elderly gentleman who had come to Harrogate to treat his gout, bringing his granddaughter Nell, the fair girl whom Alys had noticed at dinner the previous night, to keep him company.

Mr Pullen knew Sir Ralph and seemed quite unaffected by the style and manners of the lady he had married, though Alys suspected that the circumstance of his being a trifle deaf meant that he missed some of her aunt's more vulgar utterances.

The two girls immediately struck up a friendship, though their situations could not have been more different. Nell was her grandfather's heiress and would have a London season when she turned eighteen, while Alys was destined never to be out at all – unless this brief sojourn counted as her debut.

But they soon discovered that they shared a taste for Gothic romances, and Alys confided in Nell her ambition to complete one of her own.

The days quickly fell into an agreeable pattern, consisting of morning visits to take the water at the Sulphur Well in Low Harrogate, promenading the Assembly Rooms or the gardens, and visiting the shops and libraries. As well as the Pullens they made several new acquaintances, and soon felt quite at home there, something Alys would have thought quite impossible when she first arrived.

Only one cloud marred her enjoyment of this idyll when, on their fourth visit to the Assembly Rooms, she had the misfortune to catch the eye of the new Lord Rayven.

Attired in one of the demure but modish white muslin gowns fashioned by Miss Grimshaw's clever hands, her large grey eyes sparkling and the green ribbon threaded through her curls setting off their chestnut hue to perfection, she was promenading the room with Lady Basset.

Her aunt's head-dress of purple and orange ostrich feathers and the exceedingly low décolletage of her over-trimmed gown, in combination with the flushed cheeks and slightly unsteady gait of someone who had partaken rather too liberally of the brandy before setting out, might have singled her out for comment in less mixed company. Here, however, Alys was happy to note several even greater quizzes of both sexes, including one elderly man wearing rouge, a powdered wig and spangled coat.

The musicians were striking up for a country dance at one end of the room, where Nell, squired by a portly general who had taken a fancy to her, was taking her place in the set. Alys did not envy her: it was already hot and would grow more so later as the room filled.

Looking with interest at the assembled throng, many of whom were by now familiar to her, her eyes fell upon the tall figure of a man: indeed, he was of such a height that once her eyes were turned in that direction it would have been hard to miss him.

Why, it is Raymundo Ravegnac, to the life! was her first astonished thought, for he had the black hair, sallow complexion and hawk-nosed face of her villain, though marred by a scar running down one cheek ... *and* a very sardonic expression in his dark eyes when he caught her staring.

Alys blushed and looked away instantly, though consigning that interesting scar to memory as a useful addition to Raymundo's appearance! She was determined not to turn in his direction again, but was severely discomfited when, only a few minutes later, he had himself introduced to them by the Master of Ceremonies.

After one startled, fleeting glance Alys merely curtsied, eyes averted, but Lady Basset exclaimed in delight, 'Lord Rayven? Lud, to think that we should meet you, when it was only a few days ago that we were being shown around Priory Chase by your housekeeper!'

He muttered something under his breath that Alys did not quite understand, then said with the strangest emphasis, 'Indeed? I am sorry I was not then at home, *Lady* Basset,' as if he was incredulous that she should be entitled to call herself any such thing – and when Alys saw the vulgar and flirtatious way her aunt behaved in his presence, she could hardly be surprised.

'As to that, my lord,' Lady Basset said, simpering and pretending to hide her blushes behind her fan, 'I am sure I would not have ventured to *force* myself on you, had you been at home.'

'No force would have been required to meet two such delightful visitors, I assure you,' Lord Rayven replied imperturbably.

Lady Basset continued in this vein until Alys was ready to sink from mortification, especially since she knew she had brought this ordeal on to her own head by catching his lordship's attention in the first place.

She kept her eyes downcast and refused to be drawn into the conversation, such as it was, until Lord Rayven happened to mention that he had been advised to apply the waters of the sulphur spring to a sabre cut on his arm, which was not healing as fast as it might.

'You would be better advised to pack it with cobwebs, for that is a sovereign way to promote a clean and healthy wound and fast healing. I have never known it fail,' she said decidedly, unable to resist giving her advice.

He turned to her, eyebrows raised, as if amazed to hear that she could speak at all, let alone with such directness. 'Perhaps, Miss Basset—'

'Weston. I am Miss *Weston*,' Alys interrupted. 'Lady Basset is . . . is my aunt. By marriage.'

'Miss Weston, I would gladly take your advice, but where would I obtain such a large supply of cobwebs?'

'The further reaches of your own cellars should provide a more than adequate number. My gown was quite covered in them when I came out.'

'You explored my *cellars?*'

'Indeed I did, and they are quite delightful,' Alys replied, her face rapt and her expressive, large grey eyes growing luminous with the memory. 'I am sure I have never enjoyed anything half so much in my life.'

He stared down at her, as if puzzled. 'Extraordinary,' he muttered, before Lady Basset again claimed his attention.

Alys began to wish she had disclaimed *any* relationship with Lady Basset, but to her infinite relief, after a few more moments he bowed and walked off. Alys gazed after him absently, thinking that he still looked very much the soldier he had been until so recently. There was something about the proud way he held himself and the rather military cut of the coat across his broad shoulders....

As if he felt her regard he suddenly turned his head and favoured her with a brooding, half-frowning glance, his dark-blue eyes holding hers, until her heart began to pound so much that she felt dizzy. Then he turned on his heel and strode off, leaving Alys wishing for the second time that the ground would open up and swallow her.

Lady Basset, observing this exchange, teased her on making a conquest and could talk of nothing else but his asking to be introduced to them.

'Oh no – I am sure he was merely piqued by my rudeness in staring at him,' Alys said, fervently hoping that this would be the end of the acquaintance. He looked to be several years her senior and was immeasurably above her in rank and wealth: what interest could he have in a callow miss, with no fortune, connections or even beauty?

'And Papa most expressly warned me against having anything to do with Lord Rayven, so should news reach him of this encounter, he will be extremely angry.'

'Oh, pooh!' Lady Basset said airily. 'Major Weston has no power to dictate to whom *I* may speak, and so I will tell him.'

'Well, I daresay we will not see Lord Rayven again, and there will be an end of the matter,' Alys said hopefully.

'Why? Did you not think him a fine figure of a man? You are very hard to please! He is not precisely handsome, perhaps, but very striking and of a commanding presence. I only wish I might have seen him in uniform, for I am sure I would have been in ecstasies of admiration.'

Alys could only be deeply grateful that she had not.

When the two girls were standing together later, sipping lemonade and fanning themselves, Alys described the encounter, especially the amazing coincidence of Lord Rayven's resembling her villain to a quite extraordinary degree. 'Except that I have given *my* villain brown eyes and perhaps it would be less commonplace to change them to dark blue, like his? And Lord Rayven has a scar across his cheek that would make an interestingly sinister addition, too.'

Nell agreed. 'He was pointed out to me yesterday when we were coming away from the library and he does indeed look just the part – and so tall and forbidding that it would put me in a quake to speak to him. Neither does he sound in the least agreeable.'

'Agreeable? No, he was certainly not *that* – I did not like his manner in the least, and his singling me out in such a way has made my aunt quiz me on the subject until I could scream. But I do not suppose I will ever see him again, or if I do that he will favour me with more than a common bow in passing, so she will very soon forget all about him.'

'It is a pity Lord Rayven did not turn out to be that divinely fair young man we saw the other day, getting into a post-chaise,' Nell giggled. 'Such a profile! And I wish my hair was as golden.'

'He *was* a veritable Adonis. I may have him for Malvina's betrothed, Alfonz, for if the villain is dark, the hero should be fair: equalling good and bad.'

Nell looked at her admiringly. 'You are so much cleverer than I, Alys! Pray, will you read me a little more of your novel after dinner? I swear I did not sleep for hours last night, imagining that a ghostly monk was standing over my bed!'

'Be grateful that my intention is marriage,' said Raymundo Ravegnac.

'But I am betrothed to Alfonz Montroth – he will seek my release!'

He uttered a bark of laughter that chilled Malvina to the bone. 'Do not look for rescue there! Who do you think it was who betrayed you into my hands? How came we to find your secret trysting place, if he did not lead us there?'

'How indeed?' Alys muttered as, seated at her little travelling desk, she wrote furiously into the night, both disturbed and inspired by her encounter with the sardonic and discomforting Lord Rayven.

When the candles began to gutter and she went to bed, it was to dream not of the golden youth she and Nell had so briefly glimpsed, but of a darker and more brooding presence.

CHAPTER 6

Dread Excitement

The dark shadows seemed to swoop and swirl around her head and she grew dizzy with a kind of dread excitement. 'No, my beloved Alfonz would never do such a thing,' she uttered weakly. 'I know it in my heart, for he loves me.'

The Travails of Lady Malvina *by Orlando Browne*

Alys's hopes were not realized, for Lord Rayven began to frequent Harrogate only, it seemed, in order to seek her out and tease her. Although she gave him no encouragement – indeed, she was reserved in manner to the point of rudeness – Lady Basset did all in her power to throw them together, contriving embarrassingly transparent reasons for leaving them alone.

'Do you make a long stay in Harrogate, Miss Weston?' he enquired one day, as they strolled down the street together, Lady Basset having conjured up an imaginary item of shopping she must immediately obtain and requesting his lordship to walk on towards the green with Alys.

'Two weeks only,' she replied shortly. She had had perforce to take his arm, and was very conscious of the taut muscles beneath the coat of blue superfine – and also of the glances other ladies gave his tall, broad-shouldered and striking figure as they passed.

'And do you think you will achieve your *purpose* in such a short time?' He raised a dark brow. 'That is confidence, indeed.'

Alys glanced up at him, frowning, though this did little to detract from the picture of innocent prettiness she presented in her simple sprigged muslin gown and chip straw bonnet. 'Our purpose was to see if the waters would improve Lady Basset's health – and I am happy to say that she does seem better.'

'But not your *sole* purpose, surely? You have several admirers in the town, and I am convinced that old Colonel Lamphlet is trying to fix his interest with you. He gave me such a glare at the Assembly Rooms yesterday that I was in dread of being called out for my audacity in engaging you in conversation.'

'Lord Rayven, such talk as this may amuse my aunt, but it does *not* please me,' she said forthrightly, tilting her square chin upwards so that she could look him directly in the face. 'Colonel Lamphlet was merely being gallant, and I have no thought of marriage with him or anyone else.'

'Then you are entirely singular among young ladies of my acquaintance.'

Singular, Alys thought, summed up her probable destiny more aptly than he imagined!

With all the delights on offer, the distraction of new acquaintance, and the unsought and alarming attentions of Lord Rayven, it was perhaps not surprising that the end of their short visit had just begun to beckon like a grisly, skeletal hand before Alys gave much thought to poor Letty's situation.

Though Miss Grimshaw had bravely expressed her willingness to take on her duties while she enjoyed her treat, Alys knew she dreaded it. Her soft voice irritated the major and she did not have the courage to keep any kind of control over the amount he drank, or the unsuitable foods he demanded, which would make him liverish and so lead to even more explosions of rage.

No, Alys guiltily feared Letty must be having a sad time of it, and remorsefully set out to describe at length her doings for her amusement, for other than a brief note dashed off assuring her of their safe arrival, including a description of Priory Chase, she had not written to her.

So much had happened that Alys found it hard to know where to begin, or quite how much to reveal. Sitting in her small bedchamber, she mended her pen and began:

Dear Letty
I hope Papa is not proving too great a trial in my absence, but fear you will be having a very poor time of it. Do try to be firm: a hint of weakness and he will be overpoweringly odious.

The major often reminded Alys of a wolf circling an innocent lamb in his dealings with Letty: there was something so shiftily baleful in his gaze. Still, she consoled herself that, though he might rend Letty limb from limb verbally, he was incapable of offering her much in the way of physical violence.

Our first week has flown by and the second near half over. I told you of our visit to Priory Chase on our way here, did I not? But what do you think, we have now met the owner of the property himself, and he is as like any Gothic villain as you could imagine!
  Indeed, as Malvina would say, 'With a dark, intense gaze he caused a shadow to enter her soul and she shuddered, for she knew not what reason, only that she had taken an instant and unalterable dislike to the man who stood before her . . .'

Alys paused, re-read the description, then noted the words down on another piece of paper before she forgot them, for there was no telling but that her letter might go astray. She continued:

I first caught sight of the new Lord Rayven across the promenade room in Low Harrogate, a new and exceedingly elegant building, whither we had repaired after our morning visit to the Sulphur Well. (I was wearing the white muslin with the single flounce that you made for me, with new green satin ribbons, and it was much admired.)
  The water smells like bad eggs and tastes disgusting. I had only one tiny sip the first day, but Lady Basset insists on drinking a full glass every morning, though it near makes her sick. The woman in charge

of the well expects everyone to drink out of the same horn beaker, without even washing it between, but fortunately we had been warned, and I carried Lady Basset's own glass with me in my reticule, wrapped in a clean handkerchief.

But I digress, for I was about to describe Lord Rayven to you – though apart from one detail I need only tell you that he is exactly as I have described the villain, Raymundo, in my book. I was so struck by this resemblance – his black-browed, swarthy appearance, his height and something care-for-nobody about his dress (though a scar running from the corner of one eye down his cheek is a striking difference), that I am afraid I stared rudely and he caught me.

Alys blushed again in mortification even at the memory of that moment.

Oh Letty, I was covered with shame! Up went those eyebrows and, fixing me with a piercing gaze from deep-set, dark-blue eyes, he bowed slightly with a sardonic smile. Of course I looked away, quite hideously embarrassed.

I have already added that scar to Raymundo Ravegnac's appearance, though presumably Lord Rayven won his honourably in some battle, for he only recently sold out of the army. He also mentioned another cut to his arm, which is not healing so well, and I advised a cobweb poultice, which I am sure you will agree is the best remedy.

Some moments later, imagine my feelings when he had himself introduced to us! It threw Lady Basset into a perfect flutter.

I did not care for his manner, for something in his conversation and expression made me feel – like poor Malvina – rather uncomfortable. He looks to be somewhat less than thirty and I must admit that he is, if not handsome, very striking. I expect he looked even more so in his regimentals.

Lady Basset was so taken with him that she turned embarrassingly flirtatious, so that I knew not where to look. Her manners leave much to be desired when away from home, especially when gentlemen are present, but at least the company is very mixed here in Harrogate, so that until this occasion I had felt no real need to blush for my relationship with her.

She spared Letty the more mortifying elements, such as the way her Aunt tapped his lordship's knuckles with her fan and giggled if he said anything that could be remotely construed as warm, and telling him that he was a 'naughty creature'.

She tried to draw me into the conversation with his lordship, but I stayed quiet – you may be surprised to learn! – annoyed at having drawn his attention in the first place by my rude staring.

Lady Basset told him of our visit to Priory Chase. He said he was sorry to have been absent for it, but then muttered something under his breath about 'times changing since he was last in England', and 'Abbesses bringing their wares to market', that I could not understand: I do not think Priory Chase was ever a nunnery, was it?

Soon after I had given him my advice regarding the wound to his arm, to my infinite relief he bowed and walked off; but all the old tabbies of the town – including a crony of the rector's wife – were agog.

I have since begged Lady Basset not to encourage the acquaintance in any way, but he now rides or drives into Harrogate every afternoon, so our paths must cross in such a small a place. Besides, he seems to delight in seeking me out and trying to tease a few words out of me, even though I give him no encouragement. I daresay the tale will eventually reach Papa's ears and I only hope he does not have an apoplexy for he would be averse to any man singling me out, and this is the very person he warned me to avoid.

Lady Basset is harbouring the ridiculous notion that his lordship has taken a fancy to me, but my belief is that he is piqued by my lack of interest in him, and amusing himself only. Perhaps, too, after the excitements of army life, he finds being a mere viscount sadly flat! He would be better off in learning to manage his newly inherited estates, for I am sure there must be much to occupy him there.

Lady Basset keeps me so busy here that I have had little time to write except in the late evenings when she has retired; but then, there will be time enough for those amusements when I am home, for once Papa hears of Lord Rayven I am convinced he will never let me out of his sight again.

By the way, I have also espied a veritable Adonis – an exceedingly handsome young man with guinea-gold hair and eyes of the purest cerulean blue – who will make the perfect hero, though unfortunately he remains unknown to me. I saw him but once from afar, mounting into a postchaise at one of the inns.

My aunt's manners may not be all one could wish for, but her heart is good, and she has bestowed many gifts of stockings, gloves and other knick-knacks on me, with great kindness. We visit the library daily, where such small purchases may be made, and I have laid out a little of my uncle's gift in a present for you, as some small reward for keeping the ogre happy in his den in my absence. But let its nature be a surprise until my return.

Lady Basset's health seems much improved, and her colour is good. Whether that is the water, or merely a change of scene and company, I leave to you to decide.

I must go – she is calling me, for we are to make an excursion to Knaresborough to see the Dripping Well, with Mr Pullen and his granddaughter Nell, who is near my own age. I believe I mentioned them in my last note to you? Nell and I have struck up a friendship, which as you can imagine has enhanced the happiness of my stay in Harrogate.

Your affectionate Alys

'Alys!' called Lady Basset again.

'Coming, Aunt.' She sealed the letter with a coloured wafer and put it into her reticule, then tied the strings of a chip bonnet freshly trimmed with pink roses and dove-grey satin ribbons into a jaunty bow under her chin and ran down the stairs.

She was looking forward eagerly to the excursion for this was one day when she could enjoy herself without fear of Lord Rayven's sardonic presence or his deep voice in her ear, drawling the sort of near-insolent remarks the responses to which she had not been taught by Miss Grimshaw.

Nell and Alys, under the indulgent eyes of their elders, were merry as grigs all the way to Knaresborough.

CHAPTER 7

Taking the Waters

Raymundo fixed his burning, dark-blue orbs on Malvina's white and anguished countenance.

'Be mine, or this chamber will be your tomb, for there is but one way out – and that will be sealed, if you do not give me the answer I desire by the morrow.'

The Travails of Lady Malvina by Orlando Browne

Mr Pullen stayed in the carriage when they reached Knaresborough, warmly wrapped in a travelling rug and with the newspaper to amuse him, while the rest of the party went to view the Dripping Well.

They were fascinated by the strange array of objects hung there to petrify in the water and, in exchange for a few coins, an elderly man told them the history of the well, and pointed out some of the more interesting items.

'Were my cousin James here, I expect he could have lectured us at great length on the scientific explanation of the phenomenon,' Alys commented to Nell. 'I am so glad he is not!'

'Is Mr Basset of a scientific turn of mind?'

'He thinks he is, but in reality his understanding is no more than moderate.'

'Have you seen enough, girls?' Lady Basset enquired. 'Shall we take a turn along the river-bank before returning to the carriage? There seems to be quite a pretty walk there and I believe the rain will hold off a while yet.'

Alys was surprised, since her aunt did not in general care for exercise, but she and Nell were very happy to accompany her even at Lady Basset's dawdling pace.

They were enjoying the lovely prospect and the fresh air until Nell, happening to look round, espied a tall figure dressed for riding in breeches, topboots and a blue cut-away coat, striding rapidly towards them.

'Alys, look – it is Lord Rayven!' she exclaimed, clutching her friend's arm. 'What can *he* be doing here?'

'*What* indeed,' Alys said drily, for it could be no mere coincidence that brought him to this exact spot. Glancing suspiciously at her aunt, Alys surprised a momentary gleam of complacency on her face, before she greeted his lordship with expressions of surprised pleasure, which he met with a raised eyebrow and a sardonic bow.

Nell made a frightened schoolgirl's bob and Alys dropped him the slightest of curtsies before turning to Lady Basset and saying, 'Aunt, it looks increasingly like rain, perhaps we should be making our way back to the carriage? I am sure Mr Pullen will be wondering what has become of us.'

Nell, who always seemed to be struck dumb with terror in the vicinity of his lordship, squeezed her arm gratefully, but Lady Basset appeared to be about to disagree. Then one or two large drops of rain darkened the dusty path and she changed her mind, especially when she recalled that she was wearing her best bonnet. 'Perhaps we had better turn back, girls, after all,' she agreed reluctantly.

'In that case, perhaps I may be permitted to escort you to your carriage?' Lord Rayven suggested, clearly not a man to recognize a snub, and Lady Basset agreed with unbecoming alacrity. Somehow she manoeuvred it so that she walked on ahead with Nell, whose pace she declared suited her own, so that Alys had perforce to take his lordship's arm and follow on behind.

'Let us admire this admirable vista for a moment or two,' he said, restraining her when she would have set off immediately after the others. 'Or rather, let me admire you, for I had not believed until today that grey could be so becoming. Your spencer and ribbons are the exact clear shade as your very beautiful eyes. Besides, this is the first opportunity I have had to speak to you entirely alone and uninterrupted – let us not waste it.'

To her annoyance she felt herself blush at the compliment and looked about nervously, but other than the slowly receding figures of her aunt and Miss Pullen, could see no other visitors, even though there had been several earlier at the well. They were all alone under a leaden and threatening sky.

She looked up doubtfully at Lord Rayven and for just one moment the incredulous idea that he might be about to propose to her crossed her mind. Then it was as quickly dismissed: he had been attentive enough since their first meeting, it was true, but not in any lover-like way.

'Sir, there is nothing you need say to me that cannot be said before others,' she said firmly. 'Besides, the sky grows darker every minute and I am sure we are in for a downpour: I would prefer to return to the carriage *immediately*.'

'Demure as a nun's hen to the last!' he said, with a curl of his lip. 'But come, Miss Weston, you do not need to pretend to me to be anything other than what you are, and I think you and I could get on very well without the excellent *Lady* Basset.'

Alys tried – and failed – to remove her hand from his arm, for he put his other hand over it and held it firmly. 'I do not know why you always refer to my aunt in that sneering way.'

'Come, you know she is no more a lady than that mallard over there! That she has been an actress is writ plain all over her.'

'She was an actress before her marriage, but I am sure that is not a criminal offence!' Alys said tartly.

He looked down at her and smiled, a glint of admiration in his dark-blue eyes. 'You play the part of reluctant innocent so admirably that, were it not for your companion, I would perhaps have been taken in like a green 'un.'

Finally managing to pull her arm from his grasp with a great wrench, Alys turned, backing away a little and stared at him – or rather, up at him, since he was of commanding build and towered over her, even though she was above the average height.

'Sir, I do not understand your meaning, but I find the *tone* of your remarks offensive, and your manner ungentlemanly!'

'Bravo! Like *Lady* Basset, you were clearly cut out for the stage, my dear. Such big, soulful eyes and demure air.' He kissed his fingers and smiled at her in a most discomfiting way. 'A very prime article, indeed.'

'Lord Rayven,' she began again uncertainly, for in her limited experience no man had ever said such things to her and she was unsure what he meant – or, indeed, how to extricate herself. 'I would like to return to my aunt *at once*.'

'Oh, *very* good!' he applauded. 'And perhaps the bargain should be struck with her, but I thought we would deal better together, gloves off.' He moved closer and said in a low, intimate voice, 'Come, what do you say? I must return to London tomorrow on urgent business: if you go with me I will set you up in prime style in your own little establishment and, provided you do not share your favours while under my protection, you will find me generous in all ways.'

'Return to London with you ... little establishment?' Her head reeled as she stared blankly at him.

'Yes, you are a pretty little thing, and would cut quite a dash in fine gowns and jewels,' he suggested, insinuating a muscular arm about her slim waist and pulling her closer. 'I am sure your object in coming to Harrogate was to inveigle some old gentleman into marriage and I daresay with a little more encouragement Colonel Lamphlet would oblige, but take it from me, you would have much more fun in London under my protection. Come, let us seal the bargain!'

The hard, sure pressure of his kiss awoke her from a horrified trance as illumination finally dawned and, recalling half-understood passages from the letters of her aunt's worldly friend, Lady Crayling, the precise nature of the offer he was making her suddenly became clear.

Furious outrage flooded her veins in a molten, invigorating rush, and she thrust him away from her with such a mighty and most unladylike shove that it caught him entirely unawares and off-balance.

Staggering back, the heel of his boot caught the twisted root of an importunate willow, causing him to fall with an almighty splash into the river. A great cascade of displaced water suddenly shot into the air and then rained down on a gaggle of ducks, who fled, quacking indignantly.

It was fortunate that at this point the river was quite shallow. Alys stared, transfixed, as Lord Rayven slowly rose to his feet like a modern day Neptune, his wet jacket and breeches clinging modishly, if immodestly, to his admirable form. It was a vision that reminded her forcibly of the jewelled figure of a sea god she had found in her mama's jewellery box.

Damp tendrils of black hair clung to his brow, and he had an indescribable look on his face, as several conflicting emotions tried to express themselves at once: incredulity, anger, and amusement all vied together.

Amusement seemed to win. Laughing, he emptied the water out of his hat, flourished it as he bowed deeply, then, with a measuring look in his eyes that she feared boded her ill, began to wade back to the shore.

The spell of horrified fascination broke: picking up her muslin skirts she ran for dear life along the river-bank, towards the safety of the carriage.

There was no sound of pursuit, and though she looked back once, there was no sign of him, so she presumed he had thought better of whatever devilish impulse she'd seen in his eyes and had ridden straight home.

He would be, if possible, even wetter by the time he got there, for it came on to rain heavily just as Alys reached the carriage. This was fortunate, since her lame explanations for her solitary return, blazing cheeks and distracted manner were overlooked in hastening to a nearby inn, where they could shelter while taking refreshment.

Alys felt it a deep pity that a lady – especially a young lady – could not call for the brandy. And it was even more of a pity that she had not pushed Lord Rayven into the Dripping Well, where he could be hung, petrified, among all the other items, like an awful warning of what could befall so-called gentlemen who grossly insulted innocent maidens.

Lord Rayven, still grinning, waded out of the river and looked admiringly after Alys's rapidly diminishing figure, white skirts fluttering. Her gown did not seem to impede her in the least: he had not thought any young lady could run so fast.

And lady she had undoubtedly proved to be, despite being paraded about the town – and even brought to his very house! – by a woman who seemed little better than an abbess showing off her wares. If Miss Weston had been puzzlingly quiet and self-possessed, using no arts to attract other than those nature had supplied by way of beautiful and expressive grey eyes and glossy chestnut curls, he had thought it all part of their plan.

Something crackled underfoot and he picked up a letter, which she must have dropped. It was addressed to a Miss Grimshaw and, in addition to being slightly marred by the muddy imprint of his boot heel, the wafer that had sealed it was broken.

He hesitated a moment, before giving in to curiosity and opening it, hoping that it might give him some insight into Miss Weston's real character . . . which it did. It most *certainly* did.

It also showed him that, even without his crass error, she held him in unalterable dislike, comparing him with the villain in some trumpery novel she was playing at writing.

When he looked up, the flying figure had vanished beyond a turn in the pathway.

CHAPTER 8

Stormy Weather

'But I would help you escape this villainous lecher, for brother I will no longer call him,' Cornelio exclaimed, throwing himself at her feet. 'My desire for you, Cousin, arises only from love, and not from any hope of material gain. Come with me now, or regret this day forever!'

The Travails of Lady Malvina *by Orlando Browne*

When they had returned to their lodgings and were alone, Alys gave her aunt an edited explanation of what had happened.

Lady Basset was horrified, mortified and indignant by turns on her behalf, fully concurring in Alys's urgent desire to leave Harrogate immediately, if only so she could dragoon the squire into calling Lord Rayven out for his insults.

However, she calmed down overnight and after breakfast, which Alys had little appetite for, said she thought Lord Rayven would have passed the incident off as an unfortunate accident, should anyone have happened to notice it, since the truth would make him appear ridiculous. 'And it was lucky the threat of rain drove the other visitors away, so the scandal-mongers will not get to hear of it.'

'No, I do not believe anyone saw what happened, and cannot imagine that he would tell anyone of it.'

'I expect he has realized his error, Alys. How he came to be under such a dreadful misapprehension I *cannot* understand.'

Of course, Alys, not wishing to hurt Lady Basset's feelings, did not in any way suggest that her manners and dress were such as to have helped lead him to false conclusions. But when alone, she could not help but go over and over the scene, wondering if there was also something lacking in *herself*, to have invited such an insult?

But when Alys confided the whole to Nell, her friend assured her that there was nothing about her that would lead any man to think her other than a respectable girl. Then she pointed out that at least Alys need never see his lordship again, whereas *she* might very well run into him in town when she went there next season.

Somehow, this did not console Alys as much as it might.

But at least she had by now realized that the expression in his eyes when, dripping wet, he had saluted her, was both amusement *and* admiration . . . though of course the admiration of such a man was of no consequence to her whatsoever, that went without saying.

They elicited the information that his lordship had indeed left for London, and it was decided that they should continue their stay until the original departure date, rather than raise questions and conjecture by decamping abruptly. Lady Basset slowly persuaded herself that the whole incident never happened, or was but an accident, though her manner was somewhat subdued for the remainder of their sojourn in Harrogate.

In all the turmoil of emotion stirred up by this drama, Alys had not missed her letter: indeed, she had entirely forgotten about it until she received a note from Miss Grimshaw thanking her for it, and looking forward to her return.

It was a puzzle to her what had become of it, but she presumed she must have dropped it in the street and some kindly disposed person had sent it on.

The morning of their departure came, and how deeply sorry Alys was to part with her new friend. Nell felt the same, but they promised to correspond.

'You are to be my window on the big, wide world, Nell,' Alys said, embracing her as the last of Lady Basset's numerous bandboxes was carried out, 'for it is not to be supposed that I will ever travel anywhere again, so that I will relish every little detail.'

'And *you* must tell me how Malvina's adventures end, for I am quite desperate to know,' Nell returned. 'Only think how exciting it will be when it is published, and I know the author – though, of course, I will not admit it to *anyone*.'

'*If* I get it published – and then my real name must certainly stay a secret.'

Alys let down the window and waved her handkerchief for as long as she could still see her friend. Then she settled back opposite her aunt and, with her writing desk on her knees, beguiled the journey home by writing down all her impressions of her dealings with Lord Rayven as best she could, while they were still fresh in her mind.

The experience had at once angered, excited, alarmed and confused her, especially the realization that he had found her attractive, but not worthy of an honourable love. Then too, the emotions raised by being held fast in his arms and kissed so thoroughly proved hard to describe – and impossible to forget. Sometimes she fancied she felt the hard pressure of his lips on hers still. . . .

But though his tall, dark and romantically scarred person had certainly disturbed her dreams since the encounter, in them he was always the villain of the piece.

All these new experiences, mortifying though they might be, would at least enhance *The Travails of Lady Malvina*, for she felt she had gained a maturity and insight into the perfidy of the male character – as opposed to its ingrained selfishness, which she already knew all about – that she had lacked when she began the book.

At least now she had purchased her own supply of paper – for not only on fashionable trifles and a length of pretty lace for Letty, had the squire's guineas been expended.

Alys scribbled away while Lady Basset snored in her corner, exhausted by supervizing the packing of her many purchases, which threatened to engulf them at every jolt of the carriage.

'Sir,' Malvina said resolutely, though she shivered from cold and terror, 'I fear that you, too, have some motive of your own in seeking to remove me from this place to another fastness. My mind is made up, and I will not go with you. . . .'

They arrived back home in the midst of a furious thunderstorm, which was nothing, Alys discovered, to her papa's mood. He had received the whole tale of Lord Rayven's attentions from the rector, who was as much a gossip in his sanctimonious way as his wife.

Alys had barely put off her bonnet before her papa was pounding on the floor with his stick and shouting for her to come up, and when she did so she was quite afraid that he might have an apoplexy, his thin face was so suffused with rage.

'Did I not specifically order you to have nothing to do with the son of Hugo Rayven, who was the means of fleecing me out of as snug a little property as you could please?'

Alys stared at him. 'He *did*? This is the first I heard of it, for I always thought you had your way to make in the world, apart from a very small fixed income, and lived on your officer's pay and prize money, Papa.'

'Aye, so I did, till my father died.'

'Then how did this Lord Rayven's father fleece you out of your inheritance?'

'Loaded dice!' he said triumphantly, and fell back against the pillows.

While she knew that Major Weston had been a gamester, she did not know whether to believe him about the cheating. But she *did* sincerely regret the snug little property, which would have greatly added to their comfort – though if he had not lost it to Hugo Rayven, she supposed he would have gamed it away to someone else long since.

'And *this* is the man you have been flirting with!' Major Weston began again, feverishly lifting his head and fixing her with an angrily burning gaze from his one good eye. 'And, for all I know, plotting to run away with, behind my back!'

'I did no such thing, Papa – in fact, I did all that I could to discourage him.'

'Ha!' said the major. 'You think because I am tied by the leg in this accursed place that I know nothing of what you have been doing.'

'Well, if you heard that I had been flirting with Lord Rayven, or anyone else, you were misinformed,' she said calmly, 'so pray do not get into a fuss.'

But it was evident that she would never be allowed to go to

Harrogate – or anywhere else – again. As long as her papa lived she would continue here in genteel poverty, dwindling into an old maid. She had always known it was to be her lot, but now firmly put away romantic dreams she had scarce known she was harbouring – until that moment of supreme disillusionment by the river-bank.

After her papa's demise she could probably continue at the Dower House, under the squire or his heir's sufferance, in reduced circumstances – indeed, if the major continued to sell out his small capital as he had begun to, *exceedingly* reduced circumstances.

Or she might seek a post as a companion, but governessing was not an option open to her, since she was sadly deficient in such skills as Italian and the use of the globes.

Her future prospects seemed so infinitely dreary that she quite shocked Letty, to whom she had by now told the whole sorry tale of her encounters with Lord Rayven, by joking that a life of sin was beginning to have some attractions in comparison.

But there just *might* be another alternative open to her: that of supporting herself, and dear Letty, of course, by her pen. She began to apply herself to her writing with renewed vigour, polishing and reworking her prose until it was as perfect as she could make it.

Then the book was dispatched to Thomas Grimshaw in London, who agreed to undertake the task of interesting a publisher in it. Should he manage to do so, Letty was of the opinion that he would also drive a hard bargain on her behalf . . . or rather, that of Orlando Browne, for much though Alys would have liked to have seen her own name in print, she had absolutely no intention of telling Papa, should her writing meet with success.

'But if my nephew is fortunate enough to place the novel with a publisher, surely *then* you must tell the major?' Letty suggested timidly, when informed of her decision.

'Most definitely not,' Alys said decidedly. 'Should I receive any moneys for my work, then what is the point of turning them over to my father? He would only hasten *his* end, and *our* poverty, by drinking them away!'

'But, dear Alys, to deceive he who must legally have the right to—'

'He has the right to *nothing*, for he is incapable of thinking of anyone other than himself. What he doesn't know, won't hurt him –

and just think, Letty, if this novel "takes", then I will immediately write another, and another . . . and it will be all invested to support us once Papa goes to meet his Maker.'

'Us?' questioned Letty hopefully. 'You – you mean that you would want me to remain as your companion, Alys?'

'Yes of course – how would I go on without you to bear me company and lend me respectability?'

There was the sound of a pistol shot, a crashing of glass and an almost demonic howl of triumph from the garden, and they exchanged a speaking look.

'Perhaps you are right, after all,' Letty conceded. 'And we may trust Thomas to keep your secret and invest any money wisely for you.'

'Let us not count our chickens before they are hatched,' Alys said, though in her heart she was still buoyed up with the confidence of the tyro, and sure that *Malvina* would be not only published, but also an *immediate* success.

And if all her future villains turned out to be tall, dark, hawk-nosed men, prone to seizing the heroine in a rough embrace and pressing passionate kisses upon their unwilling lips – well, it was hardly to be surprised at.

CHAPTER 9

Life on the Page, 1809-1812

Malvina pushed aside the veil of ivy and stepped out into the moonlight. Freedom, at last! Yet before her, as far as the eye could see, lay a wild and craggy vista.
The Travails of Lady Malvina by Orlando Browne

No sooner had Alys completed and dispatched her first novel, than she was searching around for a subject for the next, and inspiration came in the unlikely form of James Basset.

He had been sitting with them for quite half an hour prosing on about Celestial Bodies, but now through a rain-smeared window she watched him ride away on his stout cob, as unromantic a figure of a young man as could be. Yet, if she half-closed her eyes and used a little imagination, how transformed he might become?

'Letty, what if James were really a villain,' she suddenly suggested, 'and Sir Ralph banished him to the plantation on Antigua, because of his scandalous wrongdoings?'

Miss Grimshaw's mouth dropped open, making her look like a half-witted sheep. 'A – a villain? But James is not – he could not – indeed, he is the most *proper* young man!'

'Just *pretend* it, Letty – this is a book, not real life.'

She took a hasty turn or two around the little parlour, eyes aglow with excitement. 'So, off he goes to Antigua where he ensnares an innocent and beautiful heiress. Then, on hearing of his father's death, he brings her back to his half-ruined and picturesquely remote castle.'

'But Sidlington Hall is not a castle, or *very* remote.'

Alys said patiently, 'But in my book it *will* be a castle, neglected and dank, with guttering torches along gloomy passages, dungeons, cellars and huge cavernous chimneys that howl like the voices of the dead whenever the wind blows, and—'

'Oh stop, stop!' begged Letty, her eyes round as saucers. 'I declare, I don't know where you get your terrifying ideas from in the least.'

Mary came in for the teatray and surveyed the empty plate with disgust. 'Has that great lummock etten all the cheese straws? You'd think they never fed him, up t'Hall.'

'Appearances are against him,' Alys said with a smile. 'He will bid fair to rival Lady Basset for corpulence very soon, if he goes on at this rate.'

'Eh, if I wasn't forgetting.' Mary dipped her hand into her apron pocket: 'Saul's brought this back for you, Miss Alys.'

'Oh, a letter from Nell!' She opened it eagerly, for although her friend's descriptions of her London debut sometimes made her feel quite restless, they also provided a window on to a glittering and entirely different world.

When she had read and re-read it several times, she sat down to answer it:

Dear Nell

I am indeed grateful that despite all the distractions and gaieties of your first London season, you still find the time to write to me.

While I relished every detail of your descriptions, I was particularly interested in that of Lord Byron, who sounds to me as if he would blend very easily into my notions of a villain, which as you know are to date all based entirely on Lord Rayven. And whilst we are on the subject of the infamous viscount, I am not at all surprised that he is viewed as such an eligible parti, *since he has inherited a title, great estate, a town house and presumably a fortune. But I am exceedingly amazed that he should come bang up to you at a rout, and have the insufferable insolence to ask after me! He cannot have known that I told you the whole tale of our encounter by the river in*

Knaresborough — though unless you have learnt to hide your blushes since we met, I daresay he has guessed as much now.

It was the most amazingly fortuitous circumstance, dear Nell, that you fell in love instantly with the very man already chosen for you by your family and whom you were determined to dislike. He sounds very amiable and handsome, and altogether quite good enough to marry my only friend, and so I wish you very happy.

I hear from Mr Thomas Grimshaw, who is handling my business affairs — how grand that sounds! — that the Minerva Press have rushed forward publication day and intend to puff off *Malvina* in the newspapers at any moment. I do not expect much notice will be taken of it — but still, I find it all vastly exciting and look forward to the day when I can hold the published volumes in my hands.

Your affectionate friend,
Alys

'Through the dark cellars Liliana stumbled, praying to the Lord to deliver her from the foul designs of Lord Rothskent. . . .' read Alys, in thrilling accents.

'I've never heard of anyone called Liliana,' Miss Grimshaw commented mildly, looking up from her bottomless mending basket. 'Where did you get the name from?'

'I don't know — it just popped into my head. Anyway, that is all beside the point: does *The Captive Bride of Castle Grismort* not curdle your blood?'

'Oh yes indeed, it is quite deliciously ghastly and gruesome. Do carry on and read me some more, Alys.'

'There is not much more to read. I must get on and try and finish it while my name — or rather, that of Orlando Browne — is still fresh on everyone's lips.'

Dear Nell
I am quite taken aback by what you say, for I did not expect Malvina to make such a stir, nor that people would notice Lord Rayven's resemblance to the villainous Raymundo Ravegnac. Not that he doesn't deserve it after insulting me so grossly, and he will never guess who the author is, thank goodness.

I suppose society must talk about something other than Bonaparte's encroachments and the poor King's state of health, and it might as well be my novel. If it is a great success and sells many copies, who knows how much money Mr Grimshaw may secure for The Captive Bride of Castle Grismort, *which is already well advanced.*

I will be glad of every last little detail you can provide about my maternal relatives. If my grandfather is very disagreeable, which is just what I expected from the way he behaved in casting off my mother, then Mrs Lavinia Hartwood, my great-uncle's widow, sounds pleasant enough. I am sorry that her daughter is still in the schoolroom, or you might have described her, too. I will just have to make do with the son – and you wax so lyrical on the subject of Nathaniel Hartwood, Nell, that had your heart not been so securely claimed by another, I would accuse you of having a decided tendre *for him. That he should also turn out to be the same handsome, fair man we saw so briefly in Harrogate, too! The world of the* ton *is indeed a small one.*

Your Aunt Becky is quite right in counselling you to have nothing to do with Lady Crayling – I could not sully your ears with half the things she writes to Lady Basset.

My warmest congratulations on your betrothal to Mr Rivers. He has been very frank and open with you about his rather wild youth, and earnest in his assurances that all that was behind him, but I do not suppose your grandfather would have promoted the match otherwise.

He is quite right in saying that he does not deserve you, dear Nell, but I feel sure of your future happiness.

Your affectionate friend,
Alys

Serle, Viscount Rayven, read the last chapter of The Travails of Lady Malvina with fascinated horror, then laid down the book and stared into space.

He had been told that the villain of the novel was his speaking likeness, and eventually curiosity had caused him to see for himself. He supposed Raymundo Ravegnac's appearance was not unlike his own, but there was no resemblance at all – he hoped! – to his own character.

He flicked back through the last pages: had it really been necessary to eviscerate Raymundo in such a gory and melodramatic way? Had he not already been punished enough for the assaults on the heroine's person, mainly through the resourceful inventiveness of Malvina herself? And the fierce way she had pushed him into a ravine in the previous chapter. . . .

He was reminded all at once of his encounter with Miss Weston in Knaresborough, when she had taken practical – and sudden – measures to dampen his ardour. And the letter she had dropped, in which she had said that he was the very likeness of the villain of some tale she was writing . . . though had she *named* that villain? It was too long ago to remember with any certainty.

No, the idea was too ludicrous! With a laugh he tossed the book aside: he must be mad to even suspect that any respectable young lady could be the author of such stuff – and in rejecting his advances so forcefully, respectable she had proved herself to be.

Dear Nell
Or perhaps I should now address you as Mrs Rivers? I am glad that the Lakes lived up to your expectations.

Yes, do send me Mrs More's Coelebs in Search of a Wife, *though I have no expectation of its being anything other than sober and worthy.*

Grismort is near completion and the Minerva Press are to reprint my first novel already, and are pressing me for the new one, so things go well. I do not have any difficulty in keeping my writing from Papa, since he stays mainly in his bedchamber, but Letty is in a continual quake lest someone discover who Orlando Browne is.

Lady Basset adored The Travails of Lady Malvina. *She rarely now leaves her room, for she has put on so much weight that she needs two stout servants to assist her to her feet.*

Papa is following the news of our army's movements in the newspapers and thinks he could order it all so much better himself, had he been in charge.

Your affectionate friend,
Alys

Dear Nell

I do not know what I would do without your letters, especially since the sudden sad demise of Lady Basset who, despite any little shortcomings of manner and taste, was always kind and generous to me.

I expect you will see copies of Grismort before ever I do. Lady Mallorie's Secret proceeds slowly, but I must press on, for who knows how long the vogue for such novels will last? You asked what Lady Mallorie's Secret was, and in strictest confidence it is that she is not a widow, as she pretends, but a wife fleeing with her child from a brutal and drunken husband, who married her for her fortune:

'He looked at her, and she saw at once the calculating monster hidden beneath the mask of seeming amiability and affection and was repelled.

How could she ever have been deceived in her husband's character?'

There, is that not shocking? The vile husband will recapture her, but then I fear I intend to commit murder, in order to permit her to be happy thereafter.

Your affectionate friend,
Alys

Dearest Nell

I was so sorry to hear of your disappointment, and I know it is of no consolation to say that you are very young yet, and there is plenty of time to start your family. I do so wish I was near enough to visit.

It was delightful to see you when you stopped here on your way to visit friends last month. Mr Rivers, in agreeing to make a detour of several miles just so you could spend an hour with an old friend, shows a generous and amiable disposition.

How sad the news of the King's illness is – and how shall we go on? Prince George sounds sadly profligate and, if it is not treasonable to say so, of a flibberty-gibbet character.

Your affectionate friend,
Alys

Dear Nell

It is quite decided – Thomas Grimshaw is to invest the money from my writing in the little house in Hans Town, and let it out. I count myself very fortunate to have the assistance of so trustworthy a young man – and also one who can drive a hard bargain, for I never thought to receive such sums of money for my novels. You would be quite shocked if you knew how much he attained for Lady Mallorie's Secret.

Poor Papa continues to deteriorate, so I only hope my novels carry on selling in large numbers. Thomas is of the opinion that Orlando Browne's name is now made. *I have attempted several false starts at a new book – the ideas seem to jostle in my head, then come to nothing.*

I had thought Prince George would immediately change the government for the worse once he became Regent, but from what you say, he has not done any such thing. Wiser counsels may yet prevail!

Your affectionate friend,

Alys

Dear Nell

Some quite astounding news – and funny, too, I suppose, if only the consequences had not been so unfortunate, for I have received an offer of marriage. Yes, you may stare – and so did I, when my cousin James suddenly conceived a fancy for me!

You could have bowled me over with a feather and, of course, I said no immediately and told him that my feelings for him were, and could only remain, sisterly. But he seemed unable to believe that his suit was not acceptable to me. Sir Ralph was enraged, for he had long intended that James marry our nearest neighbour's daughter when she is of age, and Papa, of course, was too much afraid of losing his patronage to show approval of the match.

Anyway, the upshot is that James is to be sent off to Antigua, where the family has an estate, and is expected to marry our neighbour's daughter on his return, which is alarmingly like the plot of Grismort *– except that James, of course, is not a villain.*

I am rather out of favour with the squire and Papa said it was clear to him that I was a cunning minx, like my mother, which seems an unkind thing to say of one who gave up everything dear to her in order to run away and marry him.

My new novel, Ravish'd by Cruel Fate, proceeds slowly, since Papa is ever frailer and more demanding. If he is not constantly watched he attempts to get out of bed, and often raves of enlisting to fight, though whether against America or Boney is unclear.

I found Byron's first cantos of Childe Harold quite scandalously thrilling, and only hope he may continue with them!
Your affectionate friend,
Alys

Dear Nell
A hasty note in reply to yours, for Papa has suffered a seizure after the rector stupidly mentioned the Prime Minister's assassination during one of his visits. The doctor has been, and thinks that the effects will pass off in time, but at present everything is at sixes and sevens.

Reading between the lines of your recent letters, I am convinced that something has occurred to render you less blissfully happy than formerly. Perhaps you fear that in taking up again with his old friends, your husband may slip back into the wild ways of his youth? But reflect that he is an older and wiser man now. Also, did you not tell me that Nat Hartwood, whom you like, is one of his particular friends?

I hope that you will confide in one who is ever your sincere friend,
Alys

'I could see that the rector thought it quite shocking that we should not be in mourning for Sir Ralph,' Letty said, as they sat in the parlour listening to Mr Franby's ponderous footsteps ascending the stairs to the invalid's chamber.

'But it would be impossible to keep the news from Papa if we did so and he has been so frail of late that the least shock could carry him off. Mr Franby must be able to see that for himself.'

'How goes your letter to your cousin?'

'I think it is almost finished – I will read it to you:

> *My dear cousin James*
>
> *It is with deep regret that I must inform you of the demise of your poor father, although this letter may cross with one from Sir Ralph's man of business, who has also written to break the news and bid you hasten home from Antigua.*
>
> *Sir Ralph's new young hunter came down with him at that tricky wall and ditch near Three Acres wood. He did not suffer, for his neck was broken in the fall.*
>
> *We have kept the news from Papa so far, since the seizure he suffered last year has left him very weak and we fear the effect on his health of losing his cousin, only friend and benefactor.*
>
> *Miss Grimshaw asks me to add her condolences to mine. Pray give our respects to your wife, whom we both look forward to welcoming to her new home. Tell her that I have had the servants thoroughly clean the Hall in readiness for her arrival, and ordered the furniture put into Holland covers. Since your mother died they have grown sadly lax, but do not fear: I intend to take charge now.*

'Poor Lady Basset! I fear we miss her sadly,' Letty said, her weak blue eyes resting mistily for a moment on Pug's plump form, prone and stertorous on a cushion.

Alys sighed. 'How quickly life changes – first Lady Basset and now Sir Ralph.'

'Mary says death always comes in threes.'

'Servants' superstition, Letty! Besides, Lady Basset has been dead these two years and more.'

'Well, I am sure I hope James's wife will prove to be as much a friend to us as his mother was, Alys.'

'Dear Letty, you are friend and companion enough for me,' Alys said affectionately, then laid down her pen. 'You know, the rector is paying rather more than his usual brief visit to Papa, for it must be quite a quarter of an hour since he—'

There was a clattering on the stairs and then the door burst open and Mary rushed in, her cap askew. 'Eh, Miss Alys, you'd best come straight away, for Rector's gone and told master about poor Sir Ralph and it's sent him in t'such a fit he's like to die!'

'Tell Saul to go straight for the doctor, Mary – he can go in Mr

Franby's gig. And tell him to be as quick as he can,' Alys ordered, making for the stairs.

But it was all over long before the doctor could be fetched.

'Mary was right, after all: deaths do come in threes,' Miss Grimshaw said after the funeral, as they sat in the parlour like a pair of large crows; though it has to be said that black suited Alys's pale skin and chestnut hair very well.

'But this death was not unlooked for – and is more in the nature of a blessed release.' Though shaken and upset, ALys could not pretend to be heartbroken by the death of one who had never shown her such signs of fatherly affection as might have endeared him to her.

Despite – or perhaps *because* of – recent tragic events, she had found fresh inspiration for her new book, which was just as well, for now she felt the whole burden of their future suddenly resting upon her shoulders. Should she fail, poor, faithful Letty must return to live as a dependent on her relatives, or find another post, and she herself would be reliant on the kindness of her cousin and his as yet unknown wife.

'You are not ... not going to write your novel *now*, are you?' faltered Miss Grimshaw as Alys seated herself purposefully before her little desk and lifted the lid.

'Of course, for there is no time to be lost, and nothing to be gained by sitting about pretending a grief I do not feel.'

'*Ravish'd by Cruel Fate* is a very *odd* sort of title, Alys. Immured as you have always been, I do not know where you get such strange fancies from.'

'But I have never been *entirely* cut off from the world,' said Alys, amused. 'What with newspapers and books and Nell's letters – not to mention that kind note from Mrs Radcliffe, when she recognized my hand in *Malvina*. I fear she is probably a better woman than I will ever be, or my heroines would not be so wilfully sure they always know what is right.'

Alys trimmed her pen and set to, writing swiftly, and hardly registered when Letty quietly left the room to see to the sending off of the remainder of their clothing to be dyed black.

Dear Nell

Well, it is all over, and we are fixed here awaiting the return of James and his new bride. It suits us well enough at present, for there is much to do both here and at the Hall, and everyone looks to me for directions. Also, the little house in Hans Town is let until early next year, so even should we wish to live there, we could not.

Yesterday, sorting Papa's effects, we discovered some letters from my grandfather, Titus Hartwood. Although I only have one side of this brief exchange of correspondence, they were clearly talking at cross-purposes. Papa was demanding the money he thought due to Mama on her marriage – which took place at Gretna – how scandalous! – but my grandfather, after berating Papa as a vile abductor among other interesting appellations, says, tellingly, 'You have removed a treasure from this house, and I will not treat with you until it is returned.'

Well, by 'a treasure' Mr Hartwood must surely have meant the golden pendant I found hidden among Mama's things, which presumably she brought away with her for some reason. But papa evidently thought he was referring to Mama herself, though how he was to return her when they were married, I cannot imagine.

I don't suppose Mama knew anything about the exchange, or she might have set Papa right, but perhaps she had got his measure by then, and would not have entrusted the treasure into his hands. It is a mystery, but if Mr Hartwood set such store by the thing, then I must endeavour to return it when I find a safe way of doing so.

Happily, my new book is at last coming along rapidly. I hope you also are feeling more cheerful now that Mr Rivers has explained that his frequent visits to Lord Chase's house are due to his forming a little Scientific Society with those of his old friends who share his interests.

Besides, you did say that he seemed quieter and more thoughtful since the tragic death of his childhood friend, Gervase Stavely, so perhaps he was a bad influence upon him? But I am, of course, very sorry for Mr Stavely's mama and younger sisters, who have been good neighbours to you in Cheshire. I believe there is a younger son, at present serving in the Peninsular?

Our foothold on life seems remarkably insecure – one must just live each day as it comes.
>Your affectionate friend,
>Alys

CHAPTER 10

Sold Out

What joy of anticipation leapt in Cicely's breast as she flew down the turret stairs to make all ready to greet him after his long absence.
  Ravish'd by Cruel Fate by Orlando Browne

'It's good to have you back, Harry, by God it is!' Serle Rayven said, shaking his friend's hand. 'But – under any other circumstances, for you know how sorry I am about Gervase.'

Captain Harry Stavely, a slight, serious, sandy-haired man who had so recently and reluctantly sold out of the Rifle Brigade on the death of his brother, nodded. 'I suppose it was always on the cards – what a fellow he was for being either up in the clouds or down in the black depths: no in-between for Ger!'

Then he looked at his tall friend and smiled. 'But it is good to see you too, Serle, for like me you will be wishing yourself back in Spain trouncing the French, rather than living comfortably at home, which is something Mama and my sisters can't understand in the least.'

'I know just what you mean, for it would have been incredible to anyone else that I had cause for regret about selling out, when I inherited the Rayven title and estates – but I did. We never thought to be anything but soldiers, did we, Harry? And now we both have responsibilities of a different kind to shoulder.'

'Yes, when Mama wrote to me telling me the news and begging me to return post haste, there was really no alternative. If only Ger had married earlier, had a family! But there, he always said he would settle down when he turned thirty, and had recently become engaged to a neighbour's daughter, so that we all hoped he was about to turn over a new leaf.'

'You are quite sure it was not just an accident?'

'He weighted his pockets down with stones,' Harry said simply.

'And he did not leave a note, saying why he took such a step?'

'No, but I have already spoken to Miss Whately, and she told me Ger visited her the day before and talked wildly of not being worthy to marry her, and said he would never be free of the dreadful things he had done in the past. Pretty much the sort of thing he wrote to me in that last letter . . . but I am sure he could not have done anything very bad!'

'He and George Rivers were part of Chase's set, I believe?' Rayven said.

'He and Rivers were close from childhood, though I know little of his other friends for we have led very different lives – but he has certainly often mentioned Lord Chase. What is he like?'

'Older – and, report says, heading straight for the devil as fast as he can go. There are many unsavoury rumours about him, Harry, not least that he has revived some kind of Hellfire Club, who meet at his house near Kew.'

Harry whistled. 'I suppose if Ger had been involved in something like that, it would account for his state of mind, though I confess I do not have the least idea of what they might do at such a club.'

'*Orgies*, I am reliably informed. Food, drink, women and quasi-magic rites, as an excuse for general debauchery. They call themselves the Brethren, and Chase is the Master.'

'Serle, *you* haven't attended one, have you?' demanded Harry, his eyes widening.

'Not I, but although the participants are masked, there is no great secret about the identity of most of them, Byron for one.'

'It sounds highly unsavoury.'

'I would have to agree with you, you old puritan, but would it be enough to account for your brother's state of mind?'

'I suppose it might, for he had fallen head over heels in love with Miss Whately, and clearly thought himself unworthy of her. . . . Now

I come to think of it, I remember him ages ago telling me in one of his letters, as if it were a great joke, that Rivers had sworn to abandon his old ways and turn over a new leaf on *his* marriage; but when I called on him he looked burnt to the socket, and I was sorry for his wife, who is a sweet, gentle creature.'

Harry's lean cheeks acquired a hint of colour and Rayven eyed his friend thoughtfully.

'Perhaps Ger was afraid that his own intentions to reform his way of life would have ended the same way,' he suggested.

'I expect that is it, and that what started out as larks and devilment soon took a darker turn, and it preyed on his mind,' agreed Harry.

'Well, let us not dwell on unhappy matters further, but go into the study and blow a cloud together, while you tell me all the news of our particular friends.'

'How the rich live!' Harry said, following him into the book-lined room and studying the effect of the rich crimson curtains and melancholy marble busts.

'It is a trifle gloomy for my taste, but I don't know quite what to do about it – the house itself is well enough, but the furnishings are old fashioned and dark. I daresay it needs a woman's touch to bring it up to date – which reminds me, did Vance ever make an honest woman of his plump *señorita*?'

'An honest woman?' exclaimed Harry with a laugh. 'Why, it turned out that she had a husband alive already in another regiment . . .'

CHAPTER 11

Changed Relations

After such joyful anticipation it was too much: Cicely fainted away. By the time her senses were restored, the castle was in the hands of strangers – and it was all too soon made clear to her that the old order had changed and nothing would ever be the same again.

Ravish'd by Cruel Fate by Orlando Browne

*D*ear Nell
You will have received my hasty note telling you of my Cousin James's return, and I must now describe to you the dismal teaparty we had with the new Lady Basset.

It lasted for barely half an hour (though it seemed longer!) during which time she interrogated me in the most vulgar and prying way imaginable as to my resources.

She is a large, roman-nosed, fair woman of about my own age, with a brusque manner, a loud voice and a shape that leads me to conclude that she is already well on the way to providing my cousin with an heir.

I can now read between the lines of what James told us yesterday of her immediate history, and perceive that she was so well and truly on the shelf that her widowed mother saw nothing for it but to take her to a different market – that of Antigua, where a fresh complexion and flaxen hair might be enough to procure her a husband.

She must have laid siege to poor James the moment she set eyes on such a prize, seized him, and now means to rule the roost. She was not at all grateful for my attempts to keep the Hall in good state for her arrival, but rather critical of anything that smacked to her of a lack of economy, by which I deduce that her mama's finances are even more straitened than ours.

Mrs Young and two unmarried sisters are to arrive at the Hall in due course, and there was a distinct gleam in her ladyship's eye when she asked me what families of consequence there were locally who could be asked to dine, and whether there were unmarried sons among them.

She seems full of energy despite her condition and means to pay a call on us tomorrow, being curious to see the Dower House, though I told her it was little but an extended cottage rather than the small mansion she might imagine. I will tell you more of her visit later, but clear it is to see that we are not about to become bosom-bows!

Your affectionate friend,
Alys

'Well!' said Lady Basset, walking into the small and rather shabby parlour next day, shadowed somewhat apologetically by her husband.

She cast a hawk-like and proprietary gaze around the room. 'This is quite cosy – and could be made exceedingly pleasant. It is certainly not a *mansion*, but neither is it merely a *cottage*.'

'It was extended for my great-grandmother, years ago,' James explained. 'That is how it became known as the Dower House.'

'And the furniture?'

'Most of the furnishings came originally from the Hall, I believe,' Alys said, 'as did the china and linen.' The latter, she reflected, being so worn it had been twice turned and was now more patchwork coverlet than sheet.

'Perhaps you would do me the kindness of showing me over the house, Miss Weston?'

It was more a command than a request, but not an unexpected one, for Alys by now had her ladyship's measure; nor was she surprised by the way she so rudely and inquisitively poked and pried about. Alys had already taken the precaution of locking her little desk and any novels – such as her own – that might cause an eyebrow to be raised into one of the presses.

Their tour took in the kitchen, where Mary regarded her in a steely manner that might have disconcerted a more sensitive woman.

'I am astonished that you have not installed a closed stove,' Lady Basset said, 'for you would find it a great saving in coals and much more efficient.'

'Nay, I've never needed nowt but what I have,' Mary said belligerently, but luckily her accent was too thick to be entirely comprehensible to Lady Basset who favoured her with a cold stare, then turned and stalked back to the parlour.

'Fetch tea, Mary, would you?' asked Alys. 'And perhaps some of those little honey cakes?'

'Tek more than honey to sweeten that one,' Mary said, 'though 'tis clear what honeypot she used to snare Mr James! But there, that's like a man.'

Lady Basset's noisy advance across the uncarpeted floor of the parlour finally awoke Pug, who had been asleep on his cushion dreaming, with twitching legs and small whimpers, of catching a rabbit. A small, very slow, *defenceless* rabbit. . . . Jolted awake, he sat up and issued a series of wheezy barks.

'I see you still have Pug, Cousin,' James said, then explained to his wife: 'When my stepmother died, Pug attached himself to Alys.'

'Indeed?' Lady Bassset contemplated the creature. 'My youngest sister, Honoria, is fond of dogs. It would make a pleasant gift to welcome her to her new home.'

'But you could not separate him from Alys now!' Letty gasped. 'Oh – pray excuse me if I sounded rude, Lady Basset, but you do not know how the poor creature pined for his mistress.'

James looked discomfited as his wife, ignoring Letty's outburst, bent down intending to lift the little dog up by the scruff and examine him further. Pug, eyes bulging indignantly at such *lèse-majesté*, lunged at her, snapping.

'The evil creature bit me!' Charlotte exclaimed incredulously, snatching back her hand.

'No, no – I daresay he was just surprised and alarmed when you bent over him,' Letty said, hurrying over and examining the injured member. 'See, the skin is not broken, for he does not have two teeth left in his head that meet!'

'So sorry,' Alys said sweetly, returning from confining Pug to the kitchen. 'I should have warned you that he is not quite at ease with strangers.'

'It is no matter,' Lady Basset said shortly. 'The creature is clearly too old and unstable to adapt to a new owner and should probably be destroyed.'

'We will *purchase* a little dog for your sister instead, how is that?' James suggested.

'You are very kind.' She drew on her gloves.

'Mary is just bringing tea: will you not stay for it?' enquired Alys.

'No indeed, I have much to do.' She looked about her again and then said, with a sly, sharp sideways glance at Alys, 'Yes, I believe Mama and the girls will be extremely comfortable here at the Dower House – but that we can discuss once they are safely with us.'

Out she sailed. James, crimsoning, ran after her, leaving a stunned silence behind him.

'Well, Letty,' Alys said, 'you see we are shortly to receive our marching orders, so it is well that we have some means of supporting ourselves elsewhere. Still, it would certainly suit us if we need not remove until April when the tenants are out of our house in London. How surprised James will be when he learns we own such a property.'

'I am glad *Ravish'd* is coming along so well now, for I do not like to leave such a long gap between new novels; but I suppose after three of them it is unlikely I will be entirely forgotten, for people will always like to be horrified and frightened.'

'It still seems very odd to me that you should be an infamous novelist, talked about by all the *ton* in London,' Letty confessed. 'Only of course they think you are a man. Why, even Mrs Franby warned me against Orlando Browne's novels – particularly *The Captive Bride of Castle Grismort*, which she said was a distasteful volume of no possible interest to any lady of delicate sensibilities!'

'She said much the same about that book by Mr Lewis, but Lady Basset bought it just the same . . . though come to think of it, it *was* rather shocking,' Alys said, with a twinkle in her grey eyes.

She went back to her manuscript, making a few corrections to the last page, and thinking how quiet it was without Papa raging in his bedchamber or shooting off his pistol in the garden. But she felt she had had enough of Little Stidding and was quite ready to live in a place where she could see faces other than those of sheep, visit lending libraries, museums and concerts, and generally amuse herself when she was not at work.

She wondered if a short visit to London in the spring would be a good idea, before they sold the Hans Town house and settled where to live permanently? She would like to see all the sights she had heard about, and was sure Letty would be glad to visit her relatives.

Lady Basset lost no time in paying another call at the Dower House, and had barely sat down before beginning, 'Miss Weston, you must excuse my plain speaking, but you now have your way to make in the world and need to cut your coat according to your cloth. First, you must instantly dismiss Miss Grimshaw, which will be an immediate economy – I cannot understand why you have not already done it. Then you should advertise for a position as governess or companion for yourself.'

'I thank you for your concern, Lady Basset,' Alys said, feeling deeply grateful that her future was not in the hands of so cold and ungenerous a woman. 'You will be delighted to learn that I am not quite the destitute orphan you think me, and in fact own a small house in a respectable part of London, to which I intend removing myself and my companion as soon as the present tenant's lease expires in the spring.'

The effect of this announcement gave her great satisfaction, for Lady Basset's jaw dropped with astonishment. 'A *house*! How is this? James did not tell me your father had property of any kind. In fact, he gave me to understand that you would be very lucky if your income came to more than a hundred and fifty pounds a year.'

'I daresay James did not know *all* of my father's business.'

'Pray, in what *part* of London is this house?'

'Hans Town.'

Lady Basset looked down her Roman nose. 'I do not believe that is where the *ton* live.'

'No, but neither is it a back-slum, and in any case, I mean to sell it and move to some small, quiet town.'

'Major Weston cannot have been open and honest in his dealings with Sir Ralph, when he came to live here at his expense,' said Lady Bassett, looking very much put out.

'I believe Sir Ralph knew how matters stood, there was no deceit,' Alys said truthfully. 'And though our income will be less than before, we will still have enough to manage on comfortably, in a modest sort of way. But I thank you for your kind concern.'

'Well!' Lady Basset said, rising to take a hasty turn or two about the small parlour, skirts swishing. 'I think you will find London prices steep – quite beyond your purse – and how you are to pay Miss Grimshaw's wages, I cannot think.'

'Miss Grimshaw is my friend as well as my companion and would stay with me whether I paid her or not.'

'Pray, *when* did you say you intended to remove to London?'

'In April, when the lease falls vacant.'

'The workmen will shortly begin to make some alterations to the Dower House in readiness for my mother and sisters. You would find yourselves uncomfortably circumstanced if you were to remain here while it was being carried out,' Lady Basset said, then added with a wintry smile, 'but James has it in mind to move you to a vacant cottage on the estate.'

Alys said nothing, biting her lip to stop the hasty words that would forever have estranged her from the Bassets. Had it been in her power, she would have removed herself and Letty instantly, but could not imagine how it could be done economically. But she could imagine what hovel her ladyship would think suitable to house them.

'I daresay you cannot have much to pack,' Lady Basset said, following some train of thought of her own.

'No, we have few possessions that cannot be taken with us,' Alys agreed. 'And you can be sure that we will waste no time in leaving, once we are able to.'

'As to that, you are a connection of my husband's and we certainly do not intend to put you out of your home, of course – merely to remove you to one more *fitting* to your present circumstances.'

When she had gone and Pug was released from bondage in the kitchen, Alys relieved her feelings by hurling a particularly hideous vase into the fireplace. Lady Basset had probably already mentally catalogued it, but let her look for it in vain when she took triumphant possession of the Dower House.

> My dear Alys
> You have been put into a quite untenable position, and I hate to think of you suffering under the tyranny of such a woman as the new Lady Basset. You and poor Miss Grimshaw cannot possibly live in some hovel on the estate until April.
> I have given the matter some thought and believe I have a solution: you must come to stay with me in the New Year. Now, do say you will, for I would like of all things to have a friend to take about with me. And of course Miss Grimshaw is included in the invitation, should she wish to accompany you.
> I have spoken of this to Mr Rivers, who says it is a capital idea, for I have become quite glum and mopish from one thing and another and having a friend to stay might cheer me up. . . .

Alys looked up from Nell's letter and said, 'There, is that not kind, Letty?'

'Indeed it is, and to invite me, too – how thoughtful, and what a sweet girl your friend is! But should you be staying with Mrs Rivers, I would welcome the opportunity to visit my relatives in London.'

'Well, this is certainly a solution, though I do hope it does not cramp the fashionable Mrs Rivers' style, having such a country dowdy as myself staying with her.'

Of necessity, both were still attired in deepest mourning, having dyed all their gowns and retrimmed their bonnets with black ribbon.

'But in London you might go into half-mourning, or even colours, for no one there will know precisely when the major died,' suggested Letty. 'I expect you will go into society with Mrs Rivers, you know, and you could not dance in your blacks.'

'Since I cannot dance, that is of no moment – and I have no desire to cut a dash in society, even if I could,' Alys said, laughing.

'But I am sure Mrs Rivers moves in the best circles, and I daresay will take you about with her.'

'Not once she has seen the shabby figure I present – I promise you, she will be very glad to leave me to my own devices while she gads about. No, I have several things I mean to do while I am staying with her, such as discussing with your nephew whether we should let my publishers into the secret of my authorship, or leave my identity a secret. Then too, I want to look over my house, visit museums, concerts, exhibitions ... the Tower with the wild beasts ... oh, *all* the things I have only heard about!'

'But if you furbish yourself up a trifle, under Mrs Rivers' aegis you might very well meet an eligible *parti*, for I am sure you are pretty enough, despite your lack of fortune.'

'I am an old maid of almost four and twenty! And in any case, I have no *wish* to get married, Letty.'

'I know you have often jokingly said so, dearest Alys, but surely—'

Alys rose and walked up and down the little parlour impatiently. 'Oh, I did have romantic dreams when I was younger, I admit, though they took a severe knock in Harrogate. But what examples of happy marriage do I have to inspire me to follow suit? Mama and Papa could not have been happy together, Lady Basset was *deeply* unhappy, and James is set to live under the cat's foot!'

'But I am sure there are many happy marriages – your friend Mrs Rivers, for one.'

'Perhaps,' Alys said dubiously, for that all was not as it should be in the Rivers household was becoming plain to her, reading between the lines of Nell's letters. 'And do not forget, should it be discovered that I am the author of such infamous novels, then there would be no hope for me at all.'

'No one need find out. And if you *should* meet some amiable, eligible man, I hope you will at least consider his offer.'

'I am unlikely to meet such a paragon, and who would marry *me*, past my prime and with barely sixpence to scratch myself with?'

'Alys, that is a most unladylike turn of phrase! And you do not look your age in the least.'

Alys laughed and thanked her, but could see that Letty still thought marriage was the ultimate prize in life; whereas she had come instead to yearn only for a little house of her very own, with no demanding, autocratic man ruling the roost. Most women needs must wait for widowhood to reward them with their independence, but hers was almost within her grasp.

'Then it is decided. I will go and stay with Mrs Rivers for a time – though *not* to husband-hunt – and you will enjoy making a visit to your nephew and his family, will you not?'

'Oh yes, I cannot wait to see the dear children. But pray, Alys, do not *entirely* close your mind to the idea of a respectable alliance should you receive an offer, for what if sales of your books fall off, or the fashion for the Gothic tale ceases, or—?'

'If that were to happen, then I would write something else,' Alys said, though such spectres frequently haunted her dreams. 'But I promise to have as good a time as I can while I am staying with Nell, if that will please you. And I will come and see you in Cheapside and tell you all about it.'

'Alys, have you thought that you might meet Lord Rayven in London?' Miss Grimshaw ventured. 'Will that not be awkward?'

'I expect he moves in very different circles, for once he inherited he became vastly wealthy and a most eligible bachelor. Nell says he is now a "buck of the first head", whatever that may be! I daresay I will not see him at all.'

'Let us hope not, but you might very well meet your maternal relatives, for although your grandfather does not now often leave his house, your aunt is in society, is she not?'

'Yes, and her daughter Arabella is out, for Nell has met her, but I daresay they will not deign to recognize me even if we should be in the same room together. I don't expect their notice – but I must say, I would like to meet Grandfather's heir, Nathaniel Hartwood,' Alys added teasingly. 'Nell says he is the handsomest man in London – and indeed, from the brief glimpse I once had of him in Harrogate, I believe she is saying no more than the truth.'

'Oh, pray do not lose your heart to someone unattainable, Alys!'

'I do not intend to lose my heart at all,' she replied, thinking affectionately that it would be odd to be separated from her quiet, kind companion after so many years together in rural isolation.

She looked forward to telling James and Charlotte of her plans in the airiest way possible at a suitable moment. It would brighten what looked likely to be a dismal Christmas, especially since the arrival of

Charlotte's mama and sisters, who frequently invaded the Dower House without a by-your-leave, to squabble over bedchambers and hangings.

Due to a sudden and obstinate burst of conscience on James's part, they set off for London in the antiquated family coach, by very easy stages. This was preferable to the stagecoach, which might have been faster, but uncomfortable and quite an expense, and it had the added advantage that they might take all their belongings with them at once.

It was a chilly February, but at least the roads were free of snow as they set off. Only James had come to see them depart, and when his stout figure was finally obscured by a turn in the drive, Letty dissolved into tears over Pug, who was clutched in her arms wrapped in an old shawl like an exceedingly ugly infant.

Alys succumbed to no such excess of sensibility but wrote her way through several counties and a succession of unexciting inns.

Suddenly, something extremely odd was happening to her characters. Simon de Lombard seemed determined to break out of his villainous mould and prove himself to be a man of honour, while behind her hero's fair face lay a dark and devious mind.

It was all strangely exciting.

Alys looked up with a sigh and stretched her stiff fingers as they approached the modest inn where they were to spend their very last night on the road.

'Letty, if Sir Walter Scott is ever to read *this* novel, I am sure he will consider my "pure vestal light" to be *quite* burnt out!'

Letty, so huddled in cloaks and shawls and scarves that only her little pink nose was easily visible, was just about to answer when there was a sudden jolt and a mighty rending of metal and wood. Then the coach tipped over, sending them tumbling to the floor in a heap.

It came to rest at an angle, one upper wheel spinning crazily, the other splintered, while the horses plunged nervously in the traces.

Inside the dark coach there was a moment's silence. Then Miss Grimshaw sat up, murmuring distressfully, 'Oh dear, oh *dear!*'

Pug sat on Alys's chest and licked her face until she pushed him off and struggled to her feet.

'Are you all right, dearest Letty?' she enquired, making her out in the gloom.

'I believe so,' she quavered. 'A little bruised, perhaps.'

'I too – but I must get out and see what the damage is. How slow they are in releasing us.' She reached up and pushed at the door above her unavailingly.

It was suddenly wrenched back from outside and a pair of strong hands was extended, into which she automatically put her own.

A deep and odiously familiar voice drawled. 'Allow me!' before ruthlessly dragging her upwards into the light.

CHAPTER 12

Bruising Encounters

> *'Simon de Lombard,' said a tall, dark-haired man of forbidding aspect, stepping forward and bowing. His eyes rested on her in a way she could not quite like, with a familiarity and almost contempt for her person.*
>
> Ravish'd by Cruel Fate *by Orlando Browne*

Alys found herself grasped rather familiarly about the waist, swung down and set on the ground next to her rescuer, dishevelled and conscious that she had lost her bonnet and her hair hung down her back. She looked up into a dark, sardonic, hawk-nosed face that lightened into amusement as he recognized her. A smile curled his lips.

'We meet again, Miss Weston.'

'Lord Rayven!'

'Yes, it is I, the wicked villain of the piece,' he declaimed rather melodramatically and she stared at him with large, startled grey eyes.

Then her wits returned and she realized he was referring to their Knaresborough encounter rather than his role in her novels. 'Pray, unhand me, sir!' she said, recovering herself to find she was the cynosure of all eyes in the busy inn yard.

'I beg your pardon, I thought you might feel faint after such a shock,' he said, removing his supporting arm. 'Allow me to introduce my friend, Mr Stavely, lately Captain Stavely of the Rifle Brigade.

Harry, this is Miss Weston, whose entirely delightful acquaintance I made some years ago in Harrogate, where I took the waters ... and even took *to* the waters. You will find her refreshingly different to other young ladies of your acquaintance, I assure you.'

The slight, sandy-haired man standing next to her rescuer smiled and bowed. 'Delighted, Miss Weston.'

'You are – still – *Miss* Weston?' said Lord Rayven. 'Now, why does that not surprise me?'

Alys gave him an indignant glare and Stavely looked with amusement from one to the other of them.

'I do not aspire to the married state, sir,' she said coldly, and he bowed.

Miss Grimshaw's voice called plaintively, from the depths of the coach, 'Alys?'

'Oh, how could I forget poor Letty?' Ignoring Lord Rayven she instead turned to Mr Stavely. 'Pray, could you assist my companion, Miss Grimshaw, out of the coach? And perhaps if she were to pass up my little dog first? He is too small to jump out.'

Pug, yapping excitedly, was handed to Alys, who tucked him under her arm. She was disappointed to see that he did not show any desire to bite Lord Rayven, or she might have put him down.

'Strange, I had not thought you the type to have a lap-dog, Miss Weston?'

'He was Lady Basset's.'

'*Was?*'

'She has been dead these three years.'

'I am sorry for your loss. You are still in mourning?' He thought how well black became her, setting off her pale skin and chestnut hair to perfection.

'I have since also lost my father,' Alys said shortly. 'I believe Mr Stavely requires your assistance in helping my companion from the coach.'

Miss Grimshaw, set down on the cobblestones, smoothed down her skirts in a flustered way. 'Oh, thank you! So kind, I declare,' she gasped, looking up gratefully at her two rescuers. 'Such a mishap!'

'Mr Stavely, allow me to introduce Miss Grimshaw,' Alys said, then added meaningfully, 'And *this*, Letty, is Lord Rayven.'

Miss Grimshaw stopped smiling and took a step back, blanching. 'Lord *Rayven*? N-not the Lord Rayven who—'

'Just a misunderstanding,' he said defensively, taken aback by her horrified expression. 'I am not the Devil incarnate, I assure you.'

'Misunderstanding? Hah!' Alys said.

'Why, what *have* you been doing to render your name so odious to these ladies, Serle?' enquired Stavely, highly amused. 'I had not thought it of you.'

'I am afraid Lord Rayven has no great opinion of my character, nor I of his, Mr Stavely,' Alys said. 'More than that would be pointless to relate. I must thank you both for your assistance, but believe we need not trouble you further. Good day.'

She turned her back and enquired of the coachman what the damage was.

'A wheel to be mended, miss.' He shot a darkling look at his lordship, still standing observing them. 'If the gentleman's curricle hadn't dashed through the arch in front of me, I wouldn't have caught the corner stone.'

'Nonsense, do not blame *me* for your poor driving,' Lord Rayven said, then he added, looking at the antiquated coach more closely, 'though from the look of it, you have not had much practice in driving such a vehicle for a considerable number of years, and so perhaps may be excused your cow-handedness.'

'I believe I have made it plain that I no longer require your assistance – or advice,' Alys said icily.

This time he took his dismissal and the two gentlemen walked into the inn where, she sincerely hoped, they were not also to spend the night. Her coachman went off to discover where the nearest wheelwright might be, while the horses, now released and calmed, were led into the stables.

As she entered the inn with Letty, the coach was being set back on to three wheels and heaved into the inn yard, so as not to block the entrance further. They were shown to a bedchamber, in which Letty insisted they sup, for fear of meeting Lord Rayven if they dined below.

But it appeared that his lordship and his friend stayed merely to refresh themselves, for she had the doubtful felicity of seeing them drive off in a most dashing way some time later from her window, whither the bustle of departure and a familiar, deep voice ordering the ostlers to "Fig 'em out!" had drawn her.

'It is Lord Rayven,' she said to Letty, who was half-dozing in front of the fire with Pug. 'They surely cannot mean to drive back to London now, for it will be dark very shortly.'

'There should be a good moon,' Letty said drowsily, then sat up a little straighter. 'Come away from the window this instant, Alys, in case he should see you.'

But it was too late: Lord Rayven said something to his friend, then looked up directly and laughingly saluted her with his whip before gathering up the reins.

She stepped back, cheeks aflame, muttering 'Show-off!' as the curricle bowled out of the archway, turned on a sixpence and vanished from sight.

'Has he gone, Alys? If so, it would be safe to take Pug for a little airing.'

'Yes, he has gone.'

'He did not appear quite the monster I imagined, though his face looks forbidding until he smiles.'

' "A man may smile and smile, yet still be a villain",' quoted Alys darkly.

'Well, if you say so, my dear . . . and of course, if he is the man who so grossly insulted you in Harrogate, then he *must* be!'

'Shakespeare – I forget which play,' explained Alys, thinking not for the first time that had she not been such a voracious reader, a governess hired for her cheapness rather than her educational attainments would have left her sadly lacking in knowledge other than that of how to induce her hens to lay, or the art of providing a good table on a limited income.

'Lord Rayven's friend Mr Stavely seemed a very pleasant young man,' Letty said.

'Yes – I wonder if he is any relation to Nell's Cheshire neighbours? But I suppose Stavely is not an uncommon name.'

'I can see how like all your villains Lord Rayven is, now I have set eyes on him, Alys, right down to that sinister scar. Let us hope he has not read any of your books, for he could not fail to recognize himself.'

'Oh, I don't suppose anyone ever does recognize themselves in books, and I should not think him the type of man to read a novel, let alone a Gothic romance, would you?' she said, though it had given her a jolt, she had to admit, when he had called *himself* a villain. 'And anyway, even should he have heard of the likeness, it would never cross his mind that I should have written them.'

'No, of course not.'

A servant scratched at the door, with a message to say that the last stage of their journey must be put off until midday tomorrow, while the wheel was mended. This was better than they had hoped, for they would still reach London in daylight.

'I think I will just jot down a few notes, while our mishap is still fresh in my mind,' Alys said, looking around her for her travelling desk with a purposeful light in her eyes. Simon de Lombard might have mysteriously re-cast himself as the hero, but she felt in the mood to have him suffer a little torture before rewarding him with Cicely's hand.

'And I, when I have walked Pug, will see if I can find the arnica, for I am bruised all over, especially my ribs.'

'Well, you *would* sew my jewellery into your stays, though I told you there was not the least need.'

'The pendant – the golden pendant,' whispered Miss Grimshaw, with a nervous look at the door.

'Oh – *that*. Yes, I suppose we must keep it safe until I can return it to the Hartwoods, but I am sure locking it into a trunk would have done just as well,' Alys said. But Letty declared her willingness to suffer any discomfort in order to protect her charge's property or virtue, in a heroic manner quite suited to the pages of a Gothic novel.

'Come, this is hopeful!' Harry Stavely quizzed his friend as they drove away from the inn. 'It is the first sign of interest I have seen you show in the fair sex since I sold out.'

'I don't know how you can say so, Harry, when you know very well I have only recently parted company with as pretty – and avaricious – an opera-dancer as ever graced the boards.'

'Oh – opera dancers!' exclaimed Harry. 'You know very well that is not what I meant.'

'No, but if you are waiting for me to fall head over ears in love with one of the society chits that are paraded for my notice, you will wait for a very long time.'

'But you must marry soon, for you are the last of the Rayvens just as I . . . I am now the last of the Cheshire Stavelys,' Harry said, a pang of loss twisting his face as he thought of his brother.

'So I must, and I mean to cast the handkerchief this very season, to some placid creature of good birth and beauty, who will be content to stay at Priory Chase and breed while I amuse myself elsewhere – and not, I assure you, to Miss Weston, who has *none* of the qualities necessary in a wife!'

Harry, who over dinner had been regaled with all the details of his friend's Harrogate acquaintanceship with Alys and her very vulgar aunt, grinned. 'Your placid creature sounds a dead bore to me. And Miss Weston is very taking even if she is not precisely beautiful – such expressive grey eyes!'

'Expressing loathing every time she looked at me, you mean?'

'But that was all a mistake – an unfortunate one, of course, but nothing you could not put right. I am sure you could win her round with a little address.'

'Are you? She was decisive enough at eighteen, but now she is a self-opinionated spinster of three or four and twenty, that might be a challenge quite beyond *my* capabilities, Harry. But I don't suppose our paths will cross, for the friend she is going to stay with is most likely to be as shabby-genteel as herself.'

'Aha! So you were interested enough to make enquiries?'

'I greased the coachman in the fist, once he had come down off his high ropes about the slur on his driving,' admitted Rayven. 'He told me she'd been living in Yorkshire with her widowed father, in a cottage on her uncle's estate, but now she has her own way to make in the world. I expect she is seeking a post as companion or governess.'

'Did you get her direction?'

'No, for I am not in the market – yet – to employ either of those,' he said drily, but all the way to London he kept thinking of a pair of large and indignant grey eyes . . . *intelligent* eyes.

The suspicions he'd once briefly entertained about the authorship of a certain novel, which at the time he had immediately dismissed as ludicrous, now crossed his mind again. She had said in the letter he had found at Knaresborough that she was writing a novel, and that he was the perfect villain – and it had to be admitted that the villain of *The Travails of Lady Malvina* bore a striking physical resemblance to himself.

Could the dowdy and country-bred Miss Weston be the notorious Orlando Browne, whose books more straitlaced mothers had forbidden their daughters to read?

Surely it was quite impossible!

Alys took it as a good omen that she finished off the very last page of *Ravish'd by Cruel Fate* just as their coach approached the great City of London, so that she could fully enjoy the astonishingly crowded and busy series of tableaux that passed the window.

As some revenge for having her hero turn out to be the villain, she had dispatched the fair but black-hearted Lucius by the expedient of having his carriage topple into a ravine. This was very satisfying, though being fond of horses she had found herself unable to allow the team pulling it to hurtle to their doom too.

It had severely taxed her brain to find a solution, but in the end her ingenuity had, of course, been equal to it.

CHAPTER 13

Quite Ravish'd

She gave a gasp of anguish and betrayal . . . her head swam dizzily, and she might have fallen, had not Simon de Lombard's strong arms drawn her back from the brink into the darkness. His warm breath stirred her hair . . . he held her pressed close, and it seemed to her disordered fancy that their hearts beat to the same rhythm, as though they were one.

Ravish'd by Cruel Fate by Orlando Browne

If Alys had feared that her friend might have turned into a sophisticated and worldly young matron in the three years since she had last seen her, any such idea was soon banished.

Nell might now be fashionably dressed and move with confidence in society, but underneath the veneer lay the sweet-natured and sensitive girl of old. Indeed, at three and twenty she looked very little different, except that her hair was cropped and dressed in feathery curls around her head and her figure, though still slight, had attained some womanly curves.

There was, though, a new sadness shadowing the blue of her eyes when she thought herself unobserved, that Alys thought was not entirely due to her so-far unfulfilled longing for motherhood.

At breakfast, which was taken at such a late hour, that country-bred Alys was quite famished, Nell fed Pug all kinds of unsuitable titbits, while expounding on the entertainments in store for her friend.

'Usually I would call on my acquaintances or receive morning callers, and then perhaps walk or drive in the park, visit the shops, go to routs, balls and parties, suppers, the theatre . . . But the season has not yet begun, so London is very thin of company. We should still be in Cheshire ourselves had not George had business in Town.'

'But that is all to the good, for I do not mean you to launch me into Society, you know,' Alys said, quite dazed. 'How your friends would stare to see you in company with such a dowd, too! No, I thank you, but I will be more than occupied in seeing the sights, attending to business and arranging where Miss Grimshaw and I are to live. And I *must* start another novel shortly, for I cannot rest on my laurels when it is now my livelihood.'

'But I am *relying* on you to give me your company when the season starts, for although I have many acquaintances, I have no *particular* friend with whom I can laugh and share secrets as we do,' Nell said plaintively. 'I have been so looking forward to it, and intend pointing out all the lions to you – like the wicked but handsome Lord Byron.'

'I *would* be curious to see the poet, I admit.'

'And so you shall, for when it becomes known that I have a friend staying with me you will be included in many invitations, though I am afraid obtaining vouchers for Almack's may be beyond your reach, for they are very particular indeed.'

Alys laughed. 'I should think not! And once your acquaintance discover my lack of wealth and family connections, they will probably think me quite beneath their touch.'

'If *I* do not think it, I don't see why they should. Besides, you *do* have perfectly unexceptional relations, even if they do not acknowledge you. As to your lack of wealth, you need not mention it at all, for no one will be ill-bred enough to ask you directly.'

'I will not *have* to mention it, for one look at me will say it all – as it did to Lord Rayven yesterday. I could see he thought me a poor, shabby-genteel thing.'

'But he did rescue you,' pointed out Nell, to whom she had briefly related the story of their accident the evening before, to account for their late arrival. 'I think that is quite romantic.'

'There is nothing remotely romantic about Lord Rayven, and his manner of speaking to me left so much to be desired that I had much rather he had left me in the coach! But his friend seemed pleasant, enough – a Captain Harry Stavely, formerly of the Rifle Brigade. I wondered if he might be a relative of your neighbours in Cheshire, for are they not called Stavely?'

'Harry Stavely?' To Alys's surprise, Nell's cheeks turned a becoming shade of pink and she looked slightly self-conscious. 'Why . . . yes, he is Gervase Stavely's brother and so has now inherited the estate. He rode over several times to speak to George about his brother this winter, for they were friends from childhood, you know, and George was much cut up about his death. Is Mr Stavely staying in Town, then?'

'That I cannot tell you, for I had little conversation with either of them. And,' she added, 'I would not feed Pug with any more sugar, for he has just been sick on the carpet.'

'Poor little thing!' cooed Nell. 'But my page will take him for a walk and then he will feel better.'

'How grand you are, with a page,' Alys said, when a gap-toothed child in livery had removed the little dog, 'even if he is not the most prepossessing of boys.'

'Oh, Sammy will improve in appearance in no time, with good feeding. I don't think he will ever be tall enough to become a footman, but already he is inches taller than when he came in.'

'Came *in*?'

'To the Benevolent Ladies Society, an Evangelical group who take small children from the worst back-slums – mostly girls, but a few boys, too – and lodge them at a house near Kew. It is in the charge of a respectable dame and they are taught the manners and skills they will need to go into service, then we try and find positions for them, like Sammy.'

'I did not know you were of an Evangelical turn of mind, Nell.'

'I am not really, except I wished to help others less fortunately circumstanced than myself, especially children, and joining the Benevolent Ladies enabled me to do that.'

'Are they orphans?'

'Some of them, but others are brought by their parents, desperate for their child to have a better life than they themselves can offer. I sometimes go out to Kew to visit them and take clothing and other necessities, so you could accompany me one day, if you wished.'

'I would like that very much, Nell,' Alys said, smiling warmly at her friend. 'Much more than going into Society, I assure you.'

'But, like me, you can do both. Alys, *do* say that you will sometimes accompany me to my engagements,' coaxed Nell.

Alys grimaced. 'Well, I suppose a little town polish would not come amiss, but I would first have to smarten myself up a bit and, as you know, my resources are limited, or I would have gone into half-mourning by now.'

'I do not think you could dance in half-mourning, so perhaps, since no one here knows the precise date of your bereavement, you might wear colours again?' suggested Nell.

'I have no objection to abandoning my mourning entirely, but I must tell you that I cannot dance.'

'I will teach you, for you might want to stand up occasionally. But let us first discuss the attaining of a suitable wardrobe for—'

'—a spinster of limited means!' interjected Alys.

'No, for a young lady making her debut in society,' Nell amended firmly.

'Not so very young and with no desire to catch a husband, which I imagine makes me fairly unique.'

'But sensible.' Nell's face clouded over.

'Mr Rivers bade me welcome very civilly yesterday,' Alys said carefully. 'He does not usually breakfast with you?'

The previous evening when she had arrived, her host had been on his way out of the house, but stayed long enough to say everything that was polite.

Alys had been shocked to see his once rubicund face now haggard, his eyes sunk into dark sockets, hardly recognizing the cheerful young bridegroom she had briefly met three years before when they had visited the Dower House.

'No, he – he is out a lot, and when he is at home he usually shuts himself into the library. That seems to be the way of married couples in his set, they barely clap eyes on each other from one day to the next,' Nell said bitterly, but Alys did not press her yet. She could perceive that her friend was not happy, but hoped that in time she would confide fully in her.

'Well, now you have me for company, Nell.'

She brightened. 'Yes, and I am sure we will have such fun! I've had a capital idea of how to replenish your wardrobe, too, if you do not dislike it. You know I have a deal of pin-money, and I am afraid I am always too inclined to buy whatever gowns and bonnets take my fancy, without thought of whether or not they will become me. And then, of course, I cannot wear them and it seems a sad waste. But our colouring is so different, that what does not suit me may well suit you. And we are much of a size, except that you are taller – but then, gowns can be let down, or have extra flounces and trimming added, after all.'

'I am not so proud as to dislike the idea, if you are sure you mean it when you say they are things that do not become you?'

But when Nell's wardrobe was displayed to her, it was clear that she had spoken the truth and was not merely trying to do her friend a kindness. 'You seem to have favoured shades of sea-green,' she said, peacocking before the mirror in a spotted muslin dress trimmed with small flat rosettes.

'Yes, and I can't think what came over me – and not just once, either, but several times. That dress looks so much better on you than it ever did on me – or it would if it were long enough. Jane, will it let down, do you think?'

'It will, and I will do it for the young lady in a trice,' agreed her maid, who had thrown herself into weeding out the garments that ill became her mistress with enthusiasm. 'Indeed, I will set about the alterations this very day.'

'You are very good – thank you,' Alys said gratefully.

'It will be a pleasure, miss.'

Nell surveyed the array with some satisfaction. 'Striped walking dress and spencer – and dove grey does become you, while it makes me look like a ghost – muslins, the Norwich shawl that was much too bright for my colouring, but so pretty. The blue silk ball gown that made me look like whey—'

'Indeed, Nell, I do not see how I would need anything else!' Alys said, overwhelmed.

'Oh, this is nothing, for you will need quite an extensive wardrobe, besides slippers, sandals, silk stockings, gloves . . . the list is endless. So now, let us go to the Pantheon bazaar where we can obtain that kind of thing at *very* little cost.'

'The Pantheon Bazaar?'

'It is the most wonderful emporium, and though it is not much frequented by the *ton*, a positive Aladdin's cave of treasures.'

'That sounds just the thing, though I must not spend too much money until I have spoken to Mr Grimshaw – Letty's nephew – who has been handling my business affairs. If you recall, he is to visit tomorrow to lay his accounts before me, and then I will have a better idea of how I am fixed. I expect he will bring the gold medallion with him, if Letty has unsewn it from her stays by now.'

Nell giggled. 'I think she has been pressed bosom to bosom with Neptune for long enough!'

'Well, she *would* do it. I must see about returning it to my grandfather.'

'It is probably very valuable, though it does not sound like the sort of ornament you would want to wear.'

'All the more reason to return it, for I am very sure I have no right to its possession. I will show it to you, when Thomas Grimshaw brings it – and he may carry back with him the revised last chapter of my new book to Letty to be copied out, and then see if he can get a good price from the Minerva Press for it.'

'Oh Alys, you are so clever, and I quite *burst* to tell everyone that you are a famous author, though I know I must not. But when people are trying to guess who this Orlando Browne might be – and *always* a man, as though a woman could not do such a thing! – then sometimes I have to keep my lips pressed together.'

'I pray you continue to do so – if I decide to live in some small quiet town, as I am inclined to do, then I will be thought quite beyond the pale if I am known as the infamous author of such shocking novels as *Ravish'd by Cruel Fate!*'

'Then let us go and be ravish'd by fashion instead,' said Nell gaily and they went out into the weak February sunshine to where the carriage awaited them.

CHAPTER 14

Death or Dishonour

Simon immovably barred the way, his burning dark eyes fixed on her face. 'Cicely,' he said softly, 'do not see me as your jailer, but as your protector.'

Ravish'd by Cruel Fate by Orlando Browne

Thomas Grimshaw presented himself next day and gave her an accounting of her business affairs. He also returned, with an amused smile, the golden ornament that had been sewn into Letty's stays.

'My aunt was in a worry that I should be robbed of it on the way here, but of course, how should anyone know that I had any such thing about my person?'

'Thank you – I suppose I must write to my grandfather and enquire whether it is indeed a Hartwood family heirloom that he would like returned to him. If so, I expect he will send a trusted servant for it, and that will be the end of the matter.'

'It must be worth a great deal of money for the gold, alone,' he suggested.

'I daresay, but I do not feel that it is mine to dispose of.' Dismissing the matter she turned to something that concerned her more: the sum they might receive for *Ravish'd by Cruel Fate*, when Letty had completed her task of copying it all out in a fair hand. 'And I do not know what I would do without her, for my handwriting is such a scrawl that no one else could read it.'

'She has told me your plans to set up house together, though she thought probably not in London?'

'No, I do not think London life would suit me even if I could afford it, which evidently I cannot.'

'Do you wish to see the house in Hans Town? It is not a modish area, but respectable. If you should decide to sell it, the current tenants are keen to buy it.'

'That would be very convenient – but first I *will* look over it, for curiosity's sake, if for no other reason,' she decided, and he arranged to take her there the very next day.

'And Letty, too, if she wishes to come, Mr Grimshaw. But it is her holiday, so should she be otherwise engaged, I will understand.'

'As to that, I believe Mr Puncheon, an old family friend, is to take her and my wife for an airing in Richmond Park tomorrow.'

'Then tell her I do not expect her – since we will not live there, it is not of any importance. I have written her a note, if you would be so kind as to take it to her, with this parcel.'

Miss Grimshaw's wardrobe was also in need of replenishment, and Alys hoped she would like the materials she had chosen for her at the Pantheon Bazaar, which had been, as Nell had promised, a positive treasure-trove of inexpensive haberdashery.

As soon as Mr Grimshaw had gone, Alys sat down and with some difficulty composed a letter to her grandfather, Mr Titus Hartwood.

Dear Sir

You may be unaware that my father died last year and, after settling his affairs, I am at present making a brief stay in Town with my friend, Mrs Rivers.

Although I have no wish to impose myself upon your notice, or that of your family, I would welcome the opportunity of returning to you an ancient and valuable golden medallion, which I think you have long wished to have restored to the family. If this is indeed so, pray tell me how this may be accomplished.

She paused for a moment, read it through, then added her plain and unadorned signature.

It was short and to the point; he would probably send someone to collect the treasured object, and that would be the end of the matter. Any further notice by her maternal relatives she neither expected nor sought, and thought it unlikely that they would even accord her a common bow in passing, should their paths ever cross.

Waking early next morning, Alys took Pug for a turn up and down the street, then set off, armed with a guidebook she had purchased the previous day, to look at the sights. Having just finished one novel, she thought she deserved a little holiday until she started the next.

She sent Sammy to fetch a hack, to his evident astonishment, and told the jarvey to take her to St Paul's. Although she knew that young ladies did not roam about town alone, she thought herself well beyond the age of needing a chaperon for such excursions as this, but it was soon borne in on her that in London this was not the case. Indeed, Nell was aghast when she walked into the breakfast parlour and told her where she had been.

'St Paul's Cathedral? *Alone*? In a hack? But – you should not – it is not at all the thing! And why did you not send for the carriage, if you *must* go?'

'I did not wish to cause any inconvenience, for it is clear to me even after such a short stay, that no one of any quality rises early!'

'*Promise* me you will take a maid with you next time.'

'Oh no – only think how bored the poor creature would be.'

'Then Sammy – take my page.'

In the end Alys agreed to this. 'And I daresay I will have seen all the most interesting things in a very few days, so you may be easy. The more fashionable parks and exhibitions I presume we will visit together.'

Later they parted company, Nell to her dressmaker and Alys to look over her house in Hans Town with Mr Grimshaw. She found it rather a narrow, mean and inelegant building and could not imagine living there, so was happy to come to an agreement with the tenants that they should purchase it.

'And once that is done,' Alys said, as they drove away, 'I can buy a small property elsewhere.'

'Do you have any idea yet where?' asked Mr Grimshaw, who was rather amused by her, even though he would have been far from happy had his own wife exhibited such independent ways.

'I had thought originally of some small spa town, for I should like to be within easy reach of libraries, shops and other entertainments. But now I find myself hankering after Yorkshire air again, so have wondered if the city of York itself might be the very place. I am sure there must be amusements enough there to please anyone, and we may come by coach to London in a trice.'

'I could look into possible properties there for you, if you wish? The prices may well be more favourable than Bath or even Cheltenham.'

'If you would be so kind. And the *outskirts* of the city, for I think it unlikely we will be able to afford to keep any kind of conveyance.'

So it was settled and he left her at the door of the Rivers' house, well satisfied that everything was in train to establish herself and Letty in a snug little property in the near future.

When Harry Stavely paid a morning call, it was with some dismay that Alys observed the blush that mantled her friend's cheeks and the slightly self-conscious way she greeted her visitor. Nell had looked pale and extinguished until that moment, but now she seemed lit by an inner glow.

'Why – Miss Weston!' he exclaimed, recognizing her.

'Mr Stavely, we meet again,' she said, glad she was wearing one of the pretty dresses that Nell had given her, rather than her shabby mourning. 'I have the advantage of you, sir, for when I described my accident to Mrs Rivers she told me who you were, while you must have had no idea that I would be making a stay with her.'

'No, but it is a very pleasant surprise to find you here, I assure you. I trust you and your companion sustained no lasting shock to the system from your accident?'

'No, I thank you, though Miss Grimshaw was a trifle bruised. Do you also make a stay in town, Mr Stavely?'

'Yes, with Lord Rayven – we are old campaigning friends, you know.'

'But I do not suppose you go out early each morning in order to look at some bit of architecture or curiosity recommended by a guidebook, as Alys does,' Nell said. 'She is quite inexhaustible! Nor did I like her to go alone, though now my page goes with her, it does not present *quite* such a strange appearance.'

'No, you should certainly not go alone, Miss Weston,' he said, looking quite shocked, for clearly he was a very serious young man. 'Do you then have a taste for antiquities?'

'I have an interest in everything new to me, antiquity or not.'

'I believe you are a bluestocking, Miss Weston. Do you also have an interest in parties and balls, like other young ladies?'

'I declare, Mr Stavely, you are unkind to tease Alys so,' Nell cried. 'Of course she is not a bluestocking!'

'I fear I am not clever enough to be ranked with those august ladies,' Alys said, 'though I do not understand why it should be thought so undesirable in a woman to possess any great degree of understanding or intellect. *I* do not mean to pretend to be stupid just to conform to such idiotic notions.'

'Er – quite,' he agreed. 'I can see that when Rayven described you as the most singular young lady of his acquaintance, he was telling only the truth.'

'Did he indeed do so?' asked Nell, intrigued.

'I expect his lordship was merely exercising his strange sense of humour at my expense,' Alys said calmly, 'it was not meant as a compliment.'

They were interrupted by the arrival of a plump, middle-aged lady and her two rather plain but good-humoured daughters and soon the conversation turned to lighter matters.

Lady Chibberly, who was very inquisitive, seated herself on the sofa next to Nell and enquired in a low voice, 'Your friend, Miss Weston, means to make a long stay with you?'

'Yes, I hope for the whole season.'

'And what of her family? From where does she come?'

'From Yorkshire, but her parents are dead.'

'She is an heiress?' Lady Chibberly asked eagerly, for she was also the mother of an adored but profligate son.

'No, although Miss Weston has a small property, her means are modest.'

'Oh . . . that is a pity, for since she is no longer in the first bloom of youth she will find it hard to get a husband without any fortune.'

'She does not intend to marry, but means instead to retire from town after this season and live quietly with a companion.'

Lady Chibberly looked surprised. 'Not marry! But there is no need for her to give up *all* hope yet, for though she is not precisely beautiful, yet there is something very taking about her expression when she is animated.'

Nell smiled. 'Perhaps some man may yet persuade her to leave off her single state, who knows?'

When they left, Lady Chibberly managed to carry off Captain Stavely with them, for she was always keen to throw her girls in the path of eligible young men.

As soon as he quitted the room Nell seemed to grow suddenly pale and extinguished again. 'There, were not Lady Chibberly and her daughters pleasant, Alys? But I fear their chatter has left me with a headache, so perhaps I will go and lie down for a while.'

'I think more than a headache ails you, Nell,' Alys said gently. 'I do not wish to pry into what does not concern me, or force a confidence you do not want to give, but something is amiss. It is my fear that your marriage, which started out so happily, is now in difficulties.'

'Oh Alys, though I know I should not burden you with my troubles, I feel I must talk to someone or go quite demented!' Nell cried, then she cast a frightened look at the closed study door and whispered, 'I never know when George is in the house or not these days – though mostly he is not. Come up to my bedchamber!'

Once there she sank down on the carved bed, her face anguished. 'You have guessed right – I am deeply unhappy, for George has slowly changed towards me and his whole character now seems so different to the man I married. I expect marriage bored him after a while, and most married couples do seem to spend much of their time apart, but I did not think George and I—'

Alys sat next to her and taking her hand patted it kindly. 'I know your marriage was arranged by your family, yet you told me yourself that they would not have proceeded with the idea had you not been willing to marry Mr Rivers.'

'No, indeed, and I felt a decided partiality from the moment I set eyes on him, and he – he said he fell in love with me instantly, too.' She gave a stifled sob and pulling out a tiny scrap of cambric edged with lace, dabbed at her eyes.

'I am quite sure he *was* in love with you, Nell, for when you came north and paid a call at the Dower House you were the picture of married happiness, and Miss Grimshaw and I were so pleased to see it. I cannot imagine what could have caused him to change, but I have myself overheard him speak roughly to you on several occasions.'

'I believe it is all the fault of his persuadable nature: he was quite wild in his youth, you know, but when he proposed he promised he had reformed his ways and would be an exemplary husband – and so, at first, he was. But slowly he was drawn back into the circle of his old friends – Gervase Stavely was also one of that set – though mainly I put it all down to Lord Chase's influence.'

'Yes, I recall you mentioning him in one of your letters. What is he like?'

'Much older, and there is just something evil about him . . . Alys, do you remember when George told me that he and his friends met together regularly, because they had formed a society?'

'Yes, for I thought it was probably just one of the kind my cousin James used to frequent – science and mystery for the credulous. He was forever conducting odd little experiments into magnetism and alchemy, but his intellect was never equal to the calculations behind them.'

'I thought so too, only then I discovered that *this* society's purpose was something far worse!' Nell said. 'One evening George insisted we attend a ball at Lord Chase's house near Kew, though I did not wish to go for I knew the company would be very mixed. Lady Crayling was there, for instance, and she is very vulgar and by no means received everywhere, but her husband is a member of Chase's set. And your relative Nathaniel Hartwood is, too, though he is so kind and charming that I am sure *he* cannot be in too deeply.'

'I suppose a man may have all kinds of friends,' Alys said. 'But do go on, this grows exciting!'

'After most of the guests had left, George sent me home in the carriage alone, with no explanation other than that he and his friends were to hold one of their mysterious meetings.'

'That was strange behaviour indeed, Nell.'

'Yes, you can imagine how astonished I was, and how little I relished driving back into London at that hour alone, despite the full moon. When I ventured to ask another lady, whose husband had also stayed behind, what might this society's interests be, she said she had learned from experience that it was better not to enquire too closely what they did, and she would advise me to do the same.'

'So you do not know what the real purpose might be?'

Nell leaned forward until her fair head was practically touching Alys's chestnut curls and whispered thrillingly, 'I believe – I have since gathered – that it is something along the lines of the infamous *Hellfire Club*!'

This disclosure fell rather flat, until she explained that this notorious society had met in the last century under the auspices of Sir Francis Dashwood for unnamed and probably unholy rites, licentious and bawdy behaviour and various undisclosed excesses. 'Apparently he had caverns and chambers excavated to hold these . . . these *orgies* in, and they even practised the Black Arts, some say.'

'Good heavens! And you know, I do recall my Aunt Basset mentioning something of the kind – she corresponded with Lady Crayling, for they used to be on the stage together, and she let fall hints in her letters that she was involved in a similar society. The Brethren, I think she called them.'

Nell nodded. 'The very same – but I am not supposed to know that, only rumours do go around. Some whisper of lewd behaviour, rituals and even *sacrifices*.'

'Sacrifices?' Alys said, startled. 'Of what?'

'Cockerels – their throats are cut and they *drink the blood*.' Nell shuddered.

Alys sat back and looked at her, wide-eyed. 'It is very hard to belieive *George* could involve himself in anything so vile.'

'I, too, found it hard to believe, but when I pressed him for an explanation he said it was merely harmless fun, but he was under oath not to tell me or anyone else what they did. And he is not himself in the least after these meetings – heavy eyed and cross, and . . . and *dismissive*, as if he knows some great secret I do not.'

'Do they always meet at Lord Chase's house?'

Nell nodded. 'Underground, rumour has it, for Templeshore House is old and there is a passage leading from the river via some ancient chambers, into the cellars of the house. Indeed, there is a Roman mosaic floor in one of the cellars which Lord Chase shows to visitors and a shell grotto decked out with strange devices.' She shivered. 'How horrible it all sounds!'

Actually, having a liking for such things, Alys felt she would love to see the ancient chambers, and especially the mosaic floor, but refrained from saying so.

'I have refused to enter Lord Chase's house since . . . and I now go everywhere alone,' Nell added forlornly.

'Not *quite* alone, it seems to me, since Harry Stavely sold out of the army and returned home,' Alys said in rallying tones. 'Clearly he has been dancing attendance on you in Cheshire this past winter, and means to do the same in London.'

Nell blushed. 'He is a good friend, nothing more.'

'No, I know you too well to think otherwise, but I could tell how much you liked him Nell – and indeed, he seems very pleasant – so you must be careful.'

'I am a married woman and, however George may treat me, I still mean to honour my marriage vows,' Nell said with dignity.

'I know George to be unkind to you, but he is surely not *violent?*'

Nell shivered. 'He is unkind to me in ways which I cannot tell to you – in intimate ways. He often does not seem to be himself on these occasions, for his eyes are quite strange – and he is always sorry afterwards if he is cruel to me. But that is not a great deal of consolation,' she added forlornly.

'No, I should think not!'

Alys said what she could to comfort her friend, but in truth there was little Nell could do but bear her lot with fortitude. Her husband might mistreat her as he liked, but she could not leave him for another without totally cutting herself off from all contact with honour, friends and family.

'What you have said simply goes to reinforce *my* long-held determination never to marry and entrust myself to the tyranny of a male, Nell.'

'But at first I was very happy, and perhaps had I had the advice of a mother ... or had the consolation of children, I might have managed better, and prevented George from falling again under such bad influences.'

'I do not think you can hold yourself to blame in any way, for it must surely be the influence of his friends, though the Brethren may not be doing anything so very bad. The rumours that have reached you might be only the inventions of malicious tongues and if their meetings are just an excuse to carouse away from censorious eyes, George will surely eventually tire of such silly pursuits and mature into a man of sense.'

Leaving her friend to rest on her bed before dinner, the hartshorn in one hand and a handkerchief moistened with lavender water over her brow, Alys went to her bedchamber and sat down at her little desk.

She had already begun to outline a new book about a penniless orphan cast adrift upon the world, the title of which was to be *Death or Dishonour*, and now she was inspired to lend it a sinister tone.

Her heroine, Drusilla, might be in the power of a cruel and rakish man who knew she was really the heiress to a fortune, yet professed to be rescuing her from her dire situation. He would be a distant relative, who might *seem* fair and good, the gentle knight riding to her rescue, yet be black-hearted in truth. Seemingly out of the goodness of his heart, he would engage her as a companion for his wife, whom he had driven mad with terror of him. . . .

Yes, she could quite see that last scene – the fair, delicate young wife rendered witless with fear of one who, in public at least, behaved to her with forbearing courtesy and affection.

She scribbled away furiously until it was time to dress for dinner, for she could not seem to resist reflecting the events and tribulations around her – though much altered, of course. Perhaps all authors did so? She determined, if Mrs Radcliffe would receive a visit from her, to ask her.

But she hoped she might find a route of escape for her heroine other than death or dishonour, even if not for poor Nell, constrained by the realities of life.

That night Alys woke from a nightmare in which she was struggling against some dark force that weighed down on her both physically and mentally.

Sitting bolt upright, panting, the revelation came to her in a moment of clarity that *all* her heroines were struggling to escape from some form of monstrous tyranny, even if only that of a selfish, but benevolent, father – but there was no escape, only the exchange of one form of tyranny for another.

Feeling oppressed she got out of bed and opened the window on to the street, at this hour briefly and mercifully silent, and wished she could soar free above the rooftops like a bird.

CHAPTER 15

Just Returns

Her father looked troubled. 'Cicely, I had thought better of you! It is no wonder that Lucius has withdrawn his request for your hand, and instead asked my permission to pay his addresses to Elizabetta.'

Cicely rose proudly to her feet. 'Then let her have him, for I think they will suit each other very well!'

Ravish'd by Cruel Fate by Orlando Browne

'You sent for me, sir?' enquired Lord Rayven, looking down with some compassion on the pain-furrowed face of Titus Hartwood, confined to his chair by a rheumatic complaint.

'Sit down!' Mr Hartwood said testily. 'Don't loom over me like that, it gives me a crick in the neck. Wait – make yourself useful and pour the brandy first.'

'It is too early in the day for me, but I will pour you a glass.'

'Namby-pamby, that's the younger generation all over. No fibre – look at that heir of mine. My younger brother William was as weak as water and his son takes after him. Handsome, mind, and charming, but no backbone – lives for pleasure.'

'That is the same for many young men,' Rayven pointed out.

'Nat's not much younger than you are, yet you have seen active service – and now you are a civilian again, you seem to occupy yourself.'

'I had a lot to learn, inheriting so unexpectedly and not having been bred to the management of a great estate, so many people depended on me for their daily bread that at first it was quite alarming. I found great want among those employed in agriculture, too, for while the value at market of their crops and animals continued to decrease, the price of the everyday staples they needed to keep their families alive rose rapidly. I find myself rather interested in farming improvements,' he added. 'Some of the new experiments are quite fascinating, don't you think?'

'No, never had a turn to be a farmer,' Mr Hartwood said dismissively. 'Politics – governing the country, not grubbing about in it – that was my game. But at least you show interest in *something*, while that cub Nathaniel has none that I can discover other than gaming, wenching, and hanging round with a damned good-for-nothing set!'

His gnarled hands clenched and unclenched on the carved arms of his chair. 'There are even rumours of Bacchanalian orgies at Lord Chase's house at Kew. You may be surprised that I know of such things, tied to this damn house as I am most of the time, but an old friend thought to warn me. They think themselves hell-born babes, I suppose, playing at secret societies like that fool Dashwood and his ilk. Pah! If only they knew!'

'Yes sir, the irony has not escaped me: your nephew play-acts, little knowing that members of his family have for generations belonged to a secret Order sharing the burden of a great secret.'

If it had come as a surprise to the new Lord Rayven that his predecessor's rather mismatched band of old cronies should expect to continue to gather at Priory Chase on a certain date every year, then it had been as nothing to his discovery of the real reason for that meeting.

'Seven families,' said Mr Hartwood now, meditatively. 'Seven members of the Order, one from each family, a line unbroken down the centuries. Keeping the secret – keeping the faith.'

'A secret I am not yet privy to,' remarked Rayven, who had found himself recruited to the Order's ranks on his return to take up his inheritance.

'You will learn it when you have served seven years faithfully and then you may find the knowledge a burden hard to bear.' He sighed. 'But who is to take my place as the representative of the Hartwoods when I am gone I do not know, for Nat has yet to prove himself anything other than a fashionable fribble.'

'Many young men are wild in their youth, yet grow sober and responsible when they turn thirty.'

'Yes, that is sometimes the case, for Charles Rayven thought much the same about his son, and yet he had started to show signs of maturity shortly before his death, thinking of marriage and taking an interest in the estate.'

'And so may your nephew settle down yet.'

'I have long wanted to think so, but I grow old and infirm and there is no sign of it.'

'Indeed, sir, I am amazed that you have managed to make the annual journey to Priory Chase every autumn these last few years.'

'I must – for who is to take my place? Three wives I have buried, and not a son to show for it!'

'I believe in the past women have been admitted as members of the Order,' Rayven suggested. 'Do you not also have a niece?'

'Yes, Arabella.' Mr Hartwood's face lightened. 'She's a pretty little thing, but just eighteen and with a head full of gewgaws, gowns and beaux. Too much of a feather-head to be burdened with serious affairs, even if I agreed with women being privy to such a secret, which I do not, whatever others in the past may have thought!'

Drumming his fingers on the arms of his chair, he frowned. 'Perhaps, if I were to marry her to the right man . . .' He shot a look at Rayven from deep-set eyes under bushy brows: 'I suppose you are not hanging out for a wife? If so, then perhaps you could stand in the Order for both our houses . . . only then the Seven would be Six, so that would not do. This situation has not arisen before, I must give it further thought.'

'I am sure Miss Hartwood is delightful,' Rayven said politely, 'but although I do intend to marry soon, I do not think giddy eighteen and sober twenty-nine go well together.'

'Perhaps not, but she's having a coming-out ball and I'll get Lavinia – William's widow, you know – to send you an invitation. Come and cast your eye over her.'

'Thank you, I will look forward to it. But going back to your problem, perhaps there is a distant relative who might be suitable?'

'Not that I know of. Of course, I've got a granddaughter, but she is out of the reckoning.'

'A *granddaughter?*' Rayven raised a surprised dark brow. 'I had no idea.'

'My only daughter ran off with a fortune hunter when she was seventeen, a gambler who lived on his soldier's pay and the throw of the dice. Much good it did him though, for I cast her off and she died soon after the child's birth.' He uttered a harsh bark of laughter. 'He wrote to me later, of course, wanting money, but I had nothing to say to him.'

'But surely your granddaughter deserved your notice?'

'She was half his, and bad blood. Of course, had she been a boy, that would have been different. Then I might have made a push to remove him from his father and have him brought up under my own eye, so I could see how he turned out.'

'So you have never met your granddaughter, sir?'

'No, but I have just this day received a letter from her, saying that since her father is dead she has come to town, and wishes to restore the Poseidon jewel to me. I knew that my daughter must have taken it, even though the blackguard she married denied all knowledge of it.'

'Well, that is good news, is it not?' Rayven said, for though he considered that the tokens the seven members of the Order assumed during their meetings were merely pointless embellishments to their purpose, he kept his opinion to himself. He had sworn eternal faith to the cause, even if he was still inclined to think that the secret he would one day learn would turn out to be of no very great moment: the location of yet another Grail or portion of the True Cross, perhaps?

'Growing up under such a father's influence, she cannot have escaped the taint,' Hartwood said. 'I suspect she has an ulterior motive in making the offer and expects to receive something equally valuable in return, if only a public acknowledgement of our relationship. She is staying with a friend for the season and, at three or four and twenty, with no money or prospects, must be scrambling after her last chance of a respectable marriage. But I will see her, if only to give her a set-down for her presumption.'

'But she *is* your granddaughter, acknowledged or not,' Rayven pointed out, 'and she may be sincere.'

'That cannot be, or why would she have waited so long to return the jewel?'

'If her father is recently dead, perhaps she has only now learned of its existence?'

'Perhaps. Well, we will see – but if Miss Alys Weston thinks to cozen an old man in his dotage, she will be much surprised.'

'*Alys Weston!*'

'Yes – can it be that you have met her already?'

'I – if it is the same person, which I suppose it must be, with such an unusual name – then yes, we are a little acquainted.'

'My daughter was called Alysaun – an old Cornish name used in her mother's family, but she was always called Alys. It seems her daughter was named for her.' For the first time a faint flicker of some softer emotion crossed his severe countenance. 'I do not suppose she bears any other resemblance to her mother. But how came you to meet her?'

'It was in Harrogate, just after I first sold out – she was paying a visit there with her aunt, a Lady Basset.'

'Yes, they were living in a grace-and-favour cottage on some relative's estate, I heard.'

'Our acquaintanceship at that time was brief,' Rayven said. That it was also a comedy of errors ending in a damp denouement, he kept to himself. 'Then recently, while on my way to town, I again met her. Her coach had had an accident and overturned, though she and her companion were unharmed.'

'Her companion?'

'A dowdily respectable older lady, whose name I am afraid I have forgotten.'

'Hmm . . . so at least she was not so lost to all sense of propriety as to jaunter about the country alone.' He shot another hard look at Rayven. 'And what do you think of her?'

Rayven, recalling a pair of large and indignant grey eyes and a determined chin, said with a sudden grin, 'Oh, I think you will find Miss Weston *quite* out of the common way!'

Hartwood stared at him consideringly. 'Will I so indeed? Yet her mother was a silly, headstrong little fool.'

'Well, Miss Weston is no fool – but headstrong, opinionated, determined – all of those I would say, yes.'

'A woman of virtue?'

'Undoubtedly.'

'Hmm ... She is staying with Mrs Rivers in Portman Square – respectable address, know the family. George Rivers is another crony of Chase and that fool nephew of mine, and presumably involved in the Brethren, as they call themselves.'

'Yes, I believe so – as was my friend Harry Stavely's brother, Gervase.'

'Killed himself, didn't he?'

'Yes, drowned. He was often of a melancholic turn of mind, but of late seemed to have had something on his conscience that led him to take so desperate a step. Harry is made of sterner stuff – he was a first class officer and will be a loss to Wellington now.'

'I suppose you both wish yourself back on the battlefield?'

Rayven's dark-blue eyes glowed. 'That we do – but there, we must accept what fate has given us.'

'Most men would be thankful, to have plump inheritances land in their laps.'

'Life in the Brigade suited us both, but I am not ungrateful and nor is Harry, except that he would rather have his brother back, hale and hearty, of course.'

'A man must do his duty in whatever sphere he is called to.'

'Very true, sir.'

'Well, I will tell you what I think of Miss Weston when I have seen her, for I have told her to bring herself and the gold Poseidon here tomorrow,' Hartwood said in a voice of dismissal, and seeing that he was tiring Rayven took his leave.

As he let himself out of the room he caught a glimpse of a fluttering pink gown vanishing around the turn of the stair. He smiled sardonically: so someone – the niece? – had been curious enough about his visit to listen at the door. But it was solid enough and she could not have heard much even with her ear pressed to the keyhole.

He drove home thinking how odd it was that Miss Weston should turn out to be Titus Hartwood's granddaughter, for he could perceive no family resemblance. But perhaps the likeness lay rather in character and some part of his stern inflexibility had been passed down to her, for he had never met any young lady with such an air of competence and of knowing just what she did – *and* didn't! – want.

He had been fighting off a strong urge to pay her a visit ever since Harry had told him that he had met her at Mrs Rivers' house, for he would enjoy teasing and provoking her. Besides, did he not deserve a little of his own back in return for his icy dipping at Knaresborough?

However, despite what she had said at their last encounter about not aspiring to marriage, her grandfather must have been correct in thinking she had come to London with that very hope in her heart. Near penniless, orphaned and alone, what else was there for her to do?

No, it would be best to steer clear of her, he decided, for fear that any attentions he might pay her be the cause of raising false expectations in her breast.

Later, when Harry arrived home in a state of high emotion far removed from his usual quiet good sense, Rayven wished his friend would also steer clear of Mrs Rivers; but as it turned out, the ill-starred pair had already come to the same conclusion.

'We are agreed that we should not meet so often, for fear of causing tongues to wag and so making her situation worse. I must leave her to her fate – yet she is an angel and I am sure her husband mistreats her!' Harry exclaimed, walking up and down the library hastily. 'She positively shrinks away when he comes into the room, and looks so afraid.'

'I am sorry for it, but I think you have made the right decision, Harry.'

'Something has altered Rivers from the man I remember, Serle. You recall I told you that when he assured me there was nothing in the meetings held by his friends that might have caused Gervase to take his life, he could not meet my eye? And this from my brother's oldest friend!'

'Mistrust him all you will, but you would still do better to keep away from his wife.'

'I must, though it will be anguish – and you can never have been in love, or you would know it,' he said with a groan. 'Serle, I long to protect her from harm, to hold her and cherish her and never let the slightest thing trouble her again.'

Rayven looked at his friend with some dismay. 'I did not realize that it had come to this pass! I admit I have never yet felt anything of *that* kind, so I daresay you are right and I have never truly been in love. But it is just as well I never married one of my earlier fancies, as things turned out, for the wife of a soldier would not at all have done as the chatelaine of Priory Chase. I owe it to my heritage to choose prudently: family, lineage, estate – all must play their part in my choice.'

'I too – but it will be very hard, when my heart belongs to another.' He summoned up a smile. 'But this is mawkish talk, is it not? How did you get on with Mr Hartwood? You know, I think it the outside of enough that you should be expected to be at the beck and call of the *last* Lord Rayven's old cronies!'

'Ah, but it turns out that Mr Hartwood is related to a mutual acquaintance, Harry – he is, in fact, Miss Weston's grandfather.'

Later, since both young men felt strangely restless, they went out to Mendoza's boxing saloon, where Lord Rayven acquitted himself so ferociously well, that his sparring partner was more than happy to see him leave again.

CHAPTER 16

Bearding Lions

Cicely retreated to her remote turret, feeling at one with the menagerie of wild beasts that were kept in the east tower, wretched in their captivity.
Ravish'd by Cruel Fate by Orlando Browne

Alys continued to take Pug for a brief airing every morning, before setting out to view those sights of interest recommended by her guidebook. Nell's page, Sammy, now accompanied her as a sop to propriety – and if people still stared at her rudely, perhaps that was just the way of Londoners?

Through trial and error she had come to realize that her guidebook was a little out of date, for several of the amusements had vanished while others, like some of the pleasure gardens, had fallen out of fashion and grown sadly shabby. Also, having dutifully viewed the exterior of several imposing buildings including the Bank of England at Cornhill and the Royal Exchange, she felt no desire to go inside them.

On the morning of her interview with her grandfather she visited the Tower, thinking it would put her in the right mood for bearding old lions in their dens. It proved to be both gloomy and melancholy, for so many terrible things had happened within those grim walls. She also found the imprisoned menagerie of wild beasts quite sad, though Sammy declared it to have been a rare treat.

She returned in time to breakfast with Nell, then sit with her in the narrow but elegant drawing-room to receive the increasing numbers of visitors who were returning to town. So far Nell's friends and acquaintances had not deigned to show much interest in her country friend, once they had ascertained that she was not a great heiress and claimed no illustrious relations, but she did like the Misses Berry, sisters no longer in their youth.

The liking appeared to be mutual, for the elder Miss Mary Berry, warmly seconded by Miss Agnes, invited her to come with Nell to their next salon. When they had departed, Nell said this was a signal honour, 'For although they are not rich, they provide no entertainment and the refreshments are meagre in the extreme, all the great, the good, the interesting, the political, the literary – oh, *anyone* of any interest – wishes to be seen at their salons. They are always enjoyable.'

'Indeed? Then I should very much like to go.'

'You will – it shall be your first public engagement and, who knows, perhaps you will then get a taste for parties.'

'I do not think so. I believe I am starting to long for the bleak moorland already, and even the gentle bleating of sheep. But I thought the Misses Berry delightful and look forward to furthering my acquaintance with them.'

'Of what were you talking so earnestly?'

'Oh – they were describing how they used to visit Sir Horace Walpole's house at Strawberry Hill, which sounds wonderfully Gothic, and that led on of course to a discussion of the *Castle of Otranto* and the rest of the genre. Although we share a preference for secret passages and chambers in the novels we read, I seem to be alone in liking *underground* ones best.'

'There is something very tomb-like about underground chambers,' Nell said with a shudder, 'and then, too, they always seem to be full of rats and spiders.'

'Well, I have no great fondness for rats myself,' admitted Alys, 'though spiders I do not mind in the least.'

'I hope you were careful not to let slip anything that might lead them to think you are an author?'

'No, and I most virtuously resisted the impulse to press them for an opinion on the works of Orlando Browne.'

'So I should hope!'

'I did not have to,' Alys said with an impish smile. 'Miss Berry confessed that she thought them quite shocking but could not forbear reading them, and her sister agreed. They said they had not the least idea who Orlando Browne might be, but apparently there has been a rumour spreading that it is a young man called Daniel Coalport.'

'Daniel Coalport? Why, he is the youngest son of one of my Aunt Becky's friends and the idlest, most foppish young man you ever saw in your life! He fancies himself a poet, and his mama paid to have a volume of his verse printed,' Nell said, 'only it did not take.'

'Miss Agnes said that he did not deny being the author when asked, just shook his head and smiled. But she was sure he was not, and just putting on airs to be interesting. It was all I could do not to tell her that he was not the author, but *myself*!'

'Oh, do say you did not!'

'No, but I think perhaps I will go with Mr Grimshaw to deliver the next manuscript to the Minerva Press, so that *they* at least will know who the real author is.'

'If you think it best,' Nell said doubtfully. 'How very surprised they will be, to be sure.'

Though outwardly self-possessed, Alys felt nervous as the carriage drew up at the door of her grandfather's imposing mansion, wondering what her reception would be. Then the servant knocked for admittance, the steps were let down and she was ushered into the marble-flagged hallway and conducted to Mr Titus Hartwood's own apartments.

'Miss Weston,' announced the manservant, opening a pair of doors on to a gloomy, lofty-ceilinged chamber, and she advanced into the room with more assurance than she felt.

Crimson brocade curtains shut out half the light and the room was hot, for a fire roared in the grate. Seated before it in a large, carved chair sat the hunched figure of an elderly man, regarding her intently from under bushy eyebrows drawn into a ferocious frown.

'Come here, girl!' he rapped out. 'I cannot get up – this damned rheumatism has me twisted into knots.'

Alys walked forward, dropped a slight curtsy and said, 'Good day, sir.' Then she stood, regarding him with undisguised curiosity.

'You resemble your mother,' he said, after a moment or two, and she thought she detected some flicker of emotion in his voice, though his stern face remained inflexible.

'Do I? I have never seen a portrait of her, so have no means of knowing, though both my father and my uncle said that she was small and delicately made – which I am not, as you see.'

'No, but your face – your eyes especially – are similar . . . though Rayven tells me you are not such a fool as your mother.'

'Rayven? Do you mean *Lord* Rayven?'

'Of course. His family and the Hartwoods have been long associated with each other: I saw him t'other day and he said he had made your acquaintance.'

Alys said nothing, though she would dearly have liked to have known what else Lord Rayven had said about her.

'You may sit down.'

Alys did so, calmly folding her hands in her lap. Her grandfather was a little alarming, it was true, but unlike her papa appeared to be unlikely to throw his snuffbox or any other missile at her head.

'So, miss, you say you have the golden Poseidon jewel in your possession?'

'Is that what you call it? I have been thinking of the figure as Neptune, though I suppose it is much the same. But indeed I do have it and will be happy to return it to you.'

'I should certainly be interested in hearing your *terms* for parting with it.'

'Terms? I am afraid I do not understand your meaning, sir – there *are* no terms. You may have it back directly.' Taking it from her reticule, still wrapped in the old bit of silk in which she had originally found it, she handed it to him.

His gnarled hands closed around it. Then, with fumbling, dry fingers that rasped against the material, he unwrapped it so that the gold and jewels gleamed dully in the firelight.

'I thought your father might have disposed of it,' he said slowly, 'for he was a fool of a gambler as well as a fortune hunter – and this was all the fortune he gained by running off with my daughter. But I suppose he knew that if he tried to sell something so distinctive, I would hear of it.'

'You do my father an injustice in thinking so, for it was concealed in a secret compartment in my mother's jewel box, and it is clear he did not know she had it. I discovered it only when he gave me the box many years later.'

'He did not know? But the letters I sent him, demanding its return—'

'Yes, I saw them when I was sorting out his belongings after his death. There was a misunderstanding – you were both talking at cross purposes for, when you demanded back the "treasure of your house", he thought you meant *Mama*.'

'Your mother was lost to me from the moment she fled for the Border, with her head stuffed full of foolish notions. And look where they brought her: to Beggar's Cross and an early death!'

Alys bit back an unwise comment on fathers who could cast aside their only child in such an unforgiving manner and instead remarked, 'I have often wondered how Mama came to have the jewel in her possession, for a young girl cannot have *worn* such a thing.'

'She loved it from first catching sight of it as a child,' he said gruffly. 'I indulged her – let her play with it. She said it was lucky. I knew when I looked for it and found it gone, that she must have it.'

'Perhaps she did wrong to take it, but you have it back now sir, and there's an end to it.'

'Yes, but what I want to know is, what do you think to gain by meekly handing over such a valuable bargaining tool, without coming to terms first? Do you think to cozen me into acknowledging you? To worm your way into my good graces? Well?' He scowled formidably at her.

A less intrepid woman – or one unused to the irascible nature of the invalid male – might have quailed in her little kid half-boots. Instead, Alys stood up and replied scornfully, 'My sole purpose in coming here today was at your request, in order to return something that belonged to you and over which I had no right of disposal. I did not desire this meeting and I require nothing from you. I wish you good day.'

She was almost at the door when his voice arrested her. 'Hoity-toity! Come back here, miss!'

She turned, eyes sparkling and her square chin tilted in a manner that Lord Rayven would have instantly recognized. 'Sir, I am not at your beck and call – or indeed, at *anyone's* beck and call. While I must give you what respect is due to your age and our relationship, I beg leave to depart from here. Nothing is to be gained by my remaining longer.'

'You are wrong, for you might have much to gain – and do not fly into the boughs again,' he added in more reasonable tones, 'but sit down and talk to me for a while. I accept your sincerity in wishing to return the jewel, but you must be a fool indeed not to see the advantages you could have got from it as a bargaining tool.'

'But I should have been a very great blackguard to have done any such thing!' She looked at him curiously. 'Still, I expect your suspicious nature arises from having spent your life in politics, which is a sad reflection on the state of government. Let me assure you that I am at a loss to think of anything I should need that you might be able to give me.'

'Then you are an even greater fool than I thought. I know your father's circumstances – he had little money, and I daresay that what was not secured was gambled away.'

'He was a chronic invalid for many years – gambling was beyond him,' Alys said, not mentioning that latterly he had tended to drink away their money rather than gamble it. 'He has left me in reduced circumstances, that is true, but there is sufficient for my needs.'

'Ha! It is as I thought – you have drawn on what meagre sum is left to fund this season in London staying with your friend, in the hopes of catching a rich husband.'

'No, indeed! After this visit to Mrs Rivers I intend setting up home elsewhere with my companion, Miss Grimshaw. I have no real taste for the sort of life Mrs Rivers enjoys – my interests are far otherwise.'

'*Every* young woman wishes to marry and though you must be quite three or four and twenty, you do not look it. You think to pull the wool over my eyes, but I know better: what other security could there be for you?'

'Fortunately I have resources enough to live comfortably, if modestly, and I ask for no more than that. You may believe me or not as you choose, but I have no desire to marry. That was not my purpose in coming to London.'

He looked at her closely. 'I cannot see where the money to maintain you is to come from – do not think that I did not have your father's affairs investigated thoroughly, when he ran off with my daughter! But perhaps some of his relatives are franking you?'

'No, both my father's cousin and his wife, who showed us many kindnesses and on whose estate we lived, are dead. But I am able to support myself, and that is all you need to know. In fact, *more* than you need to know.'

'I am your *grandfather*, girl!'

'By blood, it is true, but you cast off my mother entirely and have never made a push to know me. You are a stranger to me and I neither need nor want anything from you.'

'You are very proud! But what if *I* acknowledge *you*? You cannot gainsay me.' He sat back and regarded her assessingly. 'What a pity it is that you were not a boy!'

'So my father often remarked,' Alys said coldly, 'though who would have nursed him all these years if I had been, goodness knows.'

'Still, you are a young woman of character and with a dowry and the right connections, could make a good – possibly even a *splendid* – marriage.'

'I am sure, had I any such desire, that would be very gratifying to hear,' Alys said politely.

'If you came to live under my roof, were accepted into the family, I could make you a good match. Lavinia, my sister-in-law, is launching her daughter Bella this season and there would be nothing easier than for you to make your debut under her aegis at the same time.'

'I thank you for your offer, for I expect it is kindly meant, but having become my own mistress I do not ever intend to submit to anyone else's authority again.'

He looked at her, baffled. 'You are a very singular young woman! Pray, I suppose you have been reading *A Vindication of the Rights of Woman* and have taken all sorts of silly fancies into your head.'

'I *have* read it,' she admitted, 'and found most of it to be no more than common sense.'

'But if you do not marry, do not have children, what status will you have then? What security? What guidance?'

'I do not need guidance. Think me strange if you will, but I believe I must decline your kind offer,' she said with resolution.

'I am not used to being gainsaid – and I am your grandfather, your nearest male relative: I could have you constrained, should I wish it!'

She rose to her feet. 'You abandoned any such rights along with your daughter. And these threats do not impress me, for you would have nothing to gain but opprobrium if you behaved in such a tyrannical manner! I do not think we have any more to say to each other and, once I have disposed of my London property and purchased another in the North, you will see and hear from me no more.'

'A property?' he snapped, pouncing on the information she had not meant to let drop.

'I have a small house in town, which is let,' Alys said reluctantly.

His eyes narrowed. 'I am very sure your father did not have any property. There seems to be much you are holding back.'

'Perhaps, but I see no reason to tell you all my personal affairs. They are not your concern.'

'But now the season is starting, you are bound to meet Lavinia and Bella – not to mention my heir, Nathaniel Hartwood, who is a friend of George Rivers.'

'I suppose I will.'

'Indeed you will – in fact, I will tell Lavinia to call on you.'

'As you wish, sir.'

'Pull that bell rope,' he ordered, and when the servant answered, he summoned his family to meet her.

Mrs Lavinia Hartwood was plump, fair and foolishly amiable. 'Only fancy!' she said when the introductions were made, 'We had no notion of your existence until yesterday. Imagine our surprise!'

'Not, I hope, an unpleasant one,' Alys said, though she thought she detected some resentment in the look Miss Arabella Hartwood directed at her when she had entered the room.

'La, how tall you are, Miss Weston,' exclaimed Bella, who was a youthful version of her mama, her prettiness marred only by a faintly rabbity look about the teeth and nose. She had the all the airs of a beauty, but Alys supposed if you had a wealthy childless uncle who clearly doted on you, you could think yourself as beautiful as you pleased.

'I do not think I am so very many inches above the common height, Miss Hartwood – perhaps it is that you are so very *small*.'

'You girls need not stand on civility, I suppose, for you may call each other cousin,' Mr Hartwood said. 'Lavinia, Alys is staying with the Rivers – you are to send them cards for Bella's ball.'

Lavinia blinked. 'Of course, Titus, if you wish it.'

'What fun, Uncle Titus, to have a new cousin!' Bella cried, clapping her hands together girlishly, but another sharp sideways look at Alys belied the words.

They all sat down together, but after a few minutes of laborious conversation about how she liked London and what she had found to amuse her so early in the season, Alys began wondering whether she might make her escape.

Then the door opened and any such desire left her, for in walked the most handsome man she had ever seen. Her heart seemed to skip about in her breast when her eyes met his smiling cerulean blue ones ... But after blinking a few times, she regained her senses enough to recognize him as the golden youth of Harrogate grown up, the mirror image of so many of her heroes: in fact, her handsome cousin, Nathaniel Hartwood. His guinea gold curls were brushed into a modish style, his snowy cravat fell like a crisply frozen waterfall and the exquisite fit of his coat and pantaloons proclaimed him a very Pink of the *ton*.

'You must excuse me, sir,' he said to Mr Hartwood. 'I called to see my mother and sister, but when I heard who was above-stairs, I could not resist making the acquaintance of my cousin – if I may call her that, for second cousins as least we must be.'

'You might as well meet her now as later, I suppose,' Titus Hartwood said, 'for she is making a stay in Town.'

'I am certainly more than happy to do so.' His eyes sparkled delightfully as he took her hand in his, and smiled with such charm that Alys felt oddly breathless.

'She's staying with the Rivers for the season,' Titus Hartwood said. 'George Rivers is a friend of yours, is he not?'

'That is so, and had I already been in town I would have had the pleasure of meeting you that much the sooner, Cousin. But you must allow me to call on you tomorrow and make up for lost time.'

'I am sure Mrs Rivers will be happy to see you, sir.'

Seeing that Mr Hartwood was suddenly looking tired, leaning back in his chair with his eyes closed, she rose to go. His hooded eyes snapped open again. 'You will come to see me on Wednesday,' he said, more in demand than request.

Her chin went up. 'Should my kind hostess not have any previous engagements she wishes me to attend with her, then I will do so.'

Nat suggested that she should send Mrs Rivers' carriage away and instead take a turn in the park with him and Bella before going home.

'Oh, do let us, we can all get to know one another,' Bella said. 'How much we will have to talk about, to be sure!'

And so it was arranged, though once away from her uncle's presence Bella, sitting bodkin between them, fell silent and it was left to Nat to entertain Alys.

This he did in so lively and entertaining a manner that the time passed in a flash and she could not afterwards remember where they had driven, though she had not been so entirely dazzled as not to notice that he drove in a rather neck-or-nothing way that seemed ill-suited to the London streets.

'Well, you appear mightily taken with our new cousin,' Bella snapped, as her brother returned her home.

'Of course, for the old man seemed as determined on acknowledging her back into the family, as he was before to cut her dead, and neither of us can afford to get his back up.'

'So you were not *really* taken with her?'

'Not I,' he said, 'but we must move carefully, for our cousin could well cut us both out of the unentailed property if she gains her grandfather's favour.'

Behind his handsome face he was thinking furiously, for he had long assumed that he and Bella would inherit their uncle's wealth. Indeed, he had borrowed on the expectation, and of late his debts were becoming so pressing that he had begun to wonder about making a show of settling down, preferably with some biddable heiress, which would both please his uncle and revive his finances.

But now Miss Alys Weston had come into the equation, Titus's very own granddaughter, and it was clear to Nat that he had taken to the girl. He had not smiled at her indulgently, as he did at Bella, but instead had eyed her with a great deal of respect and interest.

'We must be careful, Bella, if she worms her way into his affections, there goes your dowry, and how could I keep up the estates without any money? No, we must be as nice as pie to our new cousin, but watch for means to discredit her in our uncle's eyes – or frighten her away.'

'Oh Nat, can it be done? You know I will do anything I can to help.'

'Keep your ears open – after all, if you had not overheard a few words of his conversation with Lord Rayven, you would not have known that Miss Weston was coming to visit today, and sent me word in advance, would you?'

'No. Nat, you did not think her pretty, did you?' she asked jealously.

'What, afraid she will steal all your beaux as well as your fortune?' he teased with brotherly cruelty.

'Not in the least, for she must be quite on the shelf – three or four and twenty!'

'True – clearly she is at her last prayers.'

'Yes, and she has such odd ideas that she must be a bluestocking, which the gentlemen hate. Do you know, she told me that she amused herself by rising early and taking her pug for a walk, and then setting off to see *monuments*.'

'Does she? Well, that is *just* the kind of thing I need to know, Bella. We will soon send her to the right-about,' he said confidently.

Titus Hartwood sat alone penning a letter to Serle Rayven, who had proved to be right in saying that he would find his granddaughter quite out of the common way.

She appeared to be a young woman of dignity, composure and some originality of mind, and while he could not condone her wilful, unfeminine independence, yet he could admire her spirit and intelligence. In fact, it was a great pity that she was not a man, for she possessed many of the qualities that he had long sought in his heir.

She and Nat had seemed pleased with one another and he wondered if Alys might have backbone enough for the two of them? It could be a solution, and though he had long intended Bella to be heiress to half of the unentailed property, there was no reason why it could not be divided between the three of them.

If he let fall a hint or two, he had a shrewd notion that Nat would quickly see which way the wind was blowing and pay court to his cousin . . . and as for Alys, he did not believe all her talk of staying single could hold against Nat's charm.

But first, he must know what she was hiding, for the source of her mysterious income might be some shameful secret he could hardly guess at.

CHAPTER 17

Concealed Passages

'My loyalties are divided,' said Simon, 'for she is my kinswoman. But if you will consent to be my bride, my allegiance will be sworn to you.'

'Can you not do what is right without such a promise? What of your knightly oaths, do they mean nothing?' Cicely said scornfully, yet she felt herself tremble under his dark and unswerving gaze. . . .

Ravish'd by Cruel Fate *by Orlando Browne*

Serle Rayven, scanning his letters over the breakfast table, looked up and said, 'This is a singular missive from Titus Hartwood, Harry! He asks me to discover, if I can, what secret Miss Weston is concealing from him about the source of her income, for he knows it to be impossible that her father could have had much to leave her.'

'An odd request indeed – but then, I don't know why you are so thick with the old curmudgeon,' his friend replied, helping himself lavishly to the ham. 'And Miss Weston may be his granddaughter, but there is no reason why *you* should take an interest in their affairs.'

'The Hartwood and Rayven families have long been associated with each other,' Lord Rayven said ambiguously.

'They may have been, but you cannot have known any of them from Adam when you inherited. Do you mean to do as the old man wants? Miss Weston seems an unusual sort of female – Mrs Rivers was complaining that she went out every morning alone, for she has a guidebook to the sights and means to work her way through it.'

'Alone?'

'Yes, and she takes a hack, you know, she will not even send for the carriage, though Nell – Mrs Rivers – has begged her to do so. But at least now she has prevailed upon her to take her page with her, which is something.'

'A page is not much protection. Such headstrong and foolish behaviour could get her into trouble.'

'Then perhaps there lies your opportunity to discover her guilty secret, by volunteering your services as her escort,' suggested Harry with a smile.

'I think that would be taking family friendship too far – and such particular interest might wake expectations in her that I have no intention of fulfilling. You know, I have sometimes had a suspicion that I know what her secret is – only to doubt my sanity in the next second. I should be more than happy to have my ideas disproved.'

'This sounds very intriguing, Serle, but I suppose you mean to tantalize me by keeping your ideas to yourself?'

'For the present, for I daresay the explanation is quite mundane and you would think I had run mad if I told you what was in my head.'

'I believe Mrs Rivers said they were to be at Miss Berry's salon tonight. Do you not also intend to go?'

'Yes, Miss Berry and her sister have always kindly included me in their invitations. Do you wish to come with me? They would make you very welcome, I am sure.'

'No, I think it best if I do not come tonight, if Mrs Rivers is to be there,' Harry said, a cloud passing over his face. 'But I might take a stroll out later and see if anyone from the Brigade is in town.'

'And I think I will go and have a word with Jarvis, for I have it in mind to set him on to watch where Miss Weston goes,' Rayven said thoughtfully. He had employed the old soldier as porter at the London house, but knew he found it slow after life on the Peninsula and would welcome a change.

When Nat Hartwood, true to his word, arrived to take Alys driving in the park, he found her alone apart from Pug, who took an instant and vociferous dislike to him.

'Mrs Rivers sends her apologies, but she is laid down upon her bed with a headache and – oh, pray hush, Pug! Sammy, do take him away and look after him until my return.'

'I am afraid I do not care much for dogs, or they for me,' Nat said with a rueful smile. 'But if the little fellow is yours, then I see I must take pains to win him round.'

'You may easily do so by offering him some choice morsel, for he is very greedy,' Alys said, returning the smile rather breathlessly, so dazzling was it.

From the top of his burnished and pomaded golden curls to the heels of his immaculately glossy topboots, he was the picture of such masculine perfection as to gladden the heart of any maiden, even one normally as unimpressionable as Alys. If his breeches clung so tightly that she wondered, most indelicately, how he would manage to sit down, and his fine blue cloth coat fitted so closely that he must have been inserted into it with some difficulty by his valet, yet the broad shouldered frame beneath it owed nothing to art and all to nature.

'I am sorry if Mrs Rivers is not feeling quite the thing. Bella, too, would have come, but begs to be excused, for she is having a morning ball with her particular friends to practise the quadrille – and, if our mother permits, the waltz.'

Since Bella's coming-out ball was to be the very next week, Alys well understood the urgency of mastering the intricate steps of the quadrille, something she herself had yet to learn.

Outside awaited a fashionable equipage into which she was tenderly assisted, and as Nat drove her through Hyde Park Alys, for the first time, knew what it was to be the centre of other women's envious regard . . . though after a while she began to wish that Nat would spend less time in returning the greetings of his many acquaintances and instead pay more attention to his pair of showy, high-stepping greys.

'It is amazing how many people already seem to know that I am Mr Hartwood's granddaughter,' she remarked, after yet another such exchange of civilities, 'and are agog to know why they have not before heard of me.'

'I am afraid my mother is the greatest gossip imaginable,' he said with a charmingly rueful smile.

'Well, it is no great secret after all and – oh, *do* pray watch that barouche, for I am sure there is not enough room to get by!'

The smile vanished. 'I am accounted no mean whip, Cousin, you need have no fear on that head.'

'Of course – it is just that I am unused to such a carriage as this,' she said hastily. Nor was she an expert on handling the reins, but she suspected that his skills were not such as would justify the vehicle in which she found herself perched so dangerously high above the ground, and the strong fear of their being overturned quite took the edge off her pleasure.

When she unexpectedly spotted a familiar, diminutive figure walking nearby in a party consisting of several children, a nursemaid and an elderly gentleman, she was glad of the excuse to ask her cousin to stop. 'It is Miss Grimshaw, my companion for many years, who is at present making a stay with her relatives – those must be some of her nephews and nieces with her.'

She waved vigorously to attract their attention and when they came up said, 'Why, Letty, I did not think to see you here! I meant to call on you in a day or two, to see how you did, but I can see for myself that you are very well. This is my cousin, Mr Nathaniel Hartwood.'

'How do you do, sir?' Letty said, casting a doubtful and flustered glance upwards. 'The weather was so fine and the children wished to fly their kites, so that when Mr Puncheon offered to escort us . . . but what am I thinking of? Allow me to introduce Mr Puncheon.'

Mr Puncheon, a portly man with a pleasant, ruddy face and silver hair, bowed and Alys said, 'I am pleased to meet you, sir, for Mr Grimshaw mentioned you as an old family friend.'

'And I have heard much of you, Miss Weston.' He favoured her with a serious, searching gaze from china blue eyes, and she wondered quite what Letty had been telling him about her erstwhile charge.

She was surprised to see that Nat acknowledged the introductions with the barest of chilly civility, and soon made an excuse of not wishing to keep his horses standing in the cool breeze to drive on.

'I have never seen Letty in such looks – her little holiday must be doing her good. Mr Puncheon seemed very amiable and a great favourite with the children.'

'He looked to me like a cit,' Nat said, as his horses took objection to a boy bowling a metal hoop alongside them and showed an alarming tendency to bolt back to their stable.

'I believe he is a retired tea merchant,' Alys said, amused at her cousin's pride, that made him look down on anyone connected with trade. 'But a perfectly respectable man.'

They turned for home, much to her relief, for the outing had not been one of unalloyed pleasure even though Nat professed himself delighted with her company.

'We are bound for the Miss Berrys' salon tonight,' she remarked as he handed her down from the carriage. (And how relieved she was to have her feet planted on firm ground again.) 'Might we see you there?'

'No, I am afraid I have a prior engagement,' he said, not mentioning that he was instead bound upon a more insalubrious party of pleasure with friends. 'How I wish, now, that I had not.'

He took her hand and favoured her with that practised smile, looking deeply into her eyes . . . but this time, strangely, her heart did not race and she was not breathless.

As she ran up the steps and into the house, she thought how brief her dazzlement by a handsome face and charming manner had been. But there was also a lingering regret, for it was as though the sun was still shining brightly, only she could no longer feel the warmth of its rays.

Fortunately, Nell, though heavy-eyed, was recovered enough to escort her that evening, and Alys found she was enjoying herself far more than she thought she would, especially once Miss Berry introduced her to a young man who was, she declared, an expert on underground drainage.

'Miss Weston,' she told him with a twinkle in her eyes, 'is exceedingly fond of underground passages, Mr Stevens, so do pray tell her of the many hidden waterways beneath London that you once described to me.'

'Oh yes, if you please, for I had no idea such things existed,' Alys begged him. 'Are they made by nature or man, and what is their purpose?'

'I believe they were sewers built by the Romans, who had expertise in such things that we have not. Their hygienic arrangements were far superior to ours. The passages cover many miles and a man may stand upright in parts of them.'

Alys, the picture of demure prettiness in an embroidered cambric dress in a becoming old-rose colour, said longingly, 'Oh, how much I should like to see those tunnels!'

'Their construction is certainly worthy of close scrutiny, but I am afraid that would be *quite* impossible for a young lady,' he said. 'In fact, I should be ashamed of myself, boring on about things of no possible interest to the fairer sex and, indeed, possibly of too unsavoury a character for their ears.'

'Not at all – I assure you I am quite fascinated,' Alys said encouragingly, for it seemed that all the interesting or exciting things in life were to be denied to her by reason of her sex. That some should be denied to her by reason of her encumbering skirts – well, *that* she could understand, for she had often found them a nuisance while clambering through the caverns in Yorkshire. But why being female should in itself preclude her from these delights, she could not fathom.

Lord Rayven, who had arrived late and, having made his way through the room, was now standing unnoticed directly behind her said, 'Ah, Stevens, but Miss Weston is not your usual delicate and swooning young lady, for she delights in dark underground places.'

Alys started and turned round as he added, 'She explored my very own cellars at Priory Chase quite thoroughly when she visited some years ago with her aunt and, I am told, penetrated even to their furthest damp and crumbling reaches. She is quite intrepid.'

'Explored your *cellars*, my lord?' began Mr Stevens, uncertain as to whether he was serious or not.

'Indeed I did,' Alys said, her eyes lighting up. 'The older parts, where they run under the abbey, are quite delightful. I used a description—'

'Yes?' Rayven said intently, as she broke off, his dark-blue eyes fixed on her face.

'I used a description of them in a letter to my companion, Miss Grimshaw,' Alys continued smoothly, aghast at how easily she had almost given herself away. 'She said it made her feel that she had been there with me, though she was very glad she had not.'

'You are singular indeed, Miss Weston,' Mr Stevens said, looking equally divided between admiration and disapproval; then he bowed and moved off.

Alys gazed after him wistfully: surely, with a little more persuasion, he might have been worked on to enable her to take just a glimpse of this fascinating underground labyrinth?

'You will not prevail on him to show you the Roman sewers, Miss Weston,' Rayven said sympathetically. 'I am afraid Stevens is a very correct young man, who would fear for your delicate sensibilities should he do so.'

'I don't think I *have* any delicate sensibilities,' Alys said absently. 'I daresay ladylike airs and susceptibilities have to be schooled into you from childhood. Besides, when you have a household to run and an invalid father demanding your constant attention, there is no time for such airs and graces.'

'I suppose not,' he agreed, thinking how well a pretty dress and a new way of arranging her dark chestnut hair had transformed her from the last time they had met. 'Do you know, Miss Weston, though you always contrive to look the part of a demure young lady, I suspect you have hidden depths . . . a bit like Stevens' underground waterways.'

Alys stared at him suspiciously. 'Likening me to a sewer can hardly be said to be a compliment, my lord.'

'I thought in your case the analogy might please you, given your interests. Tell me, do you make a long stay with Mrs Rivers?'

'She has invited me to spend the whole season with her.'

'Then I suppose that this will be only the first of many engagements.'

'Yes, for several friends of Mrs Rivers have already included me in their invitations, and though I did not come to London intending her to launch me into Society, she most earnestly wishes for my company.'

'Your interests *do* seem to differ a little from those of Mrs Rivers. Harry Stavely tells me that you venture forth most mornings to see the sights – but you really should not be driving round London with just a page for company, you know!'

'It is kind of you to concern yourself in my affairs, but that is a great nonsense, for at my age it cannot be thought improper.'

'You are very unwise and will find this great age you profess no protection, for let me tell you, you are still a *very* green girl.'

'I have long done with girlhood, and I believe I am the best judge of my own actions, my lord.'

'Then at least think of the ill light any mishap must cast upon your friend's care of you while you are residing under her roof.'

Alys glared at him in exasperation. 'There will be no mishap and I will soon have exhausted those things that interest me that are still extant, for my guide book is sadly out of date. But I have yet to visit Westminster Abbey, or the Egyptian Hall, and I am very sure Nell will not wish to go with me, for she has no interest in antiquities and curiosities.'

'Then pray allow me to offer myself as your escort,' he heard himself saying, without in the least meaning to.

'What?' She stared at him, wondering if she had heard aright.

'My curricle – and myself – will be at your command each morning.'

'*You?* But I assure you I do not need an escort, and besides—'

'I insist, Miss Weston: I am sure your grandfather would not wish you to go alone, were he to hear of it.'

'I am the only arbiter of my behaviour, Lord Rayven, and I will do as I please.'

'Then I hope it will please you to accept my escort.' He flicked open a small engraved silver box and took a pinch of snuff before looking up and adding, 'For if you do not, you will find me following you about the town in a way that may draw even more unwelcome attention to your actions.'

Indignant grey eyes met dark blue in a long, measuring exchange. What the outcome might have been was in the balance, for at this interesting point Miss Agnes Berry interrupted them.

She had brought a dandified youth with her, whom she introduced as Mr Daniel Coalport. 'I know *you* will be interested, Miss Weston, for you are a great reader of the Gothic, and Mr Coalport has a *particular* interest in the works of Orlando Browne.'

The young man bowed over Alys's hand and with mock modesty lisped, 'Oh, Mith Agnes, you should not tease me on that subject, for you know my lipth are sealed.'

'Long may they remain so!' Alys said tartly, snatching her hand back, and the young man, caught off balance, nearly fell over.

'I do not . . . get your meaning, Mith Weston?'

Lord Rayven, who had watched with fascination the swift play of emotions across Alys's mobile face, said kindly to the disconcerted youth, 'I believe Miss Weston means that she adores a mystery so much, that she prefers to imagine the author of such gems as *The Travails of Lady Malvina* as immured in some antique fortress, pen in hand. Pray, do not disillusion her.'

'Oh – of course not,' stammered the youth, and backed himself away.

'Naughty!' chided Miss Agnes with a chuckle, following suit.

'You . . . like to read novels?' Alys said cautiously, staring at Lord Rayven much as she had done at the hungry lions pacing the Tower.

'Occasionally. I am quite fascinated by the works of Mr Browne – and he, it would seem, with me – for many acquaintances have pointed out the singular parity in the appearance of that author's villains and myself.'

'In-indeed?' Alys stammered, then catching sight of Nell waving a gloved hand at her, added with relief, 'Pray excuse me, sir, I believe Mrs Rivers is ready to leave now.'

'Then until tomorrow morning, Miss Weston,' he said, and she was so keen to get away that she protested no more.

'Nell, the most annoying thing!' she said, once they were seated in the carriage. 'Mr Stavely told Lord Rayven that I go out alone every morning, and now he insists on escorting me. But surely it must be even more improper to do so with a man not related to me and one, moreover, that I know to be a libertine, for only remember the nature of the offer he made me in Knaresborough.'

'But that was a mistake, Alys, and I do not think you could call Lord Rayven a libertine, precisely. I daresay he may have a mistress in keeping, for many men do so, but I have heard no worse of him than that.'

'I think that is bad enough,' Alys said primly.

'His character is in general held to be good,' Nell assured her. 'Grandfather told me that he has made many improvements to his estates and is well regarded by his tenants, and George says he is a first rate horseman, and can drive to the inch.'

'Oh? Then I do not suppose he will overturn me, at least, which I was once or twice concerned about with my cousin. But surely it is not the thing to drive about alone with him?'

'It will be perfectly respectable in an open carriage, and I daresay he will have his groom up behind, too. How kind it is of him to offer.'

'I am not sure that kindness enters into it – in fact, I am starting to think that he delights in teasing me and perhaps only means to pay me back for pushing him into the river!'

'Or perhaps he is trying to make amends for his gross misreading of your character?'

'Well, whatever his reasoning, I expect he will soon be heartily bored and wish he had not offered himself as my escort.' She paused reflectively. 'You know, Nell, it is the oddest thing, but although he did not look as if he needed two strong men to put him into his coat, and his neckcloth was no more than moderate, yet he appeared more truly the gentleman than Nat, who struck me at first as the acme of perfection.'

She yawned. 'This has been a day of surprises and revelations, and I must go to bed as soon as we are home.'

'I too,' agreed Nell. 'I-I am glad that Mr Stavely did not accompany his friend tonight.'

'Did you expect him to? I thought you had agreed that it would be best if you avoided each other's company as much as possible.'

'Yes . . .'

'It is for the best, Nell.'

'By the by,' Nell said, after a moment's silence, 'did I mention that Miss Chibberly and I have got up a little plan to teach you the quadrille and the waltz tomorrow? Her sister Sophia is to play the music.'

'That is kind, but I do not imagine I need such skills.'

'Bella Hartwood's ball – we have received invitations for it, and you must surely mean to go?'

'Oh lord!' Alys said. 'I suppose I must.'

CHAPTER 18

Driven

Now fear also imprisoned Cecily, for the accidents that seemed to dog her footsteps were too numerous to be anything other than an attempt on her life, and she was sorely afraid.

Could she – should she – trust Simon de Lombard? His dark and silent form dogged her every footstep, though whether he was jailer or protector she had yet to determine.

Ravish'd by Cruel Fate by Orlando Browne

Alys put on one of her prettier walking dresses the next morning as armour against Lord Rayven's unwanted and sardonic presence, but it was a decision she was later to regret.

She was ready in very good time and, as usual, immediately set forth to give Pug an airing in Portman Square before leaving him with Sammy.

It was really the nicest day they had had since her arrival in London, she reflected, stepping into the quiet road with Pug and heading towards the sooty expanse of grass that passed for a garden. He had caught an intriguing scent and was tugging at his lead, and she only hoped it was not something unsavoury, for he was a changed dog these days and had developed a nose for such delicacies as old fishheads and the like. Unfortunately, he was not bright enough to realize that his only reward for such cleverness was to be bathed, a procedure he hated.

The sudden sound of hoofs and the rumble of wheels warned her of a carriage's fast approach. Looking up, startled, she glimpsed it almost upon her – the flared red nostrils of the horses, their flashing hoofs and a caped figure driving them, his face concealed by a hat pulled low and a muffler.

Reacting without thought, she scooped up Pug and flung herself aside, staggering as the vehicle rushed past, then sat down hard upon the road.

Pug must have slipped from her grasp, for he walked up and licked her face, before settling himself down next to her in a fidgety sort of way, like an old gentleman uncertain if he wished to sit on so dirty a surface. Alys was very certain that she did not, yet she seemed to have lost the power to rise to her feet.

The carriage had not stopped, or even slackened speed, and now vanished, leaving only a slatternly maid as audience to her mishap. She was standing some yards away regarding Alys with her mouth open, but as a smart curricle drew up she scurried away, as if she might be blamed for the incident.

Alys flinched, but it was merely Lord Rayven. He leapt down, tossing the reins to his groom and, stooping over her, demanded urgently, 'Miss Weston? Are you hurt? I had no very clear view of what happened, for I was just turning the corner, but I did not think you were struck.'

Alys looked up ... and it seemed a *long* way up ... to his concerned eyes.

'Come,' he said, 'can you stand? We must get you indoors again. I cannot think how you come to be out here alone in the first place.'

'Too autocratic ...' she murmured, hauled to her feet and dizzily leaning on his arm. Then she pulled herself together and stood erect, smoothing down a gown that was beyond repair and straightening her bonnet. 'I was taking Pug for a turn up and down the square, as I do every morning before I go out.'

'You should not do so.' He retrieved the end of Pug's lead and handed it to her.

'For fear of an accident?'

'Does it not strike you as odd that a carriage should almost hit the only pedestrian in the street at this time of the morning and then drive on without stopping?'

'There was a maid ... but she is gone. And I suppose the driver was so aghast at the result of his lapse of attention to the road that he was afraid to turn back. But thank you for your assistance, Lord Rayven.'

'It is as well that I was early,' he said cryptically, then added, 'I do not suppose you still mean to go out today?'

She looked at him in surprise. 'I do not see why not. I must change my dress, of course, but that will not take me more than a very few minutes, and then I wish to see Westminster Abbey. Nell says the effigies in one of the chapels are *horrid*.'

'I suppose they are, but we need not look at them.'

'Not look at them? Why, had I known about them earlier, I would have already visited the Abbey! But you cannot wish to see sights that must be commonplace to you and I will be perfectly safe there, surely, so that—'

'I will await you,' he said firmly, and he was very surprised when she did indeed run out again in little more than ten minutes, still tying the pink ribbons of her bonnet and a little hampered in that task by the ominously fat guidebook under her arm.

Lord Rayven's horses were fresh and lively, but it was a relief to see how well he handled the reins: indeed, it made her realize in comparison how very poor her cousin Nat's skills in that direction were. She stole a look at her companion's hawk-nosed and arresting, if not precisely handsome, face, and thought he looked as if he was wishing himself elsewhere.

'How quiet the town is so early – it is quite my favourite time of day. But I am sorry to drag *you* from your bed, for it seems to me that fashionable folk are out half the night and asleep most of the day.'

Mr Rivers, she had noticed, very often did not come home at all, for his candle was still on the hall table when she went out in the mornings. But she supposed Nell was only too glad not to have his company these days.

'You forget I was a soldier, Miss Weston, and so have not managed to attain the habit of sleeping late. I find my head very clear for transacting business first thing, and then often ride in the park before breakfast.'

'Then I am sorry to divert you from your usual habits, though it is quite your own fault for insisting. I cannot imagine why you do so.'

'Why, I hope to make some amends for so grossly mistaking your character in Harrogate, by rendering you this small service,' he said lightly.

'Then are you not afraid that people will think it very odd behaviour in you, should it become known that you are driving me about every morning in this fashion?'

She saw by some slight change in his expression that she had hit the nail on the head, and he was regretting his impulsive offer, for fear that she – and the world – should take his attentions to mean a warmer interest in her than he felt.

'Should anyone mention the matter, I would advise you to say that I do so at the particular request of your grandfather,' he suggested, 'and I will do the same.'

'Oh, it does not matter to me what people assume, for since I have no intention of marrying I do not fear that your actions will put off potential suitors. In fact, I will probably tell anyone vulgar enough to mention the matter, that I cordially dislike you and that you inflicted your company on me without any encouragement whatsoever.'

'Thank you, Miss Weston,' he said, rather tight-lipped.

'You are very welcome, sir. I would not for the world cause any pang of jealousy in the bosoms of those *numerous* eligible young ladies who are, I am convinced, hoping that you will cast the handkerchief in their direction.'

Since choosing a suitable bride *had* been his intention this season, he felt unreasonably annoyed – and piqued.

'It seems we understand each other,' he said shortly, and then said no more until they reached their destination.

Alys was pleased with Westminster Abbey which so early in the day had a gloomy air of importance, as if it knew many secrets she did not – which she supposed it might well do.

But the chapel with the rather decayed effigies particularly took her fancy. Lord Rayven watched her in some amusement as she carefully looked over each, before standing in the middle and murmuring, with her eyes half-closed, 'At night – illuminated only by rays of moonlight shining through the windows? If this should be the chapel of some Gothic mansion, and she is locked there, alone . . . She tells herself there is nothing to fear from the dead or from the waxen figures, but then one begins to slowly move towards her. . . .'

She opened her eyes and saw that Rayven was watching her with a very odd expression on his face. 'Oh, pray excuse me,' she said with an unconvincing laugh, 'for I have been reading too many novels, you know, so that my imagination runs away with me.'

'Yes, so I perceive. Perhaps you should read the more sober works of Miss Austen until you have recovered from such fits of fancy?'

'I very much enjoy her books already, for her heroines are sensible and she sorts out the tangles so neatly—' She stopped.

'Well, if you have seen enough, perhaps we should return home?' he suggested.

Alys cast a last lingering glance at the still figures around her, then reluctantly accompanied him out, intending to write down the scene that had occurred to her the very second she could, for it was so vivid in her mind.

Lord Rayven left her at the Rivers' house with an admonition not to walk Pug alone any more, to which she answered nothing, not meaning to let one unfortunate accident stop her – though she might, for the time being, avoid crossing the road. . . .

Alys just had time to pen a description of her accident and her impressions of the chapel at Westminster Abbey before breakfast. They would have to be written up later, for not only was she to learn the steps of the quadrille that day, but also visit her grandfather again.

An escape from under the wheels of a mysterious carriage would become an exciting new chapter in *Death or Dishonour*, a deliberate and murderous act on the part of the villainous Sir Lemuel Grosby, who wished to kill his wife and so leave the way clear to marry Drusilla who was an heiress, though she did not yet know it.

Perhaps when she snatches Lady Grosby from under the very wheels, Drusilla catches sight of the fury on Sir Lemuel's face, though he explains it as being directed at the driver. . . ?

But in her own case, of course, no one could desire her death. It had been an unfortunate accident and the driver had been too afraid of what he might have done to turn back.

*

The Misses Chibberley were both sad romps and had brought their lively younger brother with them to be her partner, so that Alys found the dancing practice somewhat exhausting – especially since she was already conscious of stiffness and bruising in places a lady was not supposed to mention from her sudden contact with the hard road that morning.

But by the end of it she thought she had a reasonable grasp of the complicated steps of the quadrille and even the rudiments of the waltz, though she did not think herself likely to ever be confident enough to take to the floor in that dance, even had she the opportunity.

She arrived at the Hartwood mansion just as a gentleman strangely attired in striped pantaloons of voluminous cut, caught in at the ankle, was coming out.

When she was shown up to her grandfather's room, she found him brooding over a fine ivory chess set.

'I do not suppose you play chess? Lord Petersham has just given me a game, but his play is damned erratic!'

'Oh, is *that* who it was I saw leaving the house?' Alys had heard of the rather eccentric peer. 'Yes, I do know the rudiments of chess, for my cousin Thomas Basset taught me, though he would play no more once I achieved proficiency at the game and always won. It was unfortunate, for I enjoyed it, and though I tried to teach it to Miss Grimshaw, my companion, she could never quite grasp it. Papa had not the patience for it.'

'Then you may give me a game,' he said, beginning to set out the pieces.

'Very well, though I warn you I am very out of practice,' she said, casting her bonnet on to a chair and sitting down opposite him. She started with caution, finding him as hard and wily an opponent as she would have expected, but soon began to gain enough confidence to give him a run for his money. He had the final victory, but it was hard fought.

'You play well – for a girl.'

'Thank you,' she said drily. 'That is a compliment indeed. I hope if you will give me a little more practice, to play even better.'

'You can come back tomorrow.'

'I am afraid I cannot; I am driving out to Kew with Mrs Rivers. She interests herself in a charitable house run by an Evangelical group of ladies, designed to take poor children and fit them for respectable occupations as servants, and I am looking forward to the visit.'

'Then the day after. I do not suppose that your days are yet so full of engagements that you cannot spare your grandfather an occasional hour of your time?'

'No, and of course if you wish it, I will come.'

'I hear that Rayven was squiring you about the town this morning.'

She stared at him in astonishment: 'How quickly news travels, but I should not be surprised when the very day after we met half London seemed to know of our relationship. But you must know that I am the most complete country bumpkin and wish to see all the sights of London, and Lord Rayven insists on going with me, though I have no need of an escort.'

'Yes, he wrote to me himself to say he was to do so, for he knew I would not like you to go alone. But your cousin Nat would do the same office.'

'Perhaps, but Nat strikes me as a man of such fashion that he would not thank you for the suggestion that he rise hours before his usual time in order to look at a lot of old tombs, buildings and museums.'

'Is that what you do?'

'Yes – this morning I much enjoyed myself in Westminster Abbey, and tomorrow—'

They were interrupted by a tap on the door and a soft voice calling, 'Uncle Titus? May I come in?'

'Ah Bella, my dear, you see Alys is here, giving me a game of chess.'

Bella pouted. 'Oh chess – I do not understand it in the least. But my cousin is so clever, it does not surprise me that she can play – in fact I suspect she is quite a bluestocking.'

'So you have said before, but I am not any such thing, unfortunately.'

'I came to thank dear Uncle for his generosity. I expect you have a mind above such things as new gowns, Cousin, but I am in transports, for I am to have the most wonderful ball dress of white satin with a pink net overdress for my come-out, and wear a blush pink rose garland in my hair.'

'You need not thank me, for I told your mother to get what you needed and send the bills to me.' His eye fell on Alys, who was neat, if not bang up to the nines, in a striped cambric gown she had had made for her by an inexpensive dressmaker found by the invaluable Jane, from materials purchased at the Pantheon Bazaar. 'I suppose you might as well do the same, Alys, for you will need a ballgown to wear for Bella's party.'

'I thank you, Grandfather, but I already have a ballgown, one rather more suited to my years than pink net and rosebuds.'

'Well, run along, both of you, I grow tired of such frippery talk,' he said, rather unfairly, Alys thought, since she had not introduced the topic of fashion in the first place.

'Nat is in the drawing-room, waiting to drive you home, Cousin,' Bella said, as soon as the doors were closed behind them. Alys noted that her fluffily girlish manner rather dropped away as soon as she was out of her uncle's sight, and thought it sad that she felt she must put on those airs in order to gain his affection.

'That is very kind, but I believe I must not trouble him again,' she said hastily.

'Oh, but he has already sent away your carriage, for he insists on having the pleasure of your company.'

'How ... delightful,' Alys said, earnestly hoping that today he might at least be driving horses over which he had *some* control.

CHAPTER 19

Peerless

'I agreed to escort my kinswoman here,' Simon de Lombard said, 'but would not have lingered so long had I not set eyes on you. To find you were betrothed to another was a cruel blow, but I soon discovered he was unworthy of you and determined to wait and ask your father for your hand on his return.'
Ravish'd by Cruel Fate by Orlando Browne

'You like my cousin Nat, don't you, Nell?' she said next day, as they drove out towards Kew to visit the Red House, as the establishment founded by the Benevolent Ladies was called.

'Yes, for he is always kind and charming *and* so very elegant! He is the only one of George's old friends who seems to be a good influence on him, and even chaffed him back to good humour on the humiliating occasion when he showed his anger with me in public.'

'I like him too – it would be hard not to, especially when he insists that nothing would please him more than the pleasure of my company if I should allow him to drive me home, as he did yesterday. But I wish he were not so very cow-handed with the reins, for I am in a constant fear that he will overturn me. Do you know, my grandfather had *already* heard of my morning sightseeing expeditions, and said he would prefer Nat to escort me rather than Lord Rayven, though I told him Nat would not thank him for the suggestion.'

'Have you thought that Mr Hartwood might hope to make a

match between you and Nat?'

Alys laughed. 'Oh Nell, I am sure he cannot have any such idea – or Nat, who is so very handsome that I can only wonder that some eligible maiden has not snapped him up in matrimony long since.'

'He *is* very popular with the ladies, but his father did not leave him any great fortune, though it is well known that he and Bella are Mr Titus Hartwood's heirs ... or it *was*, for now perhaps that has changed?'

'I do not think it: Bella in particular has been my grandfather's pet for so long that I cannot imagine her being cut out. I may be his granddaughter, but I am still little more than a stranger to him and he is baffled and angered by my wish to remain independent.'

'I believe Nat has been living on his expectations and there are rumours current that he is paying court to Miss Malfont, who is the daughter of a wealthy mill owner, so he must have outrun the fiddler. But if your grandfather decided to leave his personal fortune to you, then I can quite see that a match between you and Nat would be perfect.'

'Perfect for whom?' demanded Alys. 'This is a great deal of nonsense, Nell! I admit I was dazzled by Nat when I first met him – I would have to be made of marble not to have been – but, like all men, I can see that he has feet of clay and do not in the least wish to marry him – or *anyone*.'

'Oh well, perhaps you are right – though people will talk when it becomes known that both he and Lord Rayven are seen so often in your company.'

'There is nothing lover-like about Lord Rayven, I thank God, and I have made it plain to him that he is in no danger of my mistaking the nature of his attentions,' Alys said. 'I am glad to say we now understand each other very well. By the by, I was not much taken with Carlton House, which we saw this morning.'

Nell was looking pensive. 'Did Lord Rayven say if Mr Stavely is still staying with him? I have not seen him for some days ... though, of course, as you know, we agreed that we must part, and meet in future only as friends.'

'Nell, I am sure were you simply to lift your little finger he would come running, but you have chosen the sensible course, and must stick to it.'

Nell sighed. 'I do know. I – I told him to find some eligible lady and propose to her and I hoped I would dance at his wedding.'

Alys pressed her hand but said nothing, for there was no advice she could give in such a situation, only support when it was needed. She hardly knew how to keep her tongue between her teeth on the increasingly rare occasions when George Rivers dined at home, now she knew how he mistreated poor Nell.

'I see Sammy is up on the box,' she said, changing the subject. 'Does he like to drive out into the country?'

'Yes, I always bring him, for it is pleasant for him to spend some time with his old friends at the Red House. There is one in particular, Sarah, whom he has known since childhood. She is a very quick, sensible kind of girl of nearly fourteen, who hopes to become a lady's-maid. At present she has been helping the dame with the little ones, but I have it in mind to put her under Jane for a while to learn from her, before finding her a situation with one of my acquaintances. Perhaps she may look after you, under Jane's tutelage, while you are staying with me?'

'Why not? It would be a novelty to me to have my own abigail, and I daresay we could both learn together.'

The wall enclosing Lord Chase's gardens ran beside the road for some distance, and Alys thought wistfully of the Roman mosaic and the ancient passageway to the river leading from his cellars. Nell had told her, too, of a shell chamber he had had reconstructed from a grotto created at Twickenham by the poet Pope, which she would very much like to see.

It was a great pity that he sounded so very disagreeable!

The Red House lay well set back on the opposite side of the road. Comfortably, if plainly, furnished, it was in the charge of two middle-aged spinster sisters, plump, cheerful women in starched white caps and aprons. Order and cleanliness reigned supreme and the children all looked healthy and cheerful. Nell was obviously a great favourite with them and was quite mobbed as she distributed the little treats she had brought with her.

Alys liked Sarah, a shy, pretty girl, very much, and over the tea tray, Nell mooted the idea of appointing her as Alys's maid, under the tutelage of her own Jane.

It was fixed that she should come to them at the end of the following week, and Sarah, much excited, came to the gate to see them off just as a curricle drawn by a rather familiar pair of high-stepping grey horses was passing.

It was hastily reined in, and Nat called gaily, 'Good day Mrs Rivers – Cousin!' The smile that would once have set Alys's heart a-flutter and which now, strangely, had no effect on that organ, was bestowed upon them. 'I know Lord Chase needs no introduction to you,' he said to Nell with a bow, 'but I believe you have not met my cousin, Miss Weston, Frances?'

'How do you do,' Alys said, looking up curiously at his lordship as he extended a gloved hand that shook slightly. He was a pallid man of nearer forty than thirty, with thin lank hair and unsettlingly restless eyes, and there was something febrile about him – a sort of suppressed and unwholesome air of excitement – that she found repellent.

'I have heard of the work you good ladies are doing here,' Chase said languidly, eyeing Sarah in an appraising way. Then he smiled at her and she blushed hotly before dropping a flustered curtsy and running back into the house.

'One of your protégées, Mrs Rivers?' Nat asked.

'Yes,' Nell said shortly, as the groom who had been walking their horses approached and Sammy emerged from the house. 'Pray, excuse us – here is our carriage, and I do not wish to keep the horses standing.'

'I see what you mean about Lord Chase,' Alys said, once they were in the carriage and bowling back to London. 'How comes Nat to have such an odious friend? I took an immediate dislike to him myself and I am sure I would have done so even if I had known nothing unsavoury about him.'

'I own I did not like the way he was looking at Sarah in the least. They cannot keep young maidservants at Templeshore House, you know – no respectable young woman would go there.'

'Well, Sarah at least is safe from *that* fate, for once your Jane has trained her up, I am sure she will soon find a good post with a respectable family.'

*

Lord Rayven duly presented himself every morning, and if Alys discovered that it was much more enjoyable to be driven about by such an escort than to go alone, he, too, found himself amused by her interest in everything new to her.

He did not fulfil his professed aim of discovering the source of her income, but he did learn more of her character: she put on no airs to be interesting but was entirely natural – headstrong, opinionated and sometimes alarmingly independent in her ideas, but wholly herself.

During the rest of each day he was never quite sure where he would see her next, for the season had begun and she often accompanied Mrs Rivers to routs, salons, breakfasts, concerts and a myriad other entertainments.

For now that Mrs Lavinia Hartwood and her daughter had called on them several times, and her position as Mr Titus Hartwood's granddaughter was established by the frequency of her visits to him, she had become more of an object of interest to Society than when she had been plain unknown Miss Weston from Yorkshire.

He knew that Nat Hartwood was also often in her company and began to wonder if her grandfather had indeed decided to promote a match between them. In the eyes of the world it would be a sensible union, and he supposed Alys to be no more proof against a handsome face than the next woman, but he could not say that he either liked or trusted Nat Hartwood. He might be almost universally popular, but anyone who was a part of the Chase set could not possibly be all they appeared.

Jarvis, who was still keeping an eye on Miss Weston's movements, though there had been no revelations of any interest so far, and he was mightily bored with the task, was instructed to keep his ears open and see what he could also find out about the Brethren.

'I did warn you that the Peerless Pool was long past its heyday and no longer the resort of the *ton*,' Rayven said, as he drove Alys home from their next excursion.

'Yes, but the melancholy decay was very picturesque and interesting,' she assured him. 'I liked it much better than the gardens of

Vauxhall, where Nell and I went with a party of friends yesterday, even though they are very extensive.'

'I can hardly wait to discover what treat you have found for us to explore tomorrow, Miss Weston.'

'Why none, for I am paying an early call on an acquaintance and then afterwards I mean to see Miss Grimshaw, who is staying with relatives in Cheapside.'

'Very well – until the day after tomorrow then,' he said, handing her down from the carriage with the rare but delightful smile that most women would have found near irresistible, but that caused Alys to look at him mistrustfully.

'And pray remember me kindly to Miss Grimshaw,' he added.

'I am sure she is unlikely ever to forget you,' she said tartly. 'She was quite horrified when she learned of our excursions.'

But the thought crossed her mind like a shadow that she was fast running out of sights to see – unless she began to revisit them all, of course!

CHAPTER 20

Gentlemen Callers

'I am no longer the heiress you might have thought me, Simon – no rich prize. Even my betrothed has spurned me for another.'

'I care naught for that. Come with me – my home is far away and of a humbler kind, yet you would be mistress of all and my honoured wife.'

Ravish'd by Cruel Fate by Orlando Browne

'Well, Letty,' Alys said, kissing her cheek, 'it is good to find you alone, for it seems to me that you are so often in company with Mr Puncheon, that I suspect him of dangling after you.'

'Really, Alys – dangling after me!' Miss Grimshaw exclaimed, blushing.

'You look so handsome in that lavender gown and new cap that it would not be at all surprising. But I did not come to put you to the blush, rather to have a good coze and catch up with the news. You will never guess who I have been to visit this morning.'

'Pray, do tell me, Alys.'

'Mrs Radcliffe! I wrote asking her if she would allow me to call on her, and she kindly said I might.'

'And what is she like?'

'A lady of middle years – kindly, serious and very earnest, not at all how I had imagined her. She warned me not to overstep the boundaries of taste and propriety in my novels. I believe she rather repents of having written hers, for I am sure the author of *The Mysteries of Udolpho* cannot always have been so very *worthy*.'

'I do not know how it is in the least, since you are *quite* unworldly, my dear, but the tone of some passages in your books is decidedly warm,' ventured Miss Grimshaw, looking troubled.

'I do not suppose I would sell so well if they were not. And if they are due to my letting my imagination stray into areas where a maiden lady's should not go, then so be it. But what of you? You look very well – are you enjoying your holiday?'

A shadow crossed her companion's face. 'Yes indeed ... my nephew and his family have made me very welcome. I am quite at home here.'

'But it is not your own home, is it? Is that what troubles you? But do not worry, for Thomas is already getting particulars of houses for us in York, as I told you, so that very soon we will be settled there together and you may be easy again.'

'Oh yes, how ... how nice that will be to be sure. Only ... although your mind was set against marriage, don't you think you might, after all, reconsider? From what I hear, both Lord Rayven and your cousin Mr Nathaniel Hartwood are very attentive to you.'

Alys laughed. 'You have been listening to gossip! Lord Rayven's attentions were motivated by a desire to tease me at first, I am convinced, but now he is a little piqued by my indifference. And as to my cousin Nat, well, I was quite bowled over with him – did you ever see such a handsome man? – but it did not last more than a day or two. I do not like the way he treats animals, which is always a sure sign of character, is it not?'

'*Animals*, dearest Alys?'

'Yes, last time he came to call he kicked poor Pug out of the way when he thought no one observed him, simply for drooling over his hessians.'

'Gentlemen can be very particular about their boots, I have heard. Champagne in the blacking even, which seems a sad extravagance.'

'Perhaps, but also he treats his horses roughly, and does not speak to his groom in a way that your or I would speak to a servant. ... I don't know, it is all little things that make me feel that his character does not live up to his appearance.'

'Perhaps some other gentleman, then?'

'Dear Letty, do not worry that I mean to marry and abandon our plan of setting up home together, for I am still set on staying unwed and rely on you to lend me propriety and keep me company.'

'You are very kind,' said Miss Grimshaw, the ready tears starting to her eyes. 'You are right that I would not want to live as a pensioner here forever, even though my nephew and his family have made me more than welcome. But again, I would not in the least hold you back from making a happy marriage, should you find one worthy of your love.'

'There is no question of that.' She rose. 'Now, I believe Thomas is waiting in his study to discuss one or two business matters, so I will leave you.'

'I have near finished copying out *Ravish'd, Alys* – another day or two and it is done.'

'Good, for I mean to go to the Minerva Press with the manuscript myself and tell them who I am, so putting a stop to Mr Coalport's pretensions once and for all, for they can deny the rumours without divulging my name, you know.'

'So long as you are not seen going in,' Letty said anxiously.

'Unlikely. Have I ever thanked you for all the work you do for me, copying things out so faithfully? What would I do without you – and what in the world have I said to make you cry, dearest Letty?'

'N-nothing, do not regard it,' she sobbed, and vanished into a handkerchief.

'The young lady paid a visit to a Mrs Radcliffe,' Jarvis said, thumbing through a battered pocketbook. 'A lady novelist, she is.'

'So she is – or was – and quite a famous one,' Rayven said thoughtfully. 'I suppose you have been exerting your charms on the servants again to obtain such information, Jarvis?'

'The cooks can't bear to see a skinny man, sir, that's the way of it. But the next house Miss Weston called at, she'd been to before.'

'Yes, her companion, Miss Grimshaw, is staying with relatives in Cheapside: is that the place?'

'A very respectable family,' agreed Jarvis. 'And an uncommonly pretty maidservant a-shaking out her duster. She says the old biddy –

Miss Grimshaw – has got a caller.'

'A *caller?*'

'A retired tea-merchant called Puncheon is growing very particular in his attentions. Full of juice, he is, and a widower.'

Rayven tried, and failed, to bring Miss Grimshaw's undistinguished features to mind, then dismissed the matter. 'Did Miss Weston go home again after that?'

'Yes. Later she come out again with Mrs Rivers and got into a carriage with Mr Nathaniel Hartwood and a young fair lady. Rabbit-nosed.'

'Probably Miss Bella Hartwood.'

'Mr Hartwood seems to call often,' Jarvis commented, with a look at his master. 'Mr Rivers, he's out most nights, and looking burnt to the socket, racketing round town with his flash friends, Mr Hartwood among them.'

'Well, you can't say Nat Hartwood looks burnt to the socket – he must have sold his soul to the Devil.'

'Maybe he has, sir. You remember asking me to keep my ears open for any word about that odd set-up, the Brethren as they call themselves, that meet at Lord Chase's house near Kew?'

Rayven nodded. 'You have heard something?'

'Well, many men – and a few women – goes there, on nights when the moon is full, for some kind of unholy meeting.'

'That is pretty well common knowledge, and although they go masked, I daresay most of them know each other.'

'But what isn't so much known, sir, is there's an inner circle of the Brethren, that stays behind when the others go – and the names of George Rivers and Nathaniel Hartwood are bandied about, among others, as members of it.'

'Are they indeed? And was Gervase Stavely one of that select group, do you think?'

'So they say.'

'Captain Stavely made some enquiries into the Brethren and was assured it was a drinking and wenching club – all the usual excesses, but nothing so bad that it might cause his brother to take his own life.'

'I expect that's what most of 'em get up to – the common run of

Brethren, as you might say,' Jarvis said tolerantly, 'but there's nasty rumours going the rounds of what Lord Chase and his particular cronies might be getting up to – and them girls found dead and mutilated in the river nearby didn't rightly help matters.'

'Mutilated?'

'Raped, and carved up with symbols and stuff – and though they're the sort of drabs no one comes forward to claim, the local people have been putting two and two together, and they don't like the answer.'

'I should think not!' Lord Rayven said. 'You had better see if you can find out more, Jarvis – but without sticking your own neck out, mind!'

'I would not be entirely surprised at Chase being connected with such things, for I am told the pox has him so firmly in its grip that he is more than half crazed,' he said, retailing the information to Harry later that day. 'But I find it hard to believe that sane men would commit such foul acts.'

'Yes, and both Nat Hartwood and Rivers assured me that the meetings of the Brethren were harmless fun. In fact, Hartwood has invited me to go along on the next night of full moon to see for myself. But I do not suppose he meant me to learn of this inner circle of members,' Harry said. '*Could* it be true? And could Gervase have been involved in anything so very bad? I cannot think it of him.'

'Perhaps it is Chase alone who has been perpetrating these outrages? If Gervase found out about it, I daresay then he would feel in some part to blame,' Rayven suggested.

'Or maybe the rumours are wrong, Serle, and those poor girls were not the work of the Brethren at all? Perhaps I *will* go to their next meeting and see what goes on for myself.'

'Nothing but licentiousness and general debauchery, I should think,' Rayven said, and knowing his friend's serious character, he did not think he would find much pleasure there.

CHAPTER 21

Always the Villain

'Papa,' Drusilla said earnestly, while she sponged the sufferer's brow and rendered all the other small services that a loving heart can offer to an afflicted parent, 'I feel that there is something – some momentous secret! – that you are keeping from me. Would you not rest more easily if you shared the burden?'
                    Death or Dishonour *by Orlando Browne*

When the hired hack drew up outside the offices of the Minerva Press in Leadenhall Street, Thomas Grimshaw jumped down and assisted Alys to descend.

'Are you quite sure about this, Miss Weston?' he asked anxiously. 'Would it not be better to keep your anonymity after all?'

'I will – except to my publishers, who may put it about that that impostor, Daniel Coalport, is not the author of my books!' she said with a fiery glint in her eyes, and marched in briskly, the bulky parcel of manuscript under her arm.

Jarvis, paying off his own hack, rubbed his chin thoughtfully then commandeered a passing urchin to carry a note to Lord Rayven.

When Alys emerged some time later with Mr Lane in attentive attendance, it was to find Lord Rayven awaiting her, while his groom stood at the horse's heads.

'Ah, there you are, Miss Weston,' he said blandly. 'Had you been much longer I would have had to walk the horses.'

'Lord R-Rayven?' Alys stammered. 'What are you— I mean, *why* are you . . . were you *waiting* for me?' She cast a look behind her, but Mr Lane had vanished and the door to the Minerva office was firmly closed.

'Certainly . . . or perhaps for Mr Orlando Browne?' His dark brows raised, he observed her discomfiture. 'Unless, of course, your *companion* is this mysterious Mr Browne?'

She gathered her wits and, putting up her chin, said, 'I see that you know very well he is not. This is Mr Thomas Grimshaw, Miss Grimshaw's nephew. Thomas, this is Lord Rayven, who can have no possible interest in my affairs other than vulgar curiosity.'

'Vulgar, would you say, Miss Weston? But I believe this is not the place to discuss such matters. Perhaps you would do me the honour of taking a turn in the park to see the spring flowers?'

She stared at him, frowning, for if he had somehow guessed her secret then she must try and discover whether he meant to broadcast the information. 'Very well,' she decided.

'Miss Weston, are you sure you would not rather I called a hack to return you to Mrs Rivers' house?' asked Mr Grimshaw in a low voice.

'No, I will be quite safe with his lordship, I assure you, Thomas. He cannot have much to say to me, but it were best said in private.'

He handed her up into the carriage and watched her drive off, his concern increased by the fact that Lord Rayven had dismissed his groom. But then he smiled wryly to himself: Rayven might look as resolute a warrior as any former soldier, but if he thought to gain an advantage over Miss Weston, then he might well have met his match!

In the carriage there was silence as Rayven guided his high-spirited horses through the busy streets, but once they had entered the park Alys turned a wrathful face towards him, her eyes blazing. 'You have been spying on me! That man, the one in the frieze coat that you nodded to as we drove away – he has been watching me! I *knew* he looked familiar.'

He looked a little conscious. 'Jarvis. He is merely a former soldier-servant of mine, for whom I wished to find some employment.'

'Well, you can tell him to desist spying on me, now that you know my secret.'

'Miss Weston, you can have no notion how difficult it is for an old soldier to get work, especially one wounded as this poor fellow is – he is blind in one eye, you know, and has lost the use of an arm.'

'Then find him a job to do on your estate. You must surely be able to do that?'

'And so I mean to do eventually. I will take him back north with me next time I go, for he might help the bailiff.'

'We seem to have strayed from the subject in hand,' she said coldly. 'Pray tell me, sir, how you came to discover my authorship – and perhaps, more importantly, what you mean to do with the information?'

'I believe my suspicions were first aroused when it was drawn to my attention how closely the villain in *The Travails of Lady Malvina* resembled me – too closely for coincidence. It made me recall a certain letter of yours – one that you dropped at Knaresborough on the occasion of our unfortunate misunderstanding.'

'A – letter?'

'It was addressed to your companion, Miss Grimshaw, I think. The seal was broken in our . . . struggle,' he said, with a slight, reminiscent smile that maddened her.

'You *read* my letter? That was hardly the action of a gentleman, though I suppose it might be expected of one who had just so grossly insulted me!'

'I expect I deserved that, but I did afterwards send the letter on for you.'

'Yes, after you read it!' She only wished she could recall what she had said in it, but rather thought it had been a description of their first meeting and some very unflattering comments.

'Have *you* never read a letter you were not meant to, Miss Weston?' he said, turning his head.

'No, of course—' Then she broke off, flushing, for indeed she had on several occasions read Lady Crayling's letters to Lady Basset. 'That is beside the point: you must have known it was not meant for your eyes.'

'Perhaps not, but although I have forgotten much of it, some of the lines are burned on to my memory for ever. Indeed, had that letter not made it so plain that you had taken me in unalterable dislike, then I believe that I must have sought you out on my return from London in order to abjectly seek your forgiveness for my behaviour.'

She felt her cheeks grow hot. 'It is as well you did not, for my father would not have let you through the door. Not only did he have a profound dislike of my meeting young men, but he had already warned me before my departure for Harrogate to have nothing to do with *you* should we meet.'

'But why should he think that our paths would cross? It was pure chance that we met at all,' he said, surprised.

'We had heard that you had inherited Priory Chase, and Papa insisted that your father had been the means to ruining him.'

'My father ruined him? Come, are you sure we are not straying into the convoluted plots of one of your novels, Miss Weston?'

'No, we are not!' she snapped. 'I do not know all the circumstances, but I believe they served in the army together and were both great gamblers, and your father won Papa's estate – by cheating, he said.'

Rayven frowned in an effort of memory. 'I do seem to remember hearing something of that . . . but my father's cousin, the last Lord Rayven, paid for my schooling after my mother died, so I never got to hear the ins and outs of it. But if he had any such winnings, then he lost them again almost immediately, for he never had a feather to fly with.'

'Yes, so Papa said,' she sighed. 'And I daresay had Papa not lost them to your father at cards, it would have been to someone else.'

'And it can hardly be held to be my fault, do you think?' he pointed out gently.

'I suppose not.'

'And had I not been discouraged by your letter, I *would* have sought you out to apologize.'

'So you say, but it still does not excuse your behaviour to me in Knaresborough.'

'I was wrong, most grievously wrong. But tell me, Miss Weston, must I *always* be the villain of the piece?'

Looking up, she saw that he had turned his head again and was looking at her with a very serious expression in his dark-blue eyes.

'N-no, I have come to perceive that people in real life are never as black and white as they may seem and appearances are not a true indicator of character.'

'Then there is hope that I might redeem myself in your eyes? I assure you, I very much desire to do so.'

'If you keep the secret of my authorship, then indeed I will be ready to admit that you were not quite as bad as I once thought,' she admitted, hoping he did not read more of her novels and so discover that in *Ravish'd by Cruel Fate*, the villain somehow managed to turn into the hero and vice versa, a troubling tendency that seemed to be recurring in *Death or Dishonour*.

'I will certainly do so and I can see why you wish it, for your books seem to show a passion and experience of the world that *you* cannot possibly possess. It was what made me doubt your authorship in the first place – until I saw your face at the Misses Berrys' salon, when you depressed young Coalport's pretensions.'

'So others have said, but I daresay I have merely picked up turns of phrase from other novels I have read, particularly those of Mr Lewis – and perhaps people's imaginations provide the passages that I do not write.'

'If it became known that you were Orlando Browne, you would find yourself at the centre of a great deal of scandalized attention. But I think you should tell your grandfather the secret, for he asked me to ascertain, if I could, the source of your income; he knew your father could not have left you well provided for.'

'I will think about it, though I cannot consider the matter anyone's business but my own.' She caught sight of her cousin Nat in the distance astride a showy chestnut horse, in company with Bella, who rode a sedate grey hack, but they did not appear to have seen her for they carried on. Alys looked after them. 'I do not like the way Nat jabs at his horse's mouth. I have noticed he does so when driving, too.'

'I have no great opinion of his horsemanship or the way he handles the reins,' agreed his lordship. 'I hope my skills in that line pass muster?'

'You seem very competent,' she assured him.

'Thank you. I am sure the other members of the Four-Horse club will be delighted to hear your opinion,' he said gravely. 'I daresay we could catch up with your cousins, if you wished to speak to them?'

'No, I thank you: Bella is rather jealous of my grandfather's taking an interest in me, which I suppose is only natural, since she has been such a pet of his these several years. And Nat....'

She paused, and he glanced at her enquiringly.

'Although he is infinitely better to look at than my cousin Thomas Basset, with whom I grew up, yet his conversation is *just* as uninteresting. I suspect he only spends so much time in my company because Grandfather has told him to.'

He burst out laughing, to her astonishment, his face both softened and transformed by amusement. 'Miss Weston, I never know quite what outrageous thing you will say next! But would it not be sensible to promote a match between you? He is heir to the property and you could then be well provided for.'

'But *I* am not a piece of property to be disposed of – and even if I were in agreement with such a scheme, I am sure Nat's taste in a wife would run to someone younger, richer, better born and *much* more malleable.'

'I am sure you are quite right, as usual, Miss Weston. And indeed, we *all* hope for those very qualities in our wives.'

Alys glared at him. 'Then, since we seem to be in perfect accord, I would be very glad if you ceased interfering in my life and took me back home immediately.'

While Rayven did not tell Mr Titus Hartwood Alys's secret, he did inform him that he knew what it was, and that he hoped to persuade her to tell him herself before long. 'And I daresay you will find it amusing, rather than reprehensible, as I do.'

'I will, will I?' He directed his formidable stare at the younger man. 'I take it, it will create a scandal?'

'A little, perhaps ... but nothing to what your nephew's involvement with the Brethren will bring, if he does not cease to associate with them. There are rumours circulating of an inner circle that perform dark and unsavoury acts – even violence.'

'I, too, have been warned of this recently by old friends, so what you say does not come as a complete surprise to me,' Titus Hartwood said heavily. 'Nat is too easily led, I admit, but never vicious. If there is such an inner circle, then I am very sure he is not part of it.'

Lord Rayven said nothing, and after a moment Mr Hartwood added, 'If I were not sure that his character was, though weak, basically good, then I would not for a moment contemplate his marrying Alys.'

Rayven, who had been standing with one arm resting on the mantelpiece, gazing into the fire, turned his head and said intently, 'You have good reason to think, then, that such a match will take place?'

'Why should it not, when it would be of such advantage to both of them? Nat will see the sense of it and as to Alys – well, even if she does not, then she would have to be an unusual girl to resist my nephew's courtship!'

The upshot of all this was that Titus immediately sent for his heir and took him severely to task.

'I know you feel loyalty to your friends, Nat, but I believe it is misplaced and your good nature has led you astray. I cannot cut you out of inheriting the estate, but you will have precious little to live on if you do not reform your ways and sever those connections which will only do you harm.'

'I do not know what you have heard, Uncle, but I assure you—' blustered Nat Hartwood.

'The only assurance I want from you is that you will do what I say. Let me tell you that I intend remaking my will so that, should you marry Alys, not only will I settle your debts but you will get two thirds of my fortune after I am gone and my little Bella will have the rest.'

Nat said sullenly, 'And if I do *not* marry Alys? What then? She shows more preference for Lord Rayven's company than mine!'

'I do not think it, and in any case I am sure you have sufficient address to win her, if you exert yourself. But if you do *not* reform your ways and win her hand, then she and Bella will each have half my fortune instead – tied up securely, of course, for women are not to be trusted with money.'

White-lipped, Nat walked up and down the room, struggling to conceal his rage. 'Of course, I like my cousin very well and desire nothing more than to make her my wife,' he said after a few moments, with a tolerable assumption of his usual manner. 'And, if you wish it so much, I will cease to be a member of the Brethren, though I assure you it is perfectly harmless, whatever you have heard to the contrary.'

'Lord Chase is half mad and half foolish – that connection can do you no good.'

'As you wish, sir.' Nat Hartwood bowed and left the room, almost stumbling over Bella outside, who had been slower than usual to remove her ear from the keyhole. She seized her brother and dragged him into an antechamber.

'Did I hear aright – if you marry Alys *you* are to get two-thirds of uncle's money, and *I* only one?'

'Yes, but that will still buy you a good husband, Bella, while I must leg-shackle myself to an acidulated, opinionated spinster, or lose all!' he snapped.

'But perhaps she will not marry you, for she seems very thick with Lord Rayven, by all accounts – and if she does not, Alys and I will share Uncle's fortune and *you* will be quite cut out, Nat.'

'Of course she will marry me – if I ask her,' he said confidently. 'But I've also been paying court to old Malfont's daughter, for though she smells of the shop, my debts are so pressing that marriage to an heiress now would be of more use to me than the promise of a legacy in the future.'

'It is a great pity Alys turned up at all, for everything was perfect before she did so,' Bella said. 'I thought you were going to try and discredit her – or get rid of her by some means?'

'Oh, I *have* tried, believe me – and still have one or two ideas up my sleeve.'

Bella sighed. 'I wish she would just vanish, so that everything could be as it was before.'

So did Nat, for with a wealthy and biddable wife like Miss Malfont and a show of outward compliance to please his uncle and reinstate himself in his good opinion, he could have continued his life the way he wanted it.

No, he would rather be rid of Alys than marry her, but for the present it would seem prudent to hedge his bets and try both ways. . . .

CHAPTER 22

Bonbons

The dying man raised his head and with an anguished expression on his livid face, whispered, 'Sir Lemuel Grosby . . . my cousin! Do not—' But then, with an expression of complete astonishment – even, one would say, horror – he fell back against the pillows, breathing no more.

'Alas,' said a voice behind Drusilla, 'that I should arrive only in time to hear my cousin's last words!'

Death or Dishonour by Orlando Browne

Alys was sitting in the drawing room, wrestling with an obstinate passage in *Death or Dishonour*, while Nell, reclining on the sofa, was reading an earlier chapter.

'This is very good, Alys – but is she to marry Sir Lemuel Grosby, now that his poor wife has died in such dreadful circumstances? He may be handsome, but he is very cold and near old enough to be her father.'

'Her situation is such that it seems her only respectable option: she is orphaned and penniless. Added to this, her youth and beauty make finding a post as governess or companion unlikely. To put it plainly, she is in a hole.'

'Yes, but it seems very hard when she is barely acquainted with him. Not,' she added wryly, 'that marrying for love can be all that satisfactory either.'

'I know,' Alys said sympathetically. 'It is a pity Mr Rivers will not spend more time at his estate, for he must be better away from his friends.'

'Yes, he is always improved in the country, but I am afraid the days when my influence over him counted for anything are gone. I wish—'

But Alys was not destined to learn what she wished, for a familiar voice was heard in the hall saying gaily, 'No, do not bother to announce me. I feel myself now to be quite part of the family!' and Nat Hartwood walked in, very sure of his welcome.

At the first sound of his voice Alys had leapt across the room and snatched the manuscript from Nell's hands, and was now busily stuffing the papers back into her little desk.

'Why, Cousin, this is a surprise,' she said, closing the lid and turning around with a smile.

'But not an unpleasant one, I hope,' he said, bowing. 'Do I interrupt you? You always seem to be writing when I come to call. You must have a great correspondence.'

'I – why, yes, I do write a great many letters.' She moved away from the desk and sat down.

'Your little dog is not here, Miss Weston?' he said, looking around cautiously.

'No, he is in the kitchen, I think – he is a great favourite with the cook.'

'Ah, that is a pity, for I fear I accidentally trod on him on my last visit, and hoped to induce him to forgive me,' he said with a charming smile and the most candid of expressions in his guileless blue eyes.

Alys *almost* believed him, for he seemed so sincere . . . and yet, she had seen the incident with her own eyes.

'The real purpose of my visiting so early is to see George,' he said to Nell, 'but I simply could not resist paying my respects to two such charming ladies first.'

'I think you will find my husband in the study – he said earlier that he had a painful headache and did not wish to be disturbed.'

Nat looked at her sadly. 'Ah, but I am convinced you know the truth of these headaches and your husband's erratic temperament, do you not, Mrs Rivers?'

'I – what do you mean?' asked Nell, startled. 'What—?'

He sat down next to her on the sofa. 'If I may speak to you as a friend? You must surely have guessed by now, as I have, that poor George is quite addicted to laudanum, and though a most excellent remedy for many ills, if taken to excess it quite alters a person's temperament and undermines their health.'

'He – he does seem to take a great deal of it . . . but then, he has always been prone to these debilitating headaches, which have grown ever more frequent with the years,' Nell said, wringing her hands. 'Could this really be the cause of his change of character?'

'Yes, I suspect he has grown to rely more and more on the drug and, although I am loath to interfere, I thought I would mention the matter to you. All his friends are concerned for him, and you must endeavour to persuade him to give up, or much reduce, his intake of it.'

'I? I can do nothing – he will not listen to me!'

'Perhaps the hint would be better accepted from you or another of his friends?' suggested Alys. 'This certainly explains much about his conduct and the change in his disposition, that I found hard to understand.'

'If you think it best, I will be happy to remonstrate with him,' Nat said earnestly.

'Please – please do try it. How kind you are! And at least I now know that the change in my husband is not due to – to something I have done, but to his medicine. Perhaps, if he is weaned off it, he—'

She broke off as the subject of their conversation, having heard their voices, came into the room. The full force of what Nat had just told them struck the two ladies forcibly: George Rivers was the wreck of the healthy young man he had once been. Pasty-faced, hollow-eyed and dishevelled, a tic twitched his cheek and his brown eyes were unfocused.

'There you are, Nat! What are you doing in here? Come into the study, I have been waiting for you this age. Do you have . . . the little commission I asked you to do for me?'

'I do, and will come this instant! Cousin, perhaps you would take a turn in the park with me when I have dealt with this business matter? I believe the day to be fine – quite spring-like.' He bestowed one of his dazzlingly effulgent smiles upon Alys.

Feeling more kindly disposed to him she smiled back. 'Thank you, but on this occasion you must hold me excused: we have a prior engagement.'

'Then I will see you at Bella's coming-out ball,' he said gaily. 'And you must save at least two dances for me.'

'George, you look all to pieces,' Nat said bluntly when they were in the study with the door shut.

'One of my plaguey headaches – nothing a dose of laudanum won't cure. You did bring it?'

'Yes.' He handed over a small bottle. 'But you should not take such quantities – why, it's enough to kill a horse! It cannot be good for you.'

'Isn't "excess in everything" the Brethren's motto?' George demanded, with a wild laugh.

'Yes, but not the *entire* time, burning the candle at both ends. Look at poor Chase: going to the devil as fast as he can run.'

'That ... that's disloyalty! Treason to the Master and the Brethren.'

'No, it's common sense, and a respect for one's person. Chase was never so bad until this last dose of the pox – I believe it must be eating at his brain, for his tastes have become ever more ... *esoteric*, shall we say?'

George shuddered as he measured out drops of laudanum into a glass of water and downed it, his teeth rattling against the rim. 'You are as bad as the rest of us, Hartwood, when we meet together,' he muttered sullenly.

'Within the walls of the Temple, once the other Brethren are gone, we Masters of the Inner Circle can do anything we please – though perhaps I do not drink so deeply of the wine as the rest of you, and so whatever it is laced with has less effect.'

'That girl – the last girl, the one who—' George shuddered, then poured another dose of laudanum into his glass, which Nat reflected would have killed a man unused to the drug.

'Better not to think about it. She was just a drab; she will not have been missed. One rat out of many roaming the streets.'

'But even so, I cannot believe – I seemed to be detached, watching myself – *all* of us – do vile things to the poor creature until . . .'

Nat got up. 'We are agreed that we don't talk about what we do at the Temple – in fact, how sure are you that any of this really happened? Might you not have dreamt the whole while in a drugged stupor?'

George looked at him with a desperate hope. 'Did it not then happen? Might it all have been some kind of hallucination? But the bodies they found in the river—'

'Many dark things happen in a city's poorer areas. Best not to think too deeply, George. Look where that got Stavely.'

'Poor Ger! He was always melancholy, from a boy, but ten times worse once he fell in love and began to think that what he had done made him unfit to marry an innocent girl . . . and perhaps it does.'

'Nonsense, women are not such pure and fragile creatures as you seem to think. *You* married.'

'Yes, but I meant never to be part of the Brethren again. I swore to Nell when I proposed that I would reform my way of life, though she did not know what it had entailed. Then somehow I was drawn back.'

'We are bound by our pasts, by our oaths, and by what we have done – *together*.'

'But you said—'

Nat got up, shrugging. 'It was a bad dream? But we all return over and over to the Brethren, for we cannot resist dark pleasures, just as you, it seems cannot resist laudanum. But take care. And George—'

His haggard face was raised, yet now more smoothed out and peaceful.

'Your visitor, my cousin Miss Weston, she is always writing at something. When I walked in on them earlier she was hastily hiding a whole bundle of papers in that shabby little writing desk of hers. I am curious: take a look inside when the coast is clear, and tell me what she is scribbling, for even if it is only her impressions of her London season it may be of use to me.'

*

Nell found some comfort in the idea that the change in her husband was due not to some fault in herself, but in his over-consumption of laudanum, and hoped that he would listen to his friends and give it up.

So it was that she was in a more cheerful frame of mind when she and Alys returned from paying a visit to her Aunt Becky, who had just returned to town.

Going up to change for dinner, Alys found a little box of sugared fruits in her room, prettily tied with ribbons and bearing a card signed merely with a large and sprawling initial that she thought might be an R . . . or perhaps, she admitted to herself, *hoped* might be one. She had not seen Lord Rayven since he confronted her with the discovery of her authorship, though he had sent her a brief note saying he must go out of town.

She popped her head out of the door, and asked Nell's maid if she knew anything of it.

'No, but I will enquire, miss.'

She came back to say that it had been found on the tray in the hall and no one seemed to know when it came. 'Perhaps the second footman took it in, but he's off duty and can't be found, Miss Alys.'

'It does not matter, thank you.'

Alys opened the box and regarded the pretty looking fruits nestling in their paper cases, but she was not tempted in the least, for they reminded her too much of Lady Basset. The familiar rustling and sweet scent also seemed to stir up Pug's recollections for, sitting up, he begged with bulging eyes and drooling jaws for one of the sweetmeats.

'Oh, I suppose *one* cannot hurt,' she said, giving in, 'but no more, mind! The cook is already spoiling your figure – and, sir, your snoring at night is becoming almost unbearable.'

The sugarplum vanished in one gulp . . . only for Pug to vomit it back up on the rug almost instantly.

'There, it is too rich for your digestion, so let that be a lesson to you, Mr Greedy, and to me, not to indulge you with unsuitable foodstuffs.'

A maid brought hot water and she directed her to clear up after Pug while she began to change her dress, for they were to go out to Lady Mersham's to dine and then on to the theatre, and she knew Lord Rayven had been invited to be one of the party.

She was almost ready, with Jane having come in to put the finishing touches to her hair and dress, when Pug began to be quite ill.

'I believe it must be the sugarplum I gave him earlier – perhaps it was not good. Poor little Pug! Pray, Jane, will you have water fetched, and perhaps a hot brick might comfort him?'

Nell came in to see what the fuss was about, to find Pug clutched in Nell's arms like a baby, making little moaning noises and looking very unwell.

'He ate a bad sweetmeat, and although he brought it straight back up again, I daresay a little of the poison got into his system. But he has been sick repeatedly and cannot have anything left in his stomach. He was very thirsty, but now is merely sleepy, so hopefully he will be right as rain in the morning.'

'Oh, poor little thing!' cried Nell, gently stroking his domed head.

'I cannot leave him, I am afraid, I must stay here, for I am much attached to him.'

'Of course you must stay, but Lady Mersham is George's godmother, and a wealthy widow with no children of her own, so I am sure he will not allow me to cry off from the party. I will make your excuses, Alys.'

'Pray do. And if Lord Rayven should be there, Nell, tell him—'

'Yes?'

'Nothing – that I was detained. But I do not suppose he will notice I am not there. My grandfather asked him to discover the source of my income, you know, so now he has ascertained that, I suppose he will have no more interest in me.'

Though she *had* noticed that the old soldier, Jarvis, was still lurking about the house, especially in the mornings when she walked Pug. . . .

But when Nell popped her head in on her return late that night to see how Pug did, she brought a message from his lordship. 'Lord Rayven was sorry to hear about poor Pug, and he said he would call for you early tomorrow, in order to take the invalid out for an airing, if he should be recovered enough.'

'He did?'

'Yes, and he was most urgent that you not eat any of the sweetmeats yourself, in case they were the cause of the illness.'

'No, of course not. I have already disposed of them.'

'I am so glad Pug is better, Alys, just sleepy.'

'I knew he was on the mend the moment he sat up and looked hopeful when my supper was brought to me on a tray,' Alys said drily.

Alys ran up the steps of the Rivers' house the next day with Pug in her arms: he seemed to have enjoyed the excursion to the park in Lord Rayven's carriage, especially looking down on other, lesser dogs who had to walk instead of being driven in style.

She was a little doubtful when he made it plain that he wished to be put down and then headed purposefully in the direction of the kitchen quarters, but he did seem quite himself again.

Upstairs she was met by Jane, who, with an anxious face, asked her to go up to her mistress. 'The master has just gone out, Miss Alys, and Mrs Rivers is in great distress.'

'Straight away!' she said, untying her bonnet as she went in. 'Nell, what on earth is the matter?' She sank down on the bed next to her weeping friend and patted her shoulder. 'Is it George again? Do not cry.'

'Oh Alys, I do not deserve that you should be kind to me, for I have betrayed you!' cried Nell, lifting up a tearstained face.

'Betrayed me? How could you betray me?'

'I-I found George looking in your little desk just now, and when I asked him what he was doing, he *turned* on me! He'd found the manuscript and he-he made me tell him what you were writing – everything: Orlando Browne, the novels—'

'*How* did he make you?'

'He twisted my arm behind my back, and I thought it would break,' she sobbed, 'and I am very sorry not to be braver, but I am such a coward and . . . I was so afraid, for he was quite wild. It must be due to laudanum and drink, for he is turned into a positive *monster!*'

Alys sat back. 'So he knows . . . but why should he have been so curious?' She patted her friend's heaving shoulders and added, 'Never mind, Nell, it's no use crying over spilt milk and I certainly would not have wanted you to withhold the information at the expense of getting hurt. Perhaps George's curiosity is now satisfied, and he will say nothing about his discovery, for how can it be of any real interest to him when he is in his right mind? But I *will* speak to him on his return.'

'Oh, do not say anything that would set his back up!' Nell begged, clutching her arm. 'For if you left the house, I do not know how I would go on without you.'

'Very well, but I should like to give him a piece of my mind!'

However, when she bumped into George rather furtively crossing the hall later that day, she managed to keep her tongue within her teeth – with a great effort.

'One moment, sir: I believe you have taken an interest in my private affairs?'

He looked hangdog and defensive. 'Yes I-I believe I *should* know such a thing as that, about a guest under my roof.'

'Even though it would seem to outrage common civility to violate the privacy of my desk in order to do so? Well, sir, it is of no great moment, but I prefer to keep my authorship a secret, so must ask you not to tell anyone.'

'No, I swear on my life I will not! I do not read novels myself, you know, but I have heard of Orlando Browne's works.'

There was something unsettling in the way he looked at her that made her wonder precisely *what* he had heard. Her novels seemed to have gained notoriety on a level with those of Monk Lewis, yet she thought she had done little to deserve such a comparison.

'It was not the act of a gentleman and the offence would be compounded should you mention it to anyone.'

'No, really I will not – I was not myself and I am very sorry for it.'

'I accept your apologies, but I believe they would be better directed at your wife, whom you forced into betraying a secret.'

'There should be no secrets between husband and wife,' he said defensively, and she said no more, fearful of falling out with him to the extent that she must leave the house.

She wished she could extricate her friend from the unhappiness of her situation, but she had not yet even managed to think of a way of extricating her heroine from hers with honour, despite Drusilla's growing suspicion that her husband was responsible for his first wife's death.

While she could – and probably would – kill off Sir Lemuel Grosby, in real life things were unfortunately not so easily arranged.

CHAPTER 23

Old Loves

It was with a fast-beating heart that Drusilla heard Sir Lemuel say, 'I feel, dear Cousin, that I have come to know the sterling worth of your nature even in so short an acquaintance, so that you should not be surprised at the nature of the proposal I am about to lay before you.'

Death or Dishonour by Orlando Browne

On the morning of Bella's ball, Alys chose to revisit Westminster Abbey, which she had been longing to do.

That the expedition was by no means an unqualified success was entirely due to Lord Rayven's manner, for from the start he was both distant and curt – so very different to their last expedition together, when they had laughed over Pug's supercilious airs as he was driven through the park.

That must have been an aberration due to some kindly impulse, and her suspicion grew that he had no further interest in her, now he had discovered her secret.

Not, of course, that she cared for *that*, she told herself as they arrived back in Portman Square. No indeed! She had never desired his company in the first place.

'Lord Rayven,' she said, as he helped her to alight, 'I believe I have now visited every object of interest to me in London, and need no longer impose upon you to escort me.'

For a moment his dark, hawk-nosed face stared down at her impassively, then he replied indifferently, 'As you wish.'

Alys, not trusting herself to say more, turned away and walked into the house, blinking rapidly.

'Miss Weston,' the butler said, closing the door behind her, 'there is a' – he paused – '*gentleman* to see you. A Mr Puncheon. I have put him in the small front sitting-room.'

'Mr Puncheon?' exclaimed Alys, and thinking immediately that some mishap must have befallen Miss Grimshaw, she went quickly into the room where she found the elderly tea merchant pacing up and down in an agitated manner.

'Oh, tell me at once, sir, what is the matter? Is it Letty – Miss Grimshaw? Is she taken ill?'

'Ill? No, pray do not alarm yourself, Miss Weston, for she is very well.' He fixed his steady, china-blue eyes on her face. 'That is, she is in some distress of mind over a matter which I wish to lay before you – entirely without her knowledge, I may add.'

Alys sank down on to the nearest chair. 'If she is in any kind of distress, then you do well to tell me of it, for having been my kind companion from childhood I have both an affection and duty towards her.'

Mr Puncheon also sat down, twitching aside the skirt of his old-fashioned coat and beaming at her. 'Ah, but that is precisely it, for she too is fond of you, Miss Weston – so fond that she couldn't tell you herself for fear of disappointing you.'

'Disappointing me?' echoed Alys, puzzled. 'Pray explain, Mr Puncheon. I have noticed that she has been in low spirits lately when I have visited her, but assumed she was fretting for the time when we should be living together again.'

'She finds herself torn – quite torn! But while she is prepared to sacrifice her happiness *and* my own on the altar of duty, I have decided to lay the matter before you.'

Alys, illumination slowly dawning, exclaimed, 'Your happiness? You mean—?'

'Yes, I have asked Miss Grimshaw to be my wife, but she will not consent, for she believes you to be relying on her company and support when you set up your own establishment.'

'And – pray excuse me! – Letty *wishes* to marry you?'

'We loved each other from the moment we met,' he said simply.

'Then there is no more to be said, except to offer you both my sincere congratulations and best wishes – and to tell Letty that she is a goose to think I would wish her to accompany me at the expense of her own happiness!'

He sprung up from his seat and wrung her hand, beaming. 'Thank you, thank you! I will be off and tell her directly.'

'Do – and say that I will come and call on her shortly to wish her happy.'

When he had gone, the realization hit Alys that she had lost the future companionship of one who, even if she could not enter wholly into her interests, she was both fond of and at ease with. She could not live alone without losing her good name, but the prospect of employing some unknown female to live with her was daunting.

But Letty to marry! She must hastily revise her views of romantic love, for it had not before occurred to her that it might strike persons no longer in the first flush of youth, or even the *second*.

And she wondered whether it was too late to change the appearance of Sir Lemuel Grosby, villain of *Death or Dishonour*, to the dark, hawk-nosed likeness of the capricious Lord Rayven, who had beguiled her into liking him quite against her will, then tired of the sport. For, while she might not be able to organize her own life as she would wish, what was the point of being an author if your puppets did not dance to the tune you wished them to?

Alys was nervous as she set out for her very first ball, despite knowing that she looked her best in the sea-green silk gown and drapery of silver net that Nell had given her. And she thanked goodness that her advanced years meant she was not tied to the whites and pale tints of the debutantes, even if she was becoming tired of this particular shade of green!

Borrowed aquamarines adorned her neck and ears and sparkled in her chestnut hair, which had been brushed into a high knot of ringlets that made the most of her long neck and large grey eyes.

'What if I forget the steps of a dance and tread on my partner's feet?' she said to Nell as they awaited Mr Rivers, who had deigned to escort them that night. 'What if I have no partners at all?'

'You will not forget the steps, for we have practised them enough, and of course you will have partners – already Lord Rayven and Mr Hartwood have asked you, haven't they?'

'I think Lord Rayven has forgotten; he did not mention it last time I saw him.'

'I am sure he has not, and in any case you will scarce miss him, for you look so beautiful that you will be besieged by young men. And George will go straight to the card room, so for once, I too intend to dance and have fun,' Nell declared. She was looking exceptionally pretty in lilac gauze draperies over a balldress of white satin, her normally pale cheeks delicately flushed.

'I hope you will not dance too often with Captain Stavely, if he is there,' Alys said anxiously. 'I am amazed at how gossip speeds around the *ton* – and how it changes in the telling.'

George, who had been inserted into his tightly fitting coat with some difficulty by his long-suffering valet, at last came down the stairs, so she could say no more.

He was pale, and called for a glass of brandy before he left the house, but otherwise seemed to be in a reasonable humour, apart from impatiently drumming his fingers on the window frame as they awaited their turn to alight from the carriage.

They made their slow way up the crowded marble staircase to where their hosts awaited them and Alys grew conscious of many stares and whisperings behind fans that seemed to be directed at them, though she could not think why.

Mr Titus Hartwood was not there, and instead Nat took his place in the receiving line next to his mother. Bella was resplendent in a ballgown of pink gauze, with a wreath of silk rosebuds on her head, though her expression of delight at seeing their party was at strange variance with the triumphant look she shot at Alys when she thought herself unobserved.

'Miss Weston,' Mrs Hartwood said, the purple ostrich feathers on her turban head-dress nodding, 'my brother-in-law particularly wished to speak to you as soon as you arrived. He is in the small withdrawing room over there, which has been set up for cards.'

'Very well,' Alys said, and with a speaking glance at Nell turned away from the double doorway into the crowded ballroom that glittered with a thousand reflected candles.

She found herself face to face with Lady Chibberley and her daughters. 'Oh, good evening!' she said with a smile, pleased to find some familiar faces and was disconcerted when that lady merely gave her a hard stare and a cool nod. 'Come along, girls,' she said, hurrying them quickly past her.

As Alys, puzzled, gazed after them, Sophia looked over her shoulder and winked at her, mouthing something, before she was swallowed up into the crowd. It looked like '*Fly, all is discovered!*' But then, both the Miss Chibberlys had a very strange sense of humour – it was what she most liked about them.

Her grandfather awaited her alone in the candlelit room, which had been set out for those who preferred to play cards rather than dance. His carrying chair was placed before one of the tables and he did not smile at her, as she had grown used to, but frowned ferociously.

'Well, miss, come here where I can see you!'

She moved forward, the light catching the aquamarines in her chestnut hair. 'Good evening Grandfather. I trust your rheumatism is not too painful tonight?'

'Never mind that,' he said shortly. 'What is this I hear of you being the author of some trumpery, sensational novels?'

Lady Chibberley's reaction – even the whisperings and rude staring when they arrived – was explained. Alys faced him more calmly than she felt. 'May I ask who told you that? Was it Lord Rayven?'

She had thought first of George, but he had not seemed much interested in his discovery and besides, she could not see him rushing to lay the information before Mr Hartwood. But Lord Rayven was so very thick with her grandfather. . . .

'Never mind who was first with the news, for now, apparently, it is all around Town.'

'I am sorry you should learn of it like this, for I meant to tell you myself, the next time I visited you – not that I am in the least ashamed of it, mind.'

'You are not?'

'No, for I am a very good author, and my novels are neither

trumpery or sensational.'

'I am told they are scandalous, especially considering they come from the pen of a young and unmarried female!'

She shrugged. 'If people wish to imagine more into certain scenes than I write, well – that is not my fault. I have never heard that Byron was ever accused of writing too scandalously for his youthful and unmarried state.'

'He is a man and so the case is entirely different. But still, I am from an age when people were not, perhaps, so mealy-mouthed as today, so I will judge for myself – I have sent for copies of them all.'

He glowered at her again and she met his gaze levelly. 'And playing at novel-writing is the source of your income? It was for *that* you turned down the opportunity to become part of my household and make a respectable match?'

'Yes, for I can support myself perfectly adequately on my income if I live in quiet retirement, which I intend to do. I find most of London society boring and superficial, on the whole, though there are a few people I will miss, of course.'

'And what of your cousin Nat?'

'What of him?' she said, surprised.

'I had hoped that you and he might make a match of it.'

'A match? But I have made it plain from the start that I do not wish to wed, and I am very sure my cousin does not wish to marry *me*.'

'There you are wrong. He has assured me that he is very fond of you and asked my permission to pay his addresses to you.'

'Asked *your* permission?'

'I am your closest male relative, after all, and I admit I encouraged him.' He paused. 'Nat is essentially good-hearted, but has fallen in with a set of good-for-nothings who have been a bad influence on him. But he swears he will reform his life on his marriage – he wants only some excuse to withdraw from the society in which he finds himself, which marriage to a sensible woman will give him.'

'He should certainly do so, for those same friends have had an adverse effect upon Mr Rivers. But I am afraid I have no desire to marry Nat, even to be the means of his redemption.'

'He could also be the means of yours, for there is like to be a scandal over your novel writing and the sooner you are respectably married the better!'

'I thank you for your concern, Grandfather, and am sorry to disappoint you, but I will not marry to cover a shame I do not feel.'

'You are very set against the match, yet many women would swoon with delight to have my nephew pay his addresses to them. I hope you have not fallen for some unsuitable man, like your fool of a mother did . . . unless it is Rayven? He has frequently been in your company.'

'Where else should he have been, when you set him on to watch me?' she said acidly, though feeling her colour rise.

'He told you that? Well, it is true enough, though I did not expect him to do more than make a few enquiries into your circumstances.'

'He did not *need* to tell me, for since he seems to find me exasperating in the extreme, there could be no other reason for his attentions.'

'With that I can sympathize, but I hope you do not have a *tendre* for him.'

'Certainly not!'

'Good, for I have it in mind that he and Bella might make a match of it. She will be well dowered enough, even if I settle most of my fortune on you when you marry Nat.'

Alys said, through gritted teeth, 'Grandfather, I am not going to marry Nat or any other man, even for a share of your fortune! Let Bella and Nat inherit all, as they surely must have expected until my inopportune arrival on the scene.'

He eyed her with cold displeasure. 'I had thought you a sensible woman, despite your obstinate, independent ways, but now I see I was mistaken. You had best go back to the ballroom. I daresay the rumours of your notoriety will have gone round by now, and you must be prepared for whispers, innuendo and even, I daresay, some cuts direct – though the cloak of my name and your acknowledgement by the family will shield you from the worst of it.'

'I had rather remove my unsavoury and scandalous presence from your house!'

'Perhaps, but that would be the coward's way out – and also a sad reward for Mrs Rivers' hospitality, in leaving her to face questions alone.'

'You are right,' Alys said after a moment's pause. 'Then I *will* go through with the evening, whatever slights I must endure. But after that, I will leave London as soon as it may be arranged.'

CHAPTER 24

Besieged

Drusilla fixed her eyes on his face.

'My home is situated in a remote part of the Highlands,' Sir Lemuel said, 'and my dearest wife has long felt the want of a companion who can share with her those feminine pleasures of which I know nothing. . . .'

Death or Dishonour by Orlando Browne

Alys went out on to the landing, where only Mrs Hartwood remained to greet late arrivals, and entered the ballroom. Pausing on the threshold, her head held high but her heart in her little satin slippers, she looked about her for Nell, only to see her being led out by Harry Stavely.

'My dance, I think, Miss Weston,' said Lord Rayven's deep voice in her ear. 'I have been looking out for you this age.'

She whirled round and glared at him. 'My grandfather wished to speak with me – and I would rather *talk* with you, my lord, than dance!'

'You gratify me extremely, but might we not do both?' he said, and taking her hand drew her into a set that was forming nearby.

Arguing at a ball where the attention of most of the onlookers is already fixed on you with scandalous relish is probably *not* a good idea. Doing so in a whisper, while constantly and frustratingly being brought together and parted by the dance, is an even worse one.

'So, you have given away the secret of my authorship, Lord Rayven,' she began.

'No, I swear I did not,' he said steadily.

'You must have done, for how else should the news have spread so quickly? And what is more, you told my grandfather of it.'

'You can think that – of me?' he said, tight-lipped.

'Why not? I already had no great opinion of you, for I knew you to be a . . . a libertine and a reader of other people's private correspondence!' she hissed, flinging at his head the most hurtful things she could think of.

His hand tightened so painfully on hers that she gasped. 'Smile, Miss Weston,' he said through gritted teeth. 'The eyes of the world are upon you.'

She blinked back angry tears. 'I cannot smile to order: let them think what they will.'

The music stopped and Alys pulled her hand away and went to find Nell, who was seated at the side of the room fanning herself. Harry Stavely was just walking away and her eyes were fixed on him, so that she did not notice Alys until she plumped down on the chair next to her and whispered urgently, 'Nell, have you heard that my being Orlando Browne is common knowledge?'

'Why yes, Alys, for several *kind* persons have told me so! But Miss Mary Berry was the first and she advised us to laugh it off as though we were astonished to find anyone thought it in any way remarkable, which seems sensible, do you not think?'

What Alys thought was that her friend was in such a glow of love that she was incapable of being touched by her predicament and might herself, if she was not careful, become the object of even more avid interest to the scandalmongers.

'Nell, pray be careful not to draw attention—' she began, before her own was claimed by an entirely unknown, if slightly raffish, young man. He proved to be only the first of many men who had jumped to the erroneous conclusion that a young woman who wrote such notorious novels must be *fast*.

For the next interminable hour her waist was squeezed, she had to listen to insulting innuendoes and deflect attempts to persuade her to leave the ballroom for some quieter spot – and all under the sardonic gaze of Lord Rayven. He leaned against the wall watching her, his arms folded across his broad chest and a lock of black hair falling across his brow, looking so romantically dangerous that Lord Byron, who had just entered the ballroom, was quite struck with jealousy and only the circumstance of his being entirely mobbed by several young ladies at once saved him from the necessity of indulging in a prolonged sulk.

Just as Alys had begun to think that outright flight might be more than worth the resultant ignominy, Nat came to her rescue. She could have wept with relief when he drew her hand into his arm and said, with gentle concern, 'I have been trying to claim my dance with you, but I think perhaps you would rather go somewhere quiet and sit it out, would you not?'

'Oh yes!' she agreed gratefully. 'You – you have heard that I am that infamous author, Orlando Browne? I hope you are not very much shocked.'

'No indeed. In fact I am full of admiration,' he said, leading her to a small antechamber that had been fitted out for repairs to ladies flounces and ruffles torn during energetic dancing, and closing the doors behind them. The sound of the ballroom was suddenly reduced to a vague hum, like a disturbed hive of bees.

He seated her on a small gilt sofa and sat down next to her, taking her hand. 'But I have a confession to make, for I am afraid that it is all my fault that your secret is revealed.'

'How is this?' she said, astonished.

'You must forgive me, Miss Weston, for George let slip his discovery and *I* was so indiscreet as to tell my sister, thinking she would be as impressed by your being so well known an author as I was. But I should have known she could not keep it to herself. Indeed, I thought my uncle would quite cast you off when he first heard, he was so angry, but he quickly came to see that there was an easy way to avert any scandal.'

'So it was *you* . . .' she said slowly, barely taking in the rest of what he said.

'Yes, but do say you will forgive me, dearest Alys. In fact,' he added, seizing hold of her other hand and drawing her closer, 'say you will *marry* me, and let me give you the protection of my name.'

'What?' Her attention drawn back by these words from the contemplation of a dark, angry, scarred face that had watched her with such well-justified contempt, she attempted to release her hands.

'Oh *no* – I thank you, Nat, and I am sure your offer is kindly meant, but I have already told Grandfather that I have no desire to wed you or any other man. I do not need to,' she added simply.

'Do not *need* to?' He stared at her as if she had run mad.

'No, for I intend to continue writing my novels. But I will not be an embarrassment to the family, since I am retiring to live in the country somewhere.'

'You mean . . . you really mean, that you do not *wish* to marry?' It was clearly a concept he found hard to comprehend.

'No, for I have never seen any good come of it. I can support myself and intend to do so – and in any case, I am very sorry, but I am afraid I do not love you, Nat.'

He decided that only a show of lovemaking would overcome her resistance and seized her in his arms. 'But I love you!' he exclaimed passionately and, crushing her to him, attempted to kiss her.

'Nat, let me go!' she demanded, trying to push him away, but his superior strength made her efforts unavailing. 'What if someone should come in?'

'No one will come in – I have told one of the footmen to see to that,' he said, pushing up her chin with a ruthless hand and pressing his lips to hers. Then he jerked back with a cry, blood welling from his lip.

'You bit me!' he said with furious astonishment. 'You—'

The doors swung open, briefly letting in the sounds from the ball-room, and closed again.

'Dear me,' said Lord Rayven, taking in the scene with one swift, comprehensive glance, 'you appear to have had a slight accident, Mr Hartwood.'

'I – it is nothing,' Nat said with an effort. 'I am afraid we are having a private conversation, Rayven, if you would mind leaving us.'

'No!' cried Alys, freeing herself from his loosened grip and quickly putting as much space as possible between them. 'Our *conversation* is at an end, Nat, and I would like *you* to go!'

Nat was dabbing at his lip with his handkerchief, over which he regarded her angrily. Then, without another word, he got up and left the room. Lord Rayven stood aside to let him pass, then quickly moved forward to catch Alys as her legs gave way.

'You are faint,' he said, clasping her in his arms.

'A . . . momentary dizziness . . . it is nothing. I am better.' But her heart was beating faster than it ever had in Nat's importunate embrace.

'Has he hurt you? He did not—'

'He proposed, then tried to kiss me when I refused him, nothing more. I am glad you came in, but I am sure I could have got rid of him quite easily,' she added, sounding much more like herself.

He smiled. 'I expect you could – unless, of course, rage caused him to strangle you first, an emotion with which I could sympathize.'

For a moment, still held in his arms, they stared into each other's eyes. 'Or frustrated passion,' he added slowly, 'for you look so damned pretty tonight that there might be some excuse for him.'

Alys went pink and struggled free. 'I believe I owe you an apology, Lord Rayven,' she said smoothing down her slightly crumpled silk dress.

'In what way, Miss Weston?' He had gone back, she noted, to the Byronic pose, arms folded across his broad chest and that lock of black hair falling across his forehead.

'For misjudging you. You did not betray my secret – George Rivers told Nat, and Nat told Bella.'

'Who told everyone? Yes, your cousin Bella seems to have been busy spreading the tale all day. She must be quite exhausted, poor thing.'

'I do not know what she hoped to gain by doing so.'

'Oh, I expect she was simply motivated by jealousy – you have quite put her nose out of joint by your sudden appearance on the scene.'

'Well, I am sorry for it, but I did not intend to do so, and I have told my grandfather that I do not want his money and I am not going to marry Nat or anyone else. In fact, I am starting to think Nat is a whited sepulchre,' she said darkly. 'He looks angelic enough, and is always kind and charming, but his true nature, judging from his actions today, is far otherwise.'

'Indeed, you cannot always judge a book by its cover,' he agreed gravely.

Their eyes met again, his crinkled up at the corner in laughter, and she smiled suddenly. 'Very true.'

'How does my elderly friend Pug go on?'

'Very well.'

'I suppose you did not keep the rest of the sweetmeats?'

'No, I saw them put on to the kitchen fire myself. Sammy – Nell's page – was much aggrieved, for he has a sweet tooth, but I have promised to buy him some for himself. I suppose it was not the fault of the sender that there was one bad fruit among them.'

'You don't know who sent them?'

'No . . . I thought—' She broke off. 'No, I don't.'

'Perhaps you should receive such gifts in future with caution,' he suggested. 'Now, would you like to return to the ballroom?'

She shuddered. 'No, I feel I have had quite enough of being brave and wish nothing more than to go home. But I do not know if Nell will wish to leave so early.'

'Not if she and Harry are still in each other's pockets,' he said bluntly.

She sighed. 'I had hoped their resolution would have held. Can you not persuade your friend of the unwisdom of so openly showing his regard for Mrs Rivers?'

'No more easily than you can persuade Mrs Rivers of the unwisdom of her course,' he said. 'They must make their own decisions, but *I* will make this one for *you*, that you are going home, and under my escort.'

The men who served under his command in the Rifle Brigade would have recognized that tone of voice and obeyed, just as Alys found herself doing. She felt *much* too tired to object.

'What have you done to your lip, Nat?' Bella asked curiously.

'Never mind that,' he snapped, tired of endlessly repeating the same story of a broken wineglass. 'Listen, the old man is so taken with Alys that even the news that she writes scandalous books was not enough to sink her in his esteem.'

'How do you know?'

'He pretty well told me so, and is as eager as ever to match me with her – except that I have just asked her to marry me and she has made it very clear she will not!'

'Oh!' Bella said, glanced doubtfully at his face and looked away again.

'My uncle's likely to cut me off without a shilling unless I get rid of her.'

'Get rid of her?' Her blue eyes dilated. 'You don't mean – you *can't* mean—'

'No, no – nothing *fatal*! But I have a plan to ruin her, so that she can never come back and ingratiate herself with the old man again. I will probably need your help.'

'Of course, for there is no saying that if he starts to favour Alys even more, he may cut me out as well. But how do you mean to do it?'

'Drug her and put her on a ship bound for America. When she awakes, it will be too late for her to return, and by the time she does so, rumours will have been long circulating that she has run off with a lover.'

'Which lover, Nat? I do not know of anyone she's been seen much in company with, other than Lord Rayven!'

'There *is* no other lover, Bella,' he said impatiently. 'But once the rumour goes round, no one will believe that, and by the time she returns, her reputation will be in ruins and our uncle will have nothing more to do with her.'

'Tell me what I must do,' she said eagerly.

CHAPTER 25

Come to Grief

She could not doubt Sir Lemuel's grief at finding his wife dead in such dreadful circumstances, for, despite his chilly manner, he had shown by many small attentions his affection for her. Indeed, Drusilla had often marvelled at his patience with the irrational fancies that afflicted Lady Grosby and caused her to shrink away at his approach fearfully. . . .

Death or Dishonour by Orlando Browne

It was with some trepidation that a servant awoke George Rivers late next morning, though it was not so much the urgency of the letter in his hand that caused him to brave his master's wrath, but the coins that had accompanied it.

George, who had come home alone in the early hours with little but a hazy memory of where he had been and what he had done after leaving the Hartwoods' ball, was inclined to swear feebly, but on being told who had sent the note, sat up and held out a shaking hand.

'Bring me a pick-me-up,' he demanded, breaking the seal and opening the paper. 'Peters knows how to do the trick.' Then he focused his bloodshot eyes and read:

George
The devil's in it, for what must that madman Chase do but abduct one of the charity girls from the Red House for our private ceremonies

after the Brethren meet tonight. He told me of it as though it was the greatest jest imaginable, but this brings things too near home. Already rumours are circulating, linking us with the other girls, and we should lie low for a while, for our meetings grow dangerous – but he will not listen to reason.

However, I am at Templeshore and have now spoken to the girl, who was half out of her wits and babbling with fear. She told me that she was to come to your house tomorrow to learn to be a maid or some such to Miss Weston, and I see how I can turn that to my advantage. Pray make sure that your wife is absent from home this afternoon, so that Miss Weston is alone and I will explain all later.
N.H.

George read the note twice before the meaning penetrated the fog in his mind, assisted by the rather noxious contents of a tankard proffered by his valet.

As he swallowed the last of it, his colour fluctuated through several ghastly hues and the outcome hung in the balance. Then he gave a great belch, which seemed to give him some relief, for he declared his intention to get up.

In the breakfast parlour the ladies had also been slow to rise, and equally heavy-eyed and quiet.

Nell had danced four times the previous evening with Harry Stavely, besides allowing him to take her into supper and escort her home, after she discovered that George had already left with a group of cronies. Her rashness in allowing herself the pleasure of his company would, she knew, have to be dearly paid for. It was certain that it would come to her husband's ears eventually and, though he might not love her any more – indeed, she thought he must hate her, to treat her so – he still had a dog-in-the-manger attitude where she was concerned.

Alys had not slept until some hours after Lord Rayven had seen her home, for her mind had insisted on going over and over the scene at the ball when Nat had made his advances and Lord Rayven had come to her rescue. She could not make him out – he was kind one minute – and had he *really* said she looked pretty, or did she imagine that? – and terse the next.

He had been silent on the short drive back, seemingly deep in thought, only rousing himself to hand her down from the carriage and inform her that he would call on her next day on a matter of particular importance, when he hoped to find her alone. The prospect had not seemed to give him any great pleasure.

She had replied equally coolly that he might not find her there, since she believed Mr Grimshaw had found her just the house in York she was looking for and she meant to tell him to close the deal immediately, for she could not now wait to shake the dust of London from her feet.

Describing this exchange to Nell, she added, 'And it would be best if I were not here when he comes, for I am in dread that he means to renew the offer he made to me in Knaresborough.'

Nell put down her coffee cup and stared at her. 'Oh no – surely you must be mistaken, for your situation now is so very different – your grandfather, the fact that you are staying here with me – no, I am convinced you are wrong.'

'You saw how I was treated last night. Men think of me now as a woman of no virtue who positively *expects* their advances. I suppose I should be grateful that my cousin Nat offered me marriage, for I am quite ruined and only sorry I have involved you in such a scandal, Nell.'

'Oh nonsense. I am sure Miss Berry was perfectly right when she said you should laugh it away. It will be a seven-day wonder, you will see. And I daresay that Nat was carried away by his passion into pressing his suit more ardently than he should, and is sorry now.'

'I sincerely hope he is.'

'I still think you should stay and hear what Lord Rayven has to say, for it is my belief that he means to propose marriage to you. The alternative is unthinkable and I do not see what else of a particular nature he would wish to ask you.'

'Marriage? Ha!' Alys said with a hollow laugh. 'I know what kind of wife he is looking for and in no way do *I* fit that ideal. He even said last night that he would have understood if Nat had strangled me rather than kissed me! No, I am sure any *legal* union is the last thing on his mind – or mine. He knows my opinion of marriage.'

Nell looked at her with a faint smile. 'Do not cut off your nose to spite your face, Alys.'

'I do not know what you mean—' Alys had begun to say with dignity, when she was silenced by the unexpected appearance of George, a truly gruesome vision in a richly coloured dressing-gown that contrasted horribly with his sickly pallor.

He sank down in his chair and, spurning the coffeepot, demanded brandy.

'This early in the morning George?' Nell said timidly. 'Do you not think—'

'When I want your opinion, I'll ask for it,' he snarled, and Nell looked away, biting her lip.

Her eye fell on a letter that had lain unnoticed by her plate. Glad of some distraction from the unusual and sullen presence of her husband, she broke the wafer, opened it and read, her face gradually paling. 'Oh Alys, it is from Miss Slade at the Red House. She says that Sarah is missing and has been since yesterday.'

'*Missing?* Can I see?'

Mutely Nell passed over the letter.

'Sent on a message late yesterday afternoon, and not returned by nightfall. They have searched and can find no trace of her . . .' Alys looked up. 'What *can* have happened to her? I do not like this in the least.'

George, who had downed his brandy and was now sitting slumped in his chair, looked up at this. 'Who is this Sarah?'

'One of the young boarders at the Red House in Kew,' explained Nell. 'You must have heard me talk of them. Indeed, I mentioned to you that Sarah was to come here for Jane to train as a lady's-maid.'

'I daresay she has run off,' he answered indifferently.

'Oh no – I am sure she would not. I will send for Sammy, for they were particular friends and he might be able to shed some light on the matter.'

But Sammy, though much distressed at the news, could not help them. 'Might she have gone to visit her mother, do you think?' asked Nell.

'No, she would not go all that way alone, and besides, she was mightily pleased to be coming here tomorrow to learn to be a lady's-maid to Miss Alys,' he said.

'You may be right, but perhaps you had better go to her mother's lodgings and see if she is there. If she is, do tell her not to be nervous about her reception when she comes back; we will not be cross with her. But if you do not find her there, do not worry her mother unduly, for I expect she will have been found by now. There must be some simple explanation, such as a twisted ankle.'

'Yes, for she did not seem at all the sort of girl to run off,' Alys agreed.

'All this fuss over a street urchin, who is probably no better than she should be!' George slammed down his glass.

'But she is just turned fourteen, and a good, reliable girl, George,' Nell said quietly. 'That is why we are so anxious. I think, Alys, we had better drive out to Kew and see if there is any sign of her yet, and if—'

'You have forgotten,' George interrupted, 'you are to spend the afternoon with my godmother, Lady Mersham.'

'I do not think we picked on any particular day, for I may go any afternoon, you know – and I am persuaded, when she knows the reason—'

'There must be no excuses, I insist upon you going,' he said flatly.

'But, George—'

Seeing the thunderous expression dawning on her host's face, Alys intervened quickly.

'Yes, do go to Lady Mersham, Nell, for I am sure she will be very disappointed if you do not. I can very well go out to Kew myself.'

'But do not go alone – you must wait for Sammy to come back, at least.'

'Very well, if it will make you feel happier. It will all probably prove to be a storm in a teacup and I will find her there safe and sound.'

'I hope so indeed,' Nell said, glancing nervously at George, though he seemed to have lost interest in the subject.

Jarvis was hanging about outside the Rivers' residence, mightily bored, though he knew better than to forsake his post and risk Lord Rayven's wrath. Very particular he was, where Miss Weston was concerned, he thought indulgently, though to his way of thinking that time she was near run down by a carriage was the merest accident; and as for poisoning – well, he could not see himself why anyone should want to harm the young lady.

He watched Mrs Rivers drive off alone and her husband, who looked the worse for wear, soon follow.

That his quarry was still at home he knew, for her face appeared at the window once or twice, looking anxiously up and down the street. Then a carriage stopped outside and he became alert, for the horses pulling it were a pair of showy greys that he recognized as Nat Hartwood's.

No one got out, but a servant knocked for admittance and handed over a note. Then, only a few minutes later, Miss Weston ran out of the house, still tying the strings of her bonnet and jumped into the carriage, which immediately set off.

Jarvis, taken quite by surprise, looked up and down the road for a hack, but none was to be seen – just a boy holding a riding horse a few yards away.

He hesitated for only a moment before striding up and snatching the reins from his hands, despite his protests, and swinging himself into the saddle. 'Tell the gentleman, when he returns, that his horse has been borrowed on Lord Rayven's business!' he said and, tossing him a coin, rode off in the direction the chaise had taken, hoping he would not be hanged as a horse thief.

Alys had begun to read the letter from her cousin Nat with some reluctance, only to emit a gasp as she took in what it said: '. . . *found a young girl called Sarah here at Templeshore in great distress, but unharmed*. . . . *Fear my old friend Lord Chase has become quite unhinged and does not know what he is doing*. . . . *Wish to restore her to her friends, so pray come at once. My carriage awaits you and I have asked Bella to keep you company, for fear you do not trust my intentions after I behaved in so unmannerly a way*. . . .'

The rest of this flowery apology was lost on Alys as she flew to get her spencer and bonnet and ran out of the house.

'Oh Bella,' she exclaimed, as soon as she was in the carriage, 'I do not understand what is happening in the least, and Mrs Rivers cannot come for she is gone out, but has Nat then really found the missing child, Sarah?'

'Yes, so he wrote to me,' Bella said, 'but from old friendship with Lord Chase he wishes to avert a scandal if he can. And I was glad to be of service,' she added earnestly, 'for I feel that I have been spiteful and childish towards you, and I am very sorry for it.'

'Thank you, but you had cause to feel yourself slighted by my appearance on the scene. Yet I earnestly assure you that I do not have any expectations that my grandfather will take any further interest in me, for I have made it plain to him that I will not marry Nat, and mean instead to retire and live quietly in the country.'

'It is very kind of you, but I know I have not behaved as I should.'

'Then let us put all that behind us,' Alys said kindly. 'We are cousins after all, and should understand each other better.'

The carriage seemed to be picking up pace, and, looking out, Alys recognized landmarks. 'We are going to Kew? Is Sarah then still there – but surely not at Lord Chase's house?'

'No, but quite nearby.'

'I suppose I had better read his letter again, for I was in too much of a hurry to take it in the first time,' Alys said. But when she did, she did not find that it told her much more, apart from a lot of flowery commonplaces.

She looked up, puzzled. 'You know, it is very odd that he should send word to you, rather than directly to Mrs Rivers, who is directly concerned in the matter. In fact, the more I think about it the odder it seems. Where exactly did you say Sarah was?'

'In the grounds of Templeshore – there is a summerhouse near the gate on to the road and Nat said he would stay there with her until we arrived.'

'I do not know why Nat could not restore Sarah to the Red House himself, immediately?'

'The girl insists she will only get into a carriage if you or Mrs Rivers are in it – she is quite hysterical. Also, I believe Nat wished to consult with you and Mrs Rivers about what is best to be done to avoid scandal.'

'I do not see how it can be avoided – Lord Chase must be quite mad and should be confined. I only hope it is true that he has not harmed her.'

The more she thought of it, the stranger it all seemed, but when she asked Bella another question she begged to be allowed to be quiet and close her eyes for a little while. 'I am afraid I am one of those unfortunates in whom the motion of the carriage induces a feeling of strong malaise after only a little time.'

'I understand,' Alys said. 'It is doubly kind of you to come with me, in that case.'

Bella could not have been asleep, for she sat up once they reached the edge of Chase's estate and rapped on the panel. The carriage drew up next to a little postern gate.

'This is the spot – I recall it from a Venetian breakfast last year, when Lord Chase's sister and her husband were staying here. I was not then out, but Nat persuaded Mama to let me come. I was wearing a white muslin dress embroidered with small blue flowers...' she continued, while Alys marvelled at the recuperative powers of youth.

Alighting, they passed through the gate and found themselves on a narrow path leading through a shrubbery. It was silent except for birdsong and the slight rustle of the breeze through the leaves.

'Do you know,' Alys said, following Bella onwards, 'if this was dusk, if would be just the sort of place my heroine would be lured to on some pretext! You *are* quite sure that Lord Chase is safely—'

Some slight noise warned her – or perhaps the rushing movement of the air – but too late to avoid the blow that struck her senseless.

Bella looked with horror at the crumpled form on the ground. 'Oh Nat, I did not think you meant to hurt her! Is she dead?'

'Dead? No! As neat a bump on the head as you could wish.' He bent and picked Alys up in his arms with an ease that belied his dandified appearance. 'You have done your part, Bella. Return home, and if anyone asks you later what became of Alys, you know your story?'

She nodded, looking slightly frightened. 'Yes, that she asked me to drive with her, but then confided in me that she was to meet a lover and meant to run away with him that very day. And she made me leave her in the City, where there was a post-chaise waiting, and that is the last I saw of her – and I was too frightened to tell Mama or Uncle.'

'Very good,' he nodded. 'Stick to the story – do not be tempted to embroider it – though you may turn on the waterworks as much as you please. Now, off you go.'

Jarvis rode past the carriage until he had turned a bend in the road before tying up the horse and, after climbing over the wall, making his way back in time to see Nat Hartwood carry off the unconscious form of Miss Weston, her bonnet missing and her long chestnut hair hanging loosely.

Bella Hartwood stared after them for a moment, then turned and headed back towards the carriage; Jarvis stealthily followed her brother.

He came at last to a small folly in the shape of a temple overlooking the river and went inside and Jarvis, hard on his heels, peered cautiously round a white pillar in time to see him pass through an iron door set into the back of the building. He vanished into the darkness of some void beyond and there was the sound of a bar being drawn across the door.

Jarvis looked about him as though he expected help to be at hand, then suddenly leapt to his feet with an agility that belied his years and began to run back the way he had come.

Rayven arrived home in a fine temper and strode into the library to find Harry settled there with the newspaper.

Casting down his hat and greatcoat he exclaimed, 'Well, I have my answer, I presume!'

'She refused you?' Harry said sympathetically.

'No, she went out, even though she must have known my purpose in requesting an interview alone with her – and what is more, even that rascal Jarvis was not on duty.'

'If she has gone out, then presumably he will be following her,' Harry pointed out, laying aside his paper. 'And I have been thinking while you were gone, Serle, that perhaps Miss Weston did not know your purpose in calling on her.'

Lord Rayven stared at his friend. 'Not know? How can she possibly not have guessed?'

'Well, you made the poor girl a very different kind of offer on your first acquaintance, and since then it does not sound to me as though you have gone out of your way to make her think that you possess any warmer feelings towards her.'

'No, because I do not have any – she is the most objectionable, top-lofty, independent, stubborn—' He broke off and took a couple of hasty strides about the room. 'Warmer feelings? Most of the time I want to – to—'

'*Strangle* her, I think you said? Admit it, Serle, you love her!'

'Against my better judgement I do, but that does not mean that I have lost my senses to the point where I do not realize that she is the least suitable of wives for a man in my position.'

'At least you can offer marriage to the woman you love, which puts you in a luckier case than I. I do not know what came over me, to single out Mrs Rivers in that fashion last night. I must have been mad to be so careless of her good name.'

'Miss Weston does not find the prospect of marriage appealing,' Rayven said glumly. 'I do not think all my great estates and wealth will tempt her . . . though I was hoping my cellars might just do the trick.'

'Your cellars?' Harry said, as though his friend had run mad.

They heard the thundering of the door knocker and a commotion in the hall, then Jarvis burst into the room. He was flushed and breathless and seemed to have lost his hat. 'My lord . . . Miss Weston!'

Lord Rayven sprang up, paling. 'What is it? She isn't – speak up, man!'

'Carried off, my lord, by her cousin, Nat Hartwood,' Jarvis gasped, leaning on a chairback for support.

Harry handed him a glass and he downed the brandy in one gulp. 'Thank you, sir,' he said, steadying. 'My lord, a carriage came and Miss Weston ran out and jumped in – so I followed it – and stole a horse to do so, for there wasn't a hack to be seen.'

'Never mind that,' Rayven snapped. 'What then?'

'I followed them out to Kew. They were Hartwood's horses, I recognized those greys of his. But I had to go on past when they stopped at a gateway into Lord Chase's property and creep back. By the time I got there, Miss Hartwood was coming back along the path towards the carriage and her brother was carrying Miss Weston away – senseless.'

'But not dead?' Harry asked quickly.

'No, I am sure she was not – her head was bleeding, for one thing,' he added simply, like the old soldier he was, for the dead do not bleed.

'So, what then?' demanded Rayven, whose colour had returned along with a look that boded ill for Nat Hartwood when he caught up with him.

'I did not think I could overpower him by myself, sir,' Jarvis confessed, 'sorry though I am, but what with my arm and all . . .'

'No one would expect it of you – but go on, where did he take her?'

'To a sort of little temple building by the river, and through a door at the back of it.'

'The passageway from the river to the house,' Rayven said. 'He has taken her to the cellars of Templeshore House!'

'But what on earth can he be thinking of?' Harry exclaimed.

'Whatever it is, he will regret it,' Rayven said grimly, taking a pair of pistols from their box and loading them. 'Ring the bell – tell them to bring my horse around immediately!'

'But I'm coming with you! Just let me get my boots and—'

'There's no time to waste, Harry, follow me in the curricle as quickly as you can. We will need a carriage to bring Miss Weston back if . . . if we are in time.'

The door slammed behind him and he was gone.

'I'll go in the curricle with you, sir,' Jarvis said. 'But first, what am I to do with the horse I stole?'

'Damn the horse,' Harry said, with unusual violence.

CHAPTER 26

Stone Cold

Reliant on Sir Lemuel even for the very bread she ate, Drusilla had no means of leaving other than through his good offices in finding her another position.

This he seemed reluctant to do, though his proposal of marriage sprang, she thought, more from a desire to protect her good name than from any warmer feeling.

Death or Dishonour by Orlando Browne

Alys opened her eyes on the total, stifling darkness of the tomb and thought herself in the grip of a nightmare.

Then the discomfort of her pounding head and bruised body lying on cold, clammy stone, brought her to the realization that she really was entombed in what felt like some dark cellar or cave. Her hands were tied behind her and were numbed to useless marble.

There was no glint of light, but somewhere far off she could hear the faint, musical trickle of water, making her realize how dry her lips were. With an effort she managed to sit up, then shuffled across the floor until she came up against a wall, where she stayed, feeling sick from the ache in her head.

Some feeling slowly began to return to her hands and she could detect strange irregularities and hard protuberances in the wall behind her. Her fingers traced a large, ridged scallop shape, then another, smaller one – then the smooth curves of an oyster shell. . . .

Shells? Could she possibly be imprisoned in a *grotto*? Who had mentioned a grotto recently. . . ?

Then she remembered that it had been Nell, describing Lord Chase's house. Her mind began to clear, and she recalled perfectly well that she and Bella had come to Templeshore to rescue Sarah, only she could not remember any more than getting out of the carriage and walking through a gate. After that, it was all blackness.

If it was Lord Chase who had knocked her senseless and carried her off, then he was fit only for Bedlam.

There was a faint whimpering and a curiously muffled scrabbling in the darkness somewhere nearby.

'Bella?' Alys whispered, then louder, 'Bella, is that you?'

But the small sounds went on without pause, and Alys reflected that a weaker woman would have imagined it to be a ghost and been quite beside herself by now. She bit her lip and, ignoring the muzziness in her head, tried to think what the more enterprising of her heroines might do in such a situation. One of her earlier heroines, such as Malvina, for Cicely had shown all too much dependence on Simon in the end, even though she had resisted his dark charms until he had proved himself worthy of her.

But *she* could count on no such hero to ride to her rescue unless . . . . surely Nat had been tricked too, and could have no notion that she and Bella were prisoners here, for who knows what purpose? Or – horrid thought – perhaps the letter was a ruse thought up by Lord Chase to bring them there. But then, surely Bella knew her own brother's handwriting and the very horses that brought them here were his.

Oh, *how* she wished her head did not still ache so much, so that she could, with her usual acuity, make some sense of what had happened, and what she was to do.

'Hello?' she said again into the darkness. 'Bella, is that you? Can you hear me? Where are you?'

She became aware of a light slowly outlining a door in one wall and spilling through a small metal grille, allowing her to see that she was indeed sitting in a small, domed chamber, the walls intricately and outlandishly patterned in shells. Of Bella there was no sign, only the massive shape of a stone sarcophagus lying against one wall.

Then the door swung open with a groan of rusty hinges and a tall figure, garbed in hooded black, stood before her. Where his face should have been was a black mask, eyes glittering through the slits with an expression quite unlike Lady Malvina's gentle and monkish saviour.

'Lord Chase?' she demanded, more boldly than she felt. 'What is the meaning of this outrage? Why have you brought me to this place?'

'Not Chase. Haven't you guessed yet?' said a familiar voice, though in accents far removed from their usual languid tones, and pushing back his hood removed the mask to reveal a smiling and angelically fair face.

'Nat?' exclaimed Alys. 'But – what does this mean? Have you come to rescue me?'

'On the contrary, Cousin.'

A faint whimper reached them, and this time Alys was certain that it came from within the stone coffin. 'There is someone here with me, but that surely cannot be Bella, your own sister!'

'I thought you quicker of comprehension than this, Alys. Really, you disappoint me! But then, after almost being run down by a carriage and poisoned by sweetmeats, you were still so trusting and confiding.'

Alys stared at him as the truth hit home. '*That* was you? Then Bella—'

'At home, of course, where she should be.'

'Then – oh, my God, tell me it is not *Sarah* in the stone coffin!'

'Yes, she was a little fancy of Chase's, but rather too close to home for safety, silly fellow.'

'But why did you not let her go, when you discovered what he had done?' she demanded.

'What, and have her tell everyone of it? Besides, I quickly saw how I could use it to my advantage to lure you here.'

'And you have already tried to kill me,' Alys said wonderingly. 'But why?'

'Money, of course, fair Cousin. Fond though my uncle is of Bella, he favoured you from the minute he set eyes on you – his own granddaughter. I am the heir to the property, but his private fortune he may leave where he pleases – and he pleases to leave most of it to you.'

'I am sorry, but that was not my intention in coming to London, and I have made it plain that I do not want it.'

'Not want a fortune?' he sneered. 'Had you accepted my hand in marriage, then he would have paid my debts, and settled two thirds of his fortune on you – and, if I proved sober and respectable enough, had me accepted into an ancient Order that makes the Brethren seem the play-acting it is.'

Alys began to fear that her cousin had also run mad. '*Another* secret Order, Nat?' she said mildly. 'Do you not think it most unlikely that grandfather should be involved in such a thing?'

'That is the beauty of it: there is some great secret – perhaps a treasure – and members from each of seven families, including the Hartwoods, have sworn to guard it throughout the centuries. My father told me of it when I was a boy, for I should be the next bearer of the secret. But Bella overheard my uncle tell Rayven that, while he did not think me fit to hold that office, you, a mere woman, had the qualities he looked for.'

'But why should he tell Lord Rayven that – unless the Rayvens are one of these seven designated families, of course,' she said. 'Dear me, this grows more like one of my novels by the minute.'

'Why else should they be so thick with each other? And since you will not marry me, then I cannot risk your marrying Rayven and cutting me out altogether.'

'I do not know how many times I have to assure you that I have no interest in marrying Rayven or anyone else.'

'Just as well, since you will now never have the opportunity.'

'What do you mean to do?' she asked steadily.

'You will vanish and the rumour of your having run away with a lover will be the talk of the Town, your scandalous books raked up—'

'I don't think Grandfather will fall for that tale.'

'He will when Bella tells him that you confided in her that you felt no respect for the marriage tie and so meant to run off with a married lover to America.'

'No one who truly knows me would believe I would do anything of the kind.' She paused. 'And what, pray, *are* you intending to do with me?'

'Well, my first thought was indeed to have you carried aboard a ship bound for America – drugged, of course. But now I think a more final disposal might be better. But first, you will play a central role in poor Francis's final ceremony.'

'Ceremony?'

'Francis – our Grand Master, you know – fancies that he may achieve a closer link with the Great Beyond through union in a certain ceremony with a virgin – which I most earnestly hope you are, Cousin. Our first choice' – he cast a look at the stone coffin – 'appears to have lost her wits, which is not entirely satisfactory. Perhaps I will be merciful, and dispatch her abroad in your place. You will also make your final journey by ship, though of course you will know nothing of it, for tonight will be positively your *last* appearance.'

He seemed so amused by the idea that Alys, who had been listening in horror, suppressed any inclination to appeal to his better nature. Quite obviously he had not got one.

'Does Bella know what you mean to do?' She was glad to hear that her voice did not tremble.

'Oh no, she thinks you will be bound for America. She is a simple, trusting creature.' He picked up the candle from the ledge and began to turn away. 'Well, I just thought you might like to ponder on your fate, but I will leave you now. The Brethren will begin to arrive soon, but of course, you will not be needed until much later, for our private ceremonies take place after the majority have gone.'

'But could you not give me a sip of water first, and perhaps leave me the candle?' Alys said, despite her resolve not to plead for anything.

He looked at her bruised white face and the long hair tangled about her shoulders and frowned. 'I suppose we do need you in fair condition for the ceremony or the Master will not be best pleased. I will send a woman down to see to your needs.' He lit a candle affixed to a metal bracket in the wall. 'There, that will last an hour or two at least, if light you must have.'

She had not been alone more than a very few minutes when someone else approached.

'Lady Crayling!' Alys gasped, for although she had not been introduced to that notorious lady, she had been pointed out on several occasions.

'Yes, it is me, you little fool. I do not know how you came to get yourself into this situation, but you need not look to me for help.'

'Lady Crayling, I beg of you, for the sake of your old friend Lydia Basset, help me to escape from here!'

'I cannot – we are all sworn to keep the secrets of the Brethren for fear of the direst penalties if we do not. But this . . . no, I did not bargain for this,' she muttered.

Roughly she began to wipe the blood and dirt from Alys' face and hands, then held a horn beaker of water to her lips.

'Thank you,' Alys said quietly, when she had made her more comfortable.

The older woman looked at her and seemed to waver, but then her face hardened. 'I can do no more – drink deep from the cup when it is offered to you at the ceremony, and you will fear nothing, feel nothing.'

'Lady Crayling, there is someone else here with me, in the stone coffin yonder.'

'I know – it is a little servant girl Chase picked up. I told him it was rash to take someone local, that she would be missed, but we could not then let her go without her tattling of who had taken her.'

'But she is a child – barely fourteen!'

'I can do nothing for her – for either of you,' she said harshly. 'I am too far in now.'

She left, and Alys, feeling more alert even if chilled to the bone, considered her situation. The doorway opened on to a passage and there was no other exit from this chamber. Both her cousin and Lady Crayling had gone to the right on leaving, which presumably led to the cellars of the house.

She wondered if there was some other exit the other way, perhaps to the river, or if it merely led to the ceremonial chamber.

She shivered. She was getting stiffer and colder by the minute and, if she was going to act, had best get on with it.

The candle was out of her reach, but she studied the grotto walls nearest to the light until she found a broken edge of shell. Then she manoeuvred the rope that bound her hands behind her back until she could begin to rub them against it.

The trouble was, her hands were now so cold she could barely feel whether it was rope or flesh that was fretted by the shell, but she kept on. It was her one hope – if she could get her hands free, she might yet find a way of escape.

What seemed like hours later – and her third bit of shell – she finally felt the ropes begin to part and her hands come loose. It was exquisite agony to be able to stretch her arms in front of her, but she had barely time to savour it when there was the noise of a new arrival.

Whipping her hands behind her back and sinking to the floor, she slumped against the wall in a desolate pose, just as Nat flung open the door. 'Here's some unexpected company, Cousin – make the most of it!' he said, and a large body was thrown into the chamber, to lie lifeless on the floor.

CHAPTER 27

No More Music

Drusilla awoke to find herself lying on the cold stone floor of the chapel, with no idea of how she had got there. It was illuminated only by the weak light of the moon that shone through the narrow windows, lending a ghastly air to the ancient effigies of her husband's illustrious forebears.

Sitting up, her head spinning, she thought that one of them moved. . . .

Death or Dishonour by Orlando Browne

The door slammed and the key was turned in the lock. Alys waited only until the sound of voices and footsteps had receded down the passageway before throwing off her loosened cords and running across to the prone figure, face down on the stone floor.

She did not need to see his face to know who he was, even in the half-dark. 'Lord Rayven,' she whispered incredulously, shaking him, 'Lord Rayven!'

He did not stir, though he seemed to be breathing well enough. When she felt the back of his head, she found a large lump there – one that betokened a much severer blow than that which had knocked her out. She undid his bonds and managed to turn him partly on his side, discovering as she did so that he had not been searched, for he carried a duelling pistol in either coat pocket.

He seemed to have been in a mill, for his familiar aquiline face was now rather battered, but she thought she could guess who had finished it by creeping up behind and knocking him senseless.

Ripping off the frilled edging of her petticoat, she dabbled it in the remains of the beaker of water and gingerly dabbed at the bruise on Rayven's head, then chafed his hands, but still he did not stir.

'Heroic idiot!' she muttered, brushing away the black curls from his forehead. 'How *did* you know I was here – and did you think to tell anyone else, before you rode to the rescue?'

Then a sound behind her made her start guiltily – the child! How could she forget that there was another sufferer who also needed her assistance?

Sarah lay in the deep sarcophagus on a bed of dirty straw. Her blue eyes were wild and unfocused and she did not respond to her name other than to whimper and moan.

Alys hitched up her gown and climbed in beside her. 'Sarah!'

'No, no!' whimpered the girl, trying to draw herself back against the wall.

'Sarah, it is me – Miss Weston. Remember, you were to come and be my maid? Sarah?'

There was no response. Muttering, Alys set about untying the girl and chafing her hands, then briskly slapped her face.

With a gasp, some intelligence came back into the blue eyes, along with terror. 'Do not have hysterics Sarah,' she said quickly. 'It is Miss Weston, come to get you out of this foul place.'

'Miss Weston? Oh, Miss Weston, I must be dreaming you are here . . . I—'

'Do not waste your energy on crying, but let me help you out into the grotto, where you will find Lord Rayven.'

'L-Lord Rayven?'

'He is a friend, though at this moment somewhat incapacitated,' Alys confessed. 'Come along.'

She pushed the girl out and climbed after her, then gave her the very last dregs of the mug of water. Sarah cast fearful looks at the prone dark form on the floor.

'Miss Weston, we must leave here at once, for they mean to do dreadful things to me! Lord Chase . . . he came and gloated over what he would do to me tonight, how I would be – be the virgin sacrifice and I—'

'Not you, *me*,' Alys said. 'There has been a slight change of plan. You are merely to be shipped off abroad while I am to take your place in this unholy rite, when all except the inner circle of the Brethren are gone.'

'But what are we to do?' the girl said piteously, shaking with terror. Alys thought that as an accomplice she left a lot to be desired.

'Escape, of course. Now, if anyone should come in before we do so – though I do not expect it until later – they will barely be able to make out Rayven in that dark corner, and you may get behind the door. I will slump against the wall, so that they do not see I am untied.'

'But how then shall we escape?'

Alys went over to the barred window in the door. 'I heard them lock it each time they shut the door – but not the rattle of the key being inserted or removed and' – she inserted an arm through the bars and strained to reach down – 'I have very slender hands and wrists – unusually so, and I believe I can just reach. . . .'

Her expression concentrated, she strained on tiptoe, then there was a rattle and she withdrew her arm slowly, clutching a large key. 'There!'

'Oh, Miss Weston!' Sarah said. 'But still we have to get out and Lord Rayven is near death.'

'No he is not,' Alys said sharply, 'merely unconscious from a blow on the head. I cannot leave him, but you can escape and get help for us, if you will – we cannot be more than a mile from the Red House.'

'Alone, and in the dark, miss?'

'The dark can have no terrors comparable to all you have gone through,' pointed out Alys practically. 'Rabbits and foxes are as nothing to the creatures that inhabit *this* den. But you must leave at just the right moment, for I heard my cousin say that the two men who brought Lord Rayven here were to go back and guard the river entrance until everyone had arrived. So we must wait until the Brethren and the . . . er . . . entertainers, have passed in.'

'But what if the two men are still there?'

'If they are, I am sure I will think of something, for I will come with you thus far. In fact, we will all escape, should I manage to bring Lord Rayven to consciousness by then, but otherwise, I will come back.'

'What if they capture me?'

'Then you will be little worse off than you are now.'

She had another look at Rayven. 'If only I had more cold water to bathe his head – and he is so cold. Listen – what is that?'

The sound of feminine voices carried up the passageway. 'I believe the women who entertain the Brethren are arriving, so perhaps you had better conceal yourself, and I will sit against the wall.'

The footsteps hurried past without a pause, and once all was quiet again she attempted once more to awake Rayven.

This time he opened his eyes, scowled at her and closed them again, which she took as a hopeful sign. 'I think perhaps he will soon awake, but we cannot afford to wait. Come, I will see to your escape, for then I must have an hour or so's grace before they come for me, and the hope of the help you will bring if we cannot get out in time.'

She took the horn beaker in case she found the source of the trickling water she could hear, and after a second's thought removed one of the pistols from Lord Rayven's coat. Opening the door cautiously she peered out. Braziers lit the passage, which curved away in both directions. To their right came the faint lilt of music and raucous clamour of voices, and strange heavy scents hung in the air.

'This way!' She pulled Sarah in the opposite direction.

Cautiously they stole along the passage, and down worn steps. 'Oh, this is hideous!' Sarah said. 'What a dank, awful place.'

'It is not! Look, the brickwork in parts is quite beautiful – perhaps Roman, though it has been patched and mended roughly over the centuries. See how they have diverted this trickle of water into a basin shaped like a shell ... so pretty, if a trifle slimy. But hush, I believe we are near the entrance.'

Three steps led up to a door that was ajar, and Alys tiptoed to it and found she was looking out of a little temple down to the river. To her right, two sturdy manservants lolled against a wall, laughing at some joke; to her left, a pathway led away in the direction of the wall to where the road must lie and, hopefully, escape.

She gave Sarah a shake, pointed at the path, and patted her

briskly. 'Be quiet until you are well out of earshot, but do not fear that they will see you, for they will be looking the other way.'

Sarah looked at her mutely, eyes enormous, as Alys weighed a small and ancient piece of brick in her hand, then lobbed it as far as she could into the bushes to their right.

'Go!' she said urgently, impelling the girl out into the open as soon as the two men had leapt up and rushed off in the other direction.

'Be quick – be careful!' she hissed and Sarah fled like a startled hare in to the thicket and was gone. Fear, Alys hoped, would not only get her over the wall should the gate be locked, but give wings to her feet.

How easy it would be to follow suit, she thought longingly, before turning back resolutely and retracing her steps to the grotto, pausing as she did so to fill the horn beaker with water from the little stone basin.

Going by the noises of revelry, she still had some time to spare. Lord Rayven lay as she had left him and she moistened his lips with the water, then applied a cold compress to his head, cradling it on her lap.

She had just pressed a kiss on his brow – and if truth be told, dampened his face with a few salty tears – when he began to stir and mutter at last and his dark eyes opened and stared up at her in bewilderment. 'What . . . where. . . ?'

'Hush, Lord Rayven, it is Miss Weston. Do not try to speak until your senses return to you.'

He stared up at her speechlessly for a moment, then pulled her to him and kissed her long and hard before thrusting her away and attempting to sit up. He subsided again with a groan. 'Oh God, my head!'

'I am afraid you have taken a heavy blow,' she said. 'Were you searching for me?'

'Yes I – Jarvis – Jarvis told me. . . .' He sat up, this time successfully. 'I set off alone like a fool; there were two men guarding the entrance. I had the best of the fight, but then—'

'Someone struck you on the back of the head. I expect it was my cousin, he seems to make a habit of it.'

'He struck *you*?' He examined her bruised face in the flickering candlelight. 'He will regret that!' he said grimly.

'Possibly, but not unless we can make our escape from this place . . . hush!' The sounds of revelry grew suddenly louder as though a door had opened, and then feminine giggles heralded the return of the girls past the door.

'The meeting is breaking up – there is no time to spare,' she said urgently. 'If you are recovered enough, we must be gone, for they mean me to take part in some heathenish ceremony shortly. I assisted Sarah to get away to fetch help, but that was so long ago that I fear something has happened to prevent her.'

'Sarah?'

'The girl who was missing from the Red House . . . but of course, why should you know about that? Chase kidnapped her, but now they mean me to take her place.'

Some intelligence began to return to his eyes. 'You helped this Sarah to escape yet did not go with her?'

'I would have been very happy to go, but, of course, I could not leave you here like this.'

'I am not the hero of this piece, it seems,' he groaned ruefully, 'merely a hindrance. But you were a fool not to make good your escape when you had the chance.'

'I know it,' she said. 'However, they were too stupid to search you, so you still had your pistols in your pocket. I have one of them here.'

'Then you had best give it back, for I daresay you have no idea how to use it,' he said, trying to rise to his feet.

'Yes I do – I have two just like it in my luggage.'

'You never cease to amaze me, Miss Weston.'

'They were Papa's.'

There was the sound of loud voices approaching and Alys looked up, paling. 'We are too late, I think! Lie down again quickly – I will go with them and cause a diversion while you escape, for you are in no fit state to fight them.'

He protested, trying to struggle up, but perhaps her hands pushing him down were a little more forceful than she meant, for his head came in contact with the stone floor and he passed out. She hoped he would come round again too late for any pointless heroics . . . but in time to get some assistance before anything of an *unfortunate* nature happened to her.

Snatching up the pistol and holding it behind her back, she slumped dejectedly against the wall just as Lady Crayling swung open the door.

'I will fetch her out,' she slurred, her footing unsteady and her eyes glittering in her white face. She did not seem to notice the absence of the key in the door – Alys thought she was beyond noticing much, though she did cast a glance at the prone shape of Rayven.

'Your lover is still asleep – how boring for you! Not, of course, that you could do much with your hands tied, which is just as well, for it would have spoiled Chase's little ceremony. Stand up!'

Alys did so and Lady Crayling draped a white velvet mantle over her shoulders and fixed a vizard-mask over her face. 'Come along.'

She went with them, finding some comfort in the feel of the pistol she held behind her back when she met the gloating eyes of two masked Brethren outside. That was the one moment when, had it not been for Lord Rayven, she might have pushed past Lady Crayling and run for it.

But as she looked longingly over her shoulder a head poked around the corner and the familiar, homely, one-eyed visage of Jarvis winked at her. She blinked, uncertain if she had really seen him, then the two laughing men took her elbows and roughly propelled her along the passageway.

They could have had no idea who she was and even less idea that her hands were not bound, but clutched a deadly pistol.

Lady Crayling held aside a tapestry curtain and they thrust her forward through an open door into a scene that might have come straight from a stained-glass depiction of Hell.

The music suddenly stopped.

CHAPTER 28

Stunned by Radiant Love

'I saw all – I understand all!' cried Robert de Mondial, fervently clasping Drusilla in his arms.
'I had thought you a willing conspirator, yet now I perceive that you are just as much a victim of Sir Lemuel as my poor sister was!'
Death or Dishonour *by Orlando Browne*

Alys staggered, then regaining her balance stopped dead with astonishment, taking in what had so recently been the scene of a positive orgy. She fervently hoped it was not about to be the scene of another, with herself cast in the starring role.

The very air in the underground chamber seemed heavy with some noxious perfume that sent the senses reeling and it was hot, for many braziers burned behind screens of thin alabaster, illuminating with a hellish glow their lewd carvings. The ceiling was tented with red silk and the walls hung with tapestries, while couches, cushions and indecent sculptures were scattered, seemingly at random.

The room held only three occupants, all of whom had dispensed with their masks. George Rivers lay on a couch in a pose of abandonment, his eyes half-shut and a sheen of perspiration on his pasty face. A glass had fallen from his hand and lay on the thick rug by his side.

Nat, a taper in his hand, was in the act of lighting a lamp below what looked very like an ancient altar, except that the subject cast into dull relief by the dim flame was that of a bull. Before it lay a long and strangely ominous slab of smooth, flat-surfaced stone on which rested a curved knife.

Alys was quite transfixed with a sort of horrified fascination – until Lord Chase stood up and moved into the centre of the room before the altar, his glittering eyes fixed on her, and let his robe fall open, displaying a naked white body in a state of some excitement.

She would have recoiled, except that one of the men behind her gave her another push forwards. Under the concealing white robe, she took a firm grip on the pistol: she would shoot Chase before she let him get an inch nearer to her than he was now!

'Bring her here!' Chase commanded, but before the men behind her could seize her again, she had whirled round and backed away, bringing out the gun and holding it steadily.

They stopped, the laughter and ribald comments stilled suddenly on their lips. George, she saw out of the corner of her eye, had sat up and was staring at her as if she was a nightmare born of laudanum. Could she hope for any help from that quarter? It was worth the attempt, and she pulled off the mask and shouted, '*George!*'

'Good God, it is Miss Weston!' he exclaimed, jarred into a state of near sobriety and getting unsteadily to his feet. 'I am not dreaming – it is my wife's friend!'

'It is indeed,' Nat said. 'Thanks to you, I have managed to lure her here alone, as you see.'

'But, you cannot mean—' He looked from Chase to Nat incredulously. 'She is not some doxy plucked from the streets – you cannot do this!'

'You dare to say cannot to the Master?' thundered Chase, stepping towards him menacingly. 'What of your oath to the Brethren? This sacrifice will mean I have boundless power – I will be invincible. Do you not understand that?'

'Nat,' George said, 'tell me this is some ghastly nightmare – we cannot do this! Let me escort Miss Weston out of this place, for—'

Faster than a snake striking, Chase snatched up the knife and plunged it into George's body. His victim half-turned towards Alys, his expression astonished, then he slumped to the ground and lay still.

There was silence. Then Alys raised her pistol to arm's length and coolly shot Lord Chase.

At least, that was her intention. However, never having fired a pistol before, the shot instead went wide, ricocheted off the wall and sent a statue of Eros crashing down, most appropriately, on to Lord Chase's head.

Behind her there was a sudden scuffle and then Rayven staggered into the room and gazed about him wildly until he spotted Alys.

His bruised and bloody face was a mask of almost berserk rage, but Alys thought she had never seen a more welcome sight and made no resistance when he snatched her to him, holding her in a fierce embrace that temporarily stopped her breathing.

'Nat!' she said warningly, when his grip momentarily slackened, seeing her cousin suddenly move – but in flight, dropping the taper he was still holding and vanishing behind the altar.

'There must be another way out,' she said, 'and I've shot Lord Chase.'

'No, you only tried to shoot him: he seems to have been felled by Love,' Lord Rayven said, removing the pistol that she had been pressing into his ribcage and shoving it into his pocket.

'He stabbed George – George was trying to help me,' she shuddered.

'Serle,' Harry said, slightly breathlessly, coming into the chamber, 'they have got away and – look!'

Unobserved, the dropped taper had set fire to the rug and now a line of flames ran greedily along it and up the tapestry hangings. Beyond them, Chase was slowly crawling like some loathsome insect.

'I'll get him, sir!' Jarvis said.

'No need,' Harry replied. 'Half the neighbourhood is up in arms over the missing girl – which is what delayed us, Serle. She escaped, thanks to Miss Weston, and the mob came with the intention of freeing her and – from the sound of it – burning down Templeshore and anyone in it!'

Indeed, from above there did seem to be a great deal of clamour.

'Come, we had better go back down the passage,' Rayven said, his arm still around Alys. 'The fire is spreading.'

'But George!'

'Dead as a herring, miss,' Jarvis said cheerfully. 'You've only to look at his face.'

'Oh yes!' She felt an insane desire to giggle rise to her lips. Then the floor seemed to suddenly rise to greet her. . . .

'I never faint!' she said indignantly, swung up into Lord Rayven's arms. 'And you are not fit to carry me anywhere, my lord, pray put me down.'

'For once, let me behave like a hero, Miss Weston!'

'But—'

'But me no buts,' he snapped, and strode off down the passage. He seemed to have made a miraculous recovery.

She felt that one of her own heroines would have emerged from the temple into the ring of torchlight on her own two feet – or perhaps hand in hand with the hero – but certainly not carried by him like some helpless creature. Yet his lordship seemed very set on it . . . and actually it was rather pleasant to be held so closely in his arms and know herself safe again.

A ragged cheer went up as they came out and, as he bore her away, she saw the whole of Templeshore House lit up from within by a red glow.

'Harry,' Lord Rayven said, 'you had best drive us back in the curricle and Jarvis can take my horse, which is tied up somewhere nearby.'

'I'll find it, sir,' Jarvis said, and the two men walked off ahead of them towards the gate.

Once out of sight of the crowd, Alys said, 'I think perhaps you should put me down now, Lord Rayven. I am sure I am no lightweight, and you cannot be entirely recovered from your injury.'

'Serle.'

'I cannot possibly call you by your first name,' she protested, 'what would people think?'

'That we are engaged?' he suggested, obeying her instruction to put her down, but then instantly sweeping her off her feet into another bone-crushing embrace.

'But we are not,' she said, fending him off as much as she was able. 'I think the blow on your head has had an adverse effect on your mind, my lord.'

'*Serle*. And *you* have had an adverse effect on my good sense since the moment we met.' He cupped her face in his hands and stared down at her. 'I find you infuriating, independent, outspoken, stubborn, sure of your opinions . . . most emphatically not the sort of wife I was looking for.'

'Come to that, *I* am not looking for a husband at all,' she said indignantly. 'I—'

'I know your views on matrimony and I am prepared to sign my soul to the Devil and consign myself to living under the cat's foot for the rest of my life, if you will only say you will marry me!' he said, and silenced her with a long kiss.

CHAPTER 29

True Bliss

Dear Cousin

I am writing to you post-haste, having just received the most disturbing news from Town, informing me that you are the author of several infamous novels under the name of Orlando Browne.

I do not know how such vile and pernicious rumours get about (my dear Charlotte tells me that they are novels such as no lady of delicate sensibilities would be found reading), but I felt I must warn you that steps should be taken immediately to deny them.

I will write at more length later – indeed, I would have come to London myself, had not Charlotte's confinement been imminent, but thought to put you on your guard.

Yours in haste,

James Basset

'There has been no sign of Nat? Do you think he died in the conflagration, together with Chase, even though his body was not discovered?' Titus Hartwood asked. He seemed to have aged several years since he learned what his nephew had done.

'He may have done so,' replied Lord Rayven, 'but it is my belief that he managed to slip away, and has taken ship under another name – perhaps for America. He must know that information has been laid against him, so that he will be imprisoned should he ever return.'

Titus sighed heavily. 'I did not think him capable of such evil. And Bella, too!'

'Bella is a nothing but a silly young girl, blinded by adoration of her brother into helping him. She did not know what he intended.'

'Well, I suppose that is something. I have sent her to the country with her mother until the rumours die down.'

'Miss Weston intends to stay with Mrs Rivers as long as she is needed.'

'How is she taking her husband's death?'

'She is bearing up remarkably well,' he said drily. 'That he heroically died trying to protect Miss Weston was, of course, a great solace to her.' He might have added that the attentions of his friend Stavely had also proved invaluable in keeping up her spirits.

'Alys has not been to see me since the tragedy,' Mr Hartwood remarked.

'She was not sure whether you would wish to see her, since she thought you might in part blame her for it.'

'How can I blame her for her cousin's infamy?'

'Then I will tell her to come, sir. Indeed, I hope when she does it will be as my intended bride – if you will give us your blessing?'

'I might give it, but *will* she marry you? My granddaughter has the strangest notions of any woman I have ever met.'

'She will – on conditions, which we are still engaged in discussing. A sort of treaty, drawn up by two opposing forces, so that they may dwell alongside in reasonable harmony.'

'It does not sound like any sort of matrimony I would favour,' Hartwood said dubiously.

'I always enjoyed a good fight,' Rayven said calmly. 'It is just as well I am battle-hardened. By the way, she knows about the Order, too.'

He frowned: 'You *told* her?'

'No, your brother told Nat. He has always known and resented the fact that you did not trust him with the secret – and he told Alys when he had her captive. I believe, sir, that you must admit that she should be allowed to represent the Hartwoods in the Order, for she is twice the man of most of the other members.'

'I will give it my consideration. You are either brave or foolhardy to wish to wed her, but you have my blessing. Indeed, I would prefer the wedding to be very soon, before you recover your senses!'

'I think it is *I* who need to recover my senses,' Alys remarked, when Rayven described this conversation. 'If I *must* marry, against all my principles, why did I accept a man who is clearly of a tyrannical and overbearing disposition, so used to command that he will think he is entitled to order me about as he pleases?'

Since she was seated on the sofa beside him with her head on his shoulder and his arm around her, he did not fear that she would immediately break their engagement.

'I am butter in your hands, Alys. You know you will not lose a jot of this freedom you value so much – and you will gain the run of my cellars, though I would object if you took up permanent residence down there.'

'That is quite true,' she said, her face lighting up. 'And I have had such experiences of late as must lend considerable verisimilitude to my novels.'

She raised her head from his shoulder and fixed a pair of great, sparkling grey eyes on him in a way he found impossible to resist. 'I suppose, too, that as a married woman you could arrange for me to see the Roman sewers, could you not? I had thought of setting my next novel in London and having my heroine escape through them, but it would be invaluable to actually see them.'

'It shall be the highlight of our honeymoon,' he promised, and she returned his embrace with the fervour of true bliss.